DIVINE HART

HEATHER SHERE

Nikki

Follow your hart!

Heather Shere!

ISBN: 9781723846137

Cover Design: Rebel Graphics
Photographer: Wander Aguiar
Models: Andrew Biernat & Desiree Lynn
Proofreader: Mandi Gibala
Editor: Virginia Tesi-Carey
Developmental Editing: Kerry Heavens & Shaina Abbs

For my love,
You are the leap to my year, my perfect holiday.

Prologue

PRESTON

"Sleep well, *Detka*," I whisper to Skye's sleeping form.

I slip silently from her window and reach for my skateboard tucked out of view behind the patio furniture. When I find that it's missing, I wheel around in fear, scanning the property in the pre-dawn light. I freeze, rooted to the spot as eyes as cold as ice fix on me from their vantage point across the deck. I feel the chill of their disdain even through the burning desert night.

I turn to fully face him, a stone cold blank look plastered on my face, not wanting him to see I'm terrified inside. I don't want him to punish Skye and I don't want him to come between us. I don't want him to do so many of the things I know he is capable of to hurt us. We are so close to being together away from him that it would kill me to blow it all now.

The silence is stifling. He holds my board in one hand to prevent my escape while the other clutches a fat smoldering cigar. He looks like he has all the time in the world.

I glance across the property. Beyond the glistening pool is a fence, I know all of the properties' weak spots. If I sacrificed my board I could be gone before his ass is out of that chair. I glance back at the window. Skye. She's fast asleep with no clue we have been caught. She doesn't deserve this. She deserves a man who will protect her, not leave her to face the punishment alone. I can't bail on her now.

I look back at Bob and even though I can't see his features clearly in the pre-dawn light, his eyes gleam with satisfaction. He knows I just reached the conclusion that I'm screwed.

He waits, surely enjoying the moment, and the silence stretches on. Then he places his hand on the armrest of his chair and heaves his giant frame up to standing. I will myself not to flinch, not to show any sign of fear and for a moment we just face each other with a dozen feet between us.

Once he's let the anticipation build, he speaks. "My office. Now." It's said with a chilling note of finality before he turns toward a door at the other end of the sprawling house. I wait for him to disappear inside. He has no concern I will bolt at this point, so he doesn't even look back. He knows he has me.

I've avoided getting stuck alone with him for so long, always knowing a man like him would try to wield his power over me. Now my fate seems sealed. With heavy feet I follow his path and when I reach the door to his office, I find it open.

I step inside.

The light from a desk lamp flicks on and I wince.

"Close it," he demands.

I do as he says, careful not to make a sound. He eyes me judgmentally and makes no move.

I know he doesn't approve of me and I really don't care, but I know he's a crooked player. People in this town fear him and I love his daughter. I don't want him to have power over us. I wipe my hands on my shorts hoping my nervous gesture will go unnoticed.

"Have a seat," Bob instructs, his tone oddly polite. It sets me on edge, but not wanting to worsen my already dire situation, I obey and sit in the plush chair across the desk in his grand home office.

He skirts around his desk, sitting in his chair and leans forward, steepling his fingers and tapping them against one another.

"What are your plans for the future?" he begins abruptly.

I'm caught completely off guard. "Uhhh... like work?" I stutter, running my hand through my hair.

He leans on his desk moving forward slightly. "College? A job? My daughter?"

I open my mouth, attempting to speak and then I close it again, gulping. I've got nothing. I know which school I'm hoping to go to, but it all depends on whether I get a scholarship and if I don't, I won't be going. I don't have any plans beyond that. I know I should, but I don't, so I stare blankly at him.

"Exactly what I thought." He gives me a look of disgust. I should be used to it since he wears it whenever I'm around. Sitting back in his chair he studies me for a minute. "I have a job for you."

I'm at a loss for words, especially since I know he doesn't care for me. Hate is a better word, he hates me.

"You speak Russian, right?" He narrows his eyes with an eyebrow raised.

"Yeah, why?"

"I have some business I need taken care of in Russia, I need a man on the ground."

"Trying to get rid of me, Bob?" I know he hates the fact that his daughter and I are in love.

He smiles an unsettling smile. "There are a hundred different ways to get rid of you, boy. I'm a business man and I don't get rid of people I have a use for."

What happens to people he no longer has a use for seems implied and I swallow.

"Think of it as me giving you a chance to become something other than the desert rat you are," he says it like it's an insult but when you're a desert rat you embrace it, wearing the title with pride.

I don't have to listen to this shit, so I get up and without a word, head back toward his office door. But as my hand makes contact with the door handle, his words stop me cold.

"I can promise you enough money to get your mother out of that trailer and keep my daughter happy." His tone is smug.

I grip the door handle, taking a deep calming breath. He knew exactly what to say to get me to stop and turn to look at him with hope in my eyes.

He sneers in satisfaction when I do, then motions for me to sit back down.

He has me by the balls right now, how can I refuse? I sit down to listen to what he has to say. I mean shit, what do I have to lose?

One

PRESTON

"*Krasavets*," my mama says as she straightens my tie. Her eyes sparkle like the Pacific Ocean.

"Mama, girls are beautiful, not men." I puff out my chest.

She makes a loud humph. "If I say you're *krasavets*, then you are. Your Papa would have been so proud of you."

Seeing her eyes tear up, I pull her closer into my embrace. "Don't cry, Mama, he's watching over us now." I can't stand the sight of tears in her eyes.

"Preston Sasha Hart, you make your mama proud." Her words are muffled by my shirt.

She doesn't use my full name often. Only when she's sad or mad. Today she's sad my father isn't here with us. My father died of a massive heart attack when I was in grade school. Times were tight after that, but one thing there was always plenty of was love. I kiss the top of her head, no longer the young boy that had to reach up on tippy toes to kiss her cheek.

"We'd better get ready, Preston. They will be here soon, and we don't want to be late for your big day." She pats my cheek and collects her handbag, stopping to check herself in the hallway mirror. Always so prim and proper, her gray hair is in a perfect bun and her clothes are neat and immaculate.

My parents had me later in life; I was their miracle baby. After years of infertility, one day in their 30's they discovered mama was expecting. Not a day went by that I didn't feel like their *dorogoe ditya*, their precious child. She always smiles when she looks at me and I'd do anything to keep that smile on her face.

I turn to look at myself in the mirror over her head. I'm a clear foot taller than her and make her look so small. My dark chocolate hair is artfully blow-dried up and away from my face and I smooth it again for good measure. Papa would be so proud of me right now, if not badgering me for a shorter haircut. My eyes are a darker shade of gray-blue than my mama's, and my lips are full like my papa's. I'm the perfect mix of them both.

"Enough admiring yourself, Preston. We have to leave," Mama scolds.

We hear a horn honk outside. "They're here!"

We step out of our trailer and see Skye walking around Lea's white Audi to my front door. Skye is my girlfriend, we've been together since forever. She's my everything. She's got this wild curly hair that is as dark as mine, but with strands of caramel that frame her perfect face.

"Preston! You look incredible" Skye stops in front of Mama and kisses both her cheeks. "Good morning, Mrs. Hart. Are you ready for the ceremony?"

"How many times do I have to tell you to call me Liliya?"

"You know I can't do that."

"Where's Craig? I thought we all were driving together," I ask Skye.

Skye opens the front door of the car for my mom and whispers over the hood, "Shaina's bringing him, she just got into town."

6

"Oh! Right." I waggle my brows at Skye, making her cover her mouth to silence the giggle. We both know what they are probably up to.

The drive to the convention center where the ceremony is being held is less than five minutes. If it weren't for the stifling heat, we would be able to walk. When I imagine what hell is like, I picture this town in the summer. Hotter than the devil's breath and twice as dry. I couldn't think of anything worse than putting on a suit in this heat, even if I had one. This is probably the only graduation where you can get away with wearing board shorts and a polo under your cap and gown.

I sling my arm around Skye. "Will your parents be there?"

"Who knows? I guess they'll probably pop in to save face."

I will never understand them. They have the most amazing daughter and they act like she's just a thorn in their side. Every day that goes by since my impromptu dawn meeting with Bob, I thank my stars that I had the balls to tell him no. The money was more than tempting, but then what? Be in Bob's pocket for the rest of my life? No thanks.

Even if I could handle that and look past what illegal deeds he would almost certainly put me in the middle of, I couldn't do what he was asking of me. He wanted me to leave for a month and not tell my mom or Skye. Just disappear and leave them clueless. I couldn't figure out why that part was so important to him, but if I ever needed proof that he was crooked through and through, that was it. He wouldn't budge on it either, so I was left with no choice but to grow big enough balls to refuse him.

I had thought he would make life hell for me after that, but the last few weeks I have not seen him once. He hasn't tried to stop me seeing Skye or tried to make contact with me again. It's a little unsettling, but I'll be out of here really soon.

Shit's finally about to get real. Our adulthood begins after graduation. I was able to get into UCLA with all scholarships.

Otherwise, I wasn't going to be able to go away, there was no way we could have come up with the money. Skye and Craig will be there with me. Shaina is doing her residency at Cedars-Sinai Medical Center and Lea is going to Santa Monica College. She got into an ivy league school but it's family tradition to go to Santa Monica. I'm stoked that we are all going to be so close together.

Lea brings her car to a stop and that drags me out of my thoughts. She practically hops out of the car after she parks it and rushes around to help my mama out of the car. I see Craig walking through the crowd. His eyes crinkle with his huge smile as he sees me. I can almost hear him say, "S'up dude." Where I'm all stocky and muscular, he's lean and lanky. We all tease him that one day he'll grow into his head. He is walking side by side with Shaina and she releases his hand as soon as she spots us. I raise a brow at Craig and he just shrugs as he reaches us. Shaina and Craig have a relationship that everyone is aware of, they've just never voiced that they are a couple.

"Mrs. Hart, you look stunning." Craig grins down at my mom.

"Craig, *daragoy*, you look so handsome today."

"Just today?" He winks at her.

"Dude, stop flirting with my mom." I walk over and pop him in the back of the head.

"Hey! Watch the hair!"

"You both need to knock it off." Lea rolls her eyes in amusement.

"Chill Lea, they're just kidding. But we do need to line up, it's almost time." Skye winks at me.

"Before you go inside, can I get a picture of you all together?" My mama pulls out a new disposable camera, standing back with a soft smile on her face patiently waiting for us to gather.

I sling my arm around Skye and Craig stands beside us, pulling Shaina in front of him. Lea stands at the front, since she's shorter than us all.

"Perfect!" my mama says and snaps a picture, clicking the button to move the film forward. "Stay where you are, I want one more. Okay, smile." She looks through the viewfinder and clicks again.

"Are we good, Mama?"

"Can I get one of you and Skye?"

"You heard her, Craig, she only wants her baby boy, not your ugly mug." I playfully shove Craig out of way.

Mama blushes. "Oh, I didn't mean it that way."

Craig gives her a charming smile. "It's okay, Mrs. Hart. He has a face only a mother can love." He winks, moving out of the way.

Mama shakes her head at us. "Okay, you both look at me and smile."

I pull Skye just a tad closer, and she wraps her arms around my waist and smirks up at me.

I bend down slightly so our faces are close together, smiling down at her. "Look at Mama, *Detka*." The moment we both turn our heads toward her the camera snaps.

"You kids had better get inside, it looks like almost everyone is in already."

"Oh crap!"

"Preston! Watch your mouth," my mama scolds me.

"Sorry. Come on guys, we'd better jet." I pull Skye closer to my side, and she wraps her arms around my waist and smirks up at me. "You ready?"

"Yes, Shaina are you staying with Mrs. Hart?"

God, she's fantastic, and I'm a jackass. I should have asked that.

"Yes, we'll be as close as we can get. Come on, Mrs. Hart."

I watch as Shaina takes my mom's arm and they begin the walk into the convention center. The good thing about them coming with us is that they're here before the doors open to the public, so hopefully they will be able to get a good seat.

"Come on Preston, let's go." Skye gently tugs my hand.

The four of us walk through the parking lot toward the side entrance of the building where they have us all lining up just inside the doors in alphabetical order. We would drop Lea off at the back since her last name is Roberts, but she is the valedictorian and gets to sit right up front. I wouldn't want to be her, that's for sure. Craig and I have been sitting next to each other in everything since we started pre-school together. His full name is Craig Hardington, and I'm Hart so at least we get to keep each other company during these boring ass ceremonies.

"Okay, you both stay out of trouble." Skye slips her hand out of mine.

Lea raises her brow, then narrows her eyes slightly at Craig and me. "You guys aren't planning any pranks like flashing everyone when they call your names are you?"

Craig bursts out laughing. "Would we do that?"

"Yes! You jackasses better not do anything to ruin our day." She jabs a perfectly manicured nail at Craig.

"We don't have anything planned Lea so chill out." She's a worrywart, like I would do anything with my mom in the crowd and Craig is just as close to his mom. "I'll walk you up to your spot, Skye."

"Don't be silly, I can walk the few feet to my spot with Lea." She raises up on the tips of her toes giving me a quick kiss and walks off with Lea.

"Dude, can you believe we are graduating?" Craig grabs my shoulder and gives me a quick shake, his goofy smile filled with excitement.

"I know! It's so rad that we'll all be going to school near each other." I don't know what I would do without my friends close to me. Craig is like the brother I always wanted, and Lea is that annoying little sister that grows on you like a fungus. And Skye? Well hell, she's the oxygen I breathe.

All the kids are animated as we line up in the air-conditioned room. Time flies by as the music starts up for the procession into our seats. I just want this part over with so we can get on with the parties that are going on tonight. I hear Skye's infectious laughter and see her through the crowd laughing at Mark, our flamboyant classmate, who has a sly smirk on his face as he whispers into her ear. I'll admit I'm a bit jealous that he gets to be the one to laugh with her through this long ceremony.

"I'm talking to you." Craig waves a hand in front of my face. "Earth to Preston."

"Sorry, what did you say?"

"Would you and Skye like to drive with Shaina and me to Lea's party?"

"I think Lea is going home with her parents and leaving Skye her car."

"Cool cool... just let me know."

"Finally this damn line is moving."

As we walk into the crowded convention center, the first faces I recognize in the back are Skye's parents, her mother a shell of a woman cowering next to her bald, overweight husband. Bob is a nasty piece of work, we've all heard the whispers about him around town. Rumors that his money is dirty, and his deals aren't always on the up and up. Now I have seen it for myself and I had a lucky escape. I just need to get us away from him so he can't hurt us. I turn my head at the last second not wanting to make eye contact with him.

Craig turns and elbows me. "There's Shaina and your mom,

up front with my parents." He points to the first row where our families are parked.

My mom spots us, and she practically bounces on her feet as she waves to us. My only goal in life is to be a man she can be proud of, she deserves that and I feel like today is a big step toward that.

Finally, we get to our seats and go through the motions of the ceremony. I hope Lea doesn't quiz me on what her speech was about, since I only joined in the crowds clapping and of course, had to catcall her to make her turn a few shades of red. The evil look she threw Craig and I said we'll suffer for it later, but it's well worth it.

The principal starts calling the names at last, and I'm glad that it's almost a done deal so I can take off this sweatbox red robe.

"Skye Divine," the principal announces, and she walks across the stage and poses for a picture and smiles out to us. She doesn't mind the yelling Craig and I are doing, she just turns slightly red and regally walks off the stage.

It seems like an hour goes by as they call name after name and finally our row is motioned to stand. We walk to the side of the stage and Craig's name is called. He struts out across the stage; that's when I notice the room has big screen TV's so parents and friends can actually see close ups of their loved one's faces. Craig's goofy ass grin flashes up.

"Preston Hart." At the sound of my name my feet move. I shake hands with the principal and see the camera off to the side. Looking directly into it, I mouth, "I love you, mama!" as I walk off stage.

I hear a few 'awwwws' and I smile even broader.

"What the hell, Preston? Showing us all up by mouthing to your mama."

"You're just mad you didn't think of it, Craig."

"Damn straight I am. That's some major brownie points right there."

We sit back down, and a cry goes up behind us. People are calling for paramedics. I try to see what is going on, but everyone is doing the same and I can't get a look. Staff are moving toward the crowd and security is already on the scene trying to keep the crowd back some. Suddenly, I see a flash of Shaina's red hair down on the floor.

"Fuck, I think that's Shaina." Craig's already pushing his way through the crowd.

I have a sick feeling in the pit of my stomach as I follow him, pushing through the crowd to where Shaina is on the floor performing CPR. I turn cold and panic hits me. I begin shoving people out of my way. When I can't get through the aisle, I climb over the chairs. My foot slips through a chair, and I kick it to the side almost going down with it. I have to get to them; I can't see who she's working on, but I don't see my mama. "Mama, where are you!?" I call out to her, hoping she hears me and comes to find me.

A strong arm blocks my way, and I feel as though I've hit a brick wall.

"Slow down, kid. You can't come any further," the convention center's security guard says, holding me back with one arm.

"My mom's over there, I need to get to her."

"Let the paramedics take care of the emergency first, then I'll let you though."

"Shaina!" I shout as they raise the gurney and she comes up with it, still performing CPR.

She looks up, not missing a beat on her chest compressions. "Get to the hospital, I'm doing all I can," she yells back and gives her patient her full attention.

That's when I go cold. There on the gurney, lifeless, is my mama.

The hospital is like most buildings in Palm Springs, brown stucco that blends in with the browns of the desert. The only color is the blue of the sky and green of the palm leaves. Skye pulls Lea's car around to the entrance. "Go, I'll park the car."

I sprint into the building and immediately a security guard yells, "No running, kid!"

I wave him off and slow to a brisk walk up to the counter where a lady greets me with a smile. "My mom was just brought in, Liliya Hart, can I see her?"

"One moment while I check the patient list." She starts shuffling papers around in no hurry, and I just want to grab her and shake her. It can't be that hard to find someone that just came in.

"She came in an ambulance," I state with more calmness than I feel, hoping to speed her along.

She pushes her glasses up and looks at me above the rims. "Car accident or convention center?" Not an ounce of compassion is on her face.

"Is that how you have them filed away?" I can't help the venom in my tone. "Convention center."

She shuffles for a minute more. "Are you related?"

I have to resist the urge to stop her from touching things on her desk and scream in her face HELP ME! "Yes, I just told you. I'm her son," I say between gritted teeth.

"Can I see your ID?"

Snatching the cap off my head and keeping my curse words to myself, I unzip my gown. Reaching into my back pocket, I find it empty, *shit*. "I forgot my wallet. I didn't think I would need it today."

"I'm sorry, sir. Without ID we can't release any patient

information," she states in that cold authoritative tone as if I were a child.

I lean over the desk with my hands flat on the counter. "It's my fucking mother! Where is she?" I growl into the woman's face.

She lifts a hand. "Security."

Great, just what I need. I look back to the weedy man coming out from the desk by the front door, the same one that told me not to run.

"Alright, son, what's the problem?" he asks, putting his hands on his hips about his belt, the look is almost comical.

"My mom is back there." I point at the double doors that lead to the treatment areas.

He gives me an understanding look and looks at the lady behind the desk. "Car accident or convention center?"

What the hell is wrong with these people? "Her name is Liliya Hart, and she was *at* my graduation." I'm so fed up with how they are treating me I'm on the verge of breaking down and crying.

He snaps a finger then points at me. "Gotcha, so what's the issue?"

"He doesn't have his license, so we can't confirm his identity."

I throw up my hands and turn away from the desk. It's rare that I lose my temper, but I am a word away from doing just that. Before I can go off, Skye walks in the door, scanning the room until her eyes stop on me. My rage quickly fades. I can concentrate on my mom with Skye near me. Taking long strides, I walk across the lobby, meeting her halfway.

"How's she doing?" she says with worry.

"I have no clue, Tweedle-Dee and Tweedle-Dumb won't tell me a thing without my ID, which I've left at home. We're going to have to go get it before they let me see her." I can feel a lump starting to form in my throat at the thought of wasting another fifteen minutes before I find out anything.

She frowns and tosses a nasty look at the lady behind the counter. "Oh yeah, your mom handed your wallet to me when she got in the car, so I threw it in my bag just in case." She fishes through her big ole hobo bag and pulls out my wallet.

"Oh, Skye, you're a lifesaver!" I pull her to me and swiftly kiss her cheek, then put her hand in mine and walk with her back to the desk.

I push my ID onto the counter. "Can you *please* let me know how my mother is doing?" I plead with the woman behind the counter.

She takes my identification and taps something into the computer. "If you can have a seat I will have someone come out and talk to you."

"Is she ok?" I squeeze Skye's hand, waiting.

"I don't have any medical information. I'll get a nurse right out to talk to you," she coldly states.

I feel a tugging on my hand and look down into Skye's eyes wondering if the desolation I feel is showing on my face.

"Come on, let's go wait."

I blindly follow her into a secluded corner and sit down. I brace my elbows on my knees and hold my head in my hands waiting for someone to come out to speak to us. Skye is rubbing my back trying to comfort me, no words are needed at a time like this. The wait is going to kill me.

"Mr. Hart?"

I jump to my feet and turn looking at Skye, motioning for her to come.

She shakes her head. "I'm not family, I'll just wait here for you."

I frown at her and lean down and grab her hand. "You're our family, I need you."

"Okay." She takes my hand and squeezes it while we both walk up to the nurse who is calling my name.

"Mr. Hart?" she directs the question at me this time.

"Yes, can I see my mother?"

"I'm Angel, let's go to a private room so we can talk." She proceeds to direct us into a room right behind the emergency doors.

I squeeze Skye's hand, then quickly soften my grip so I don't hurt her. She squeezes mine back in return and rubs my upper arm.

"Is she okay? Can I see her?" I ask as I pass her going in the room. She doesn't answer me, she just pauses and closes the door.

"Not just yet. Right now we are trying to stabilize her."

"What does that mean? I can't lose her." I choke back the boulder that's in my throat.

"We are doing our best. Your mother had a heart attack. We're trying to get her stabilized to get the specialist in to evaluate her."

"Is she awake?" Skye rests her hand on mine.

"No, she isn't awake. Let me be perfectly clear, Mr. Hart. She has almost slipped away twice. The specialist is on his way to do more testing, they may have to operate. It's touch and go right now, but please know we are doing everything we can to give your mother the best care possible." She at least has empathy in her voice as she's explaining this to us.

"Slipped away?" I manage to choke out.

"Yes, your friend performed CPR successfully on the scene to reestablish a heart rhythm, but again in the ambulance, paramedics had to resuscitate her. Your mother's condition is critical, but she is in good hands, Mr. Hart."

"Okay, will I be able to see her soon?" I feel like I'm a broken record, I just keep repeating myself.

"We'll let you know when we can get her stabilized, then we can let you have a brief visit with her."

I nod my head and squeeze Skye's hand again. This is a nightmare that I want to wake from.

"What we need to do right now is have you fill out a health history for her, and also provide us with copies of her insurance card if you have it with you. I'll send in our administrative assistant to help you fill it out. She can also answer any questions you might have about your mother's care."

"Okay," I murmur. She leaves Skye and myself in this stark, cold room with only a few chairs around a table and nothing else but the white walls. I choke up. "They had to revive her twice, Skye." I turn slightly to face her, not trying to hide the tears I feel filling my eyes.

"Oh, Preston. I'm so sorry. I don't know what to say." She cradles my face and then throws her arms around my neck.

"Just hold me." I'm not ashamed, I need her. I lean my forehead against her shoulder and cry. Something I have not done since my father passed.

I'm not sure how long we've been sitting like this when there is a soft knock on the door. I pull away and see a wet spot on Skye's shirt. "Sorry," I murmur.

"Don't be." She uses her thumb to wipe the wetness from my cheeks.

"Come in," I call out.

An older lady with a hospital uniform comes in. "Mr. Hart?"

"Yes, that's me." I turn to face her as she sits down at the table and sets her paperwork down.

"My name is Jasmine, I'm here to help you fill out the admitting paperwork for your mom. Do you know her medical history?"

"Uhhh, she's had no issues that I know of." I look over to Skye since her and mom spend a lot of time together. "Did she ever mention anything to you?"

"No, the only thing she would mention is being healthy as a horse."

"That's ok, do you have a copy of her insurance card?"

"We don't have health insurance." I feel doom in the pit of my stomach.

"Do you know if she qualifies for Medicare?" Jasmine sits very still with her pen ready to write down my answer.

"I don't, we never looked into it. Is my Mom even old enough for that?"

She looks down at her paperwork. "Oh I see, no, she won't qualify for Medicare because of her age." She pauses to collect herself and offers an apologetic smile. "In that case, Mr. Hart, we will get her stabilized here but once she is stable, we will have to transfer her to the county hospital."

"County? But won't her doctors be here?" I run my hands through my hair nervously.

"She will get all new doctors and possibly free care at County," she says reassuringly, but I know she is placating me.

"Will they have specialists there?" I'm confused about how healthcare works and why she has to move, but I know it's all to do with money...money we don't have.

"I'm not sure who the other hospital has on staff, but they will take good care of her. I can get you in touch with a patient care advocate. They will be able to talk you through everything." She starts scooping up her paperwork.

"Is there anything we can do to keep her here?" I don't want her to go there, that's where we lost my Dad.

"You can pay cash, up front. Is that a possibility?

"No." I sigh.

"Ok, once they have her stabilized we will let you know about moving her."

She picks up her stuff and walks out of the room. That's it. No insurance, no help.

As soon as the door shuts, I turn to my side and look at Skye. "She's going to die if they move her. I don't know what to do."

"Stay positive, we'll figure something out. I'll be right back. I'm going to let the gang know what's going on."

I nod my head and hide my face in my hands. I hate feeling this helpless. *Fuck* she had a heart attack.

Two

SKYE

As I leave the room, I hear the lady that was helping with paperwork at the counter talking in hushed tones. I pause for a moment to eavesdrop on the conversation.

"Angel, I wish there was something we could do. We both know if they move her she is as good as dead." Jasmine rubs her temples and has a weary expression on her face.

"Well they can't pay for her care and don't have insurance, so there is no way we can treat her here."

They both stop talking when they see me standing off to the side. Looking at both of them, I see looks of sympathy and pity shining in their eyes. I nod to them and walk into the waiting room, searching in my purse for my cell phone, hoping it still has a charge.

Perfect, forty percent.

The phone rings, once, twice...

"Skye?" Lea's voice is high-pitched.

"Hey." I'm suddenly choked up, I can be real and weak with Lea.

"What's wrong with Liliya?"

"She had a heart attack. They've had to bring her back twice. But Lea, they don't have insurance."

"Fuck."

"Yeah, they're now talking about stabilizing her and sending her to County Hospital." We both know how bad County can be. Lea lost a cousin years ago at that hospital, they gave her someone else's medication. I know that can happen anywhere, but between Preston's father and Lea's cousin, it's left a bad taste in all of our mouths.

"I hate to mention this, Skye, but...would your parents help?"

"I can't ask, Lea. My father would love that way too much."

"Some things are worth it, Skye, just saying." Her voice tried to soften the blow she just dealt me.

"I gotta go." I don't even wait for her to say goodbye. I just end the call.

I stare out into the room, leaning back against the furthest wall from everyone and see nothing but sickness and sadness. I slowly crouch into a sitting position and hug my knees, thinking. I know we have the money to help Liliya, and she and Preston mean the world to me, but I know what it will cost me to ask. What I wouldn't give for a loving parent like Preston's mom.

A baby crying brings me out of my thoughts. I can't sit out here all day wallowing in self-pity. Lea is right; some things are worth a little self-sacrifice. Before I lose my nerve I do something I never thought I would do, I call a number I've never dialed before.

"Skye?"

He answered faster than I expected, in fact I didn't think he would answer at all, so now it feels as if my mouth is filled with cotton balls. I can't seem to say anything.

"Skye is that you? Is everything alright?" For a second it actually sounds like he cares. It makes me wonder if I misdialed.

I swallow hard and steel my nerves. "Dad?"

I can see him in my head all smug, waiting for me to tell him what it is I'm calling for.

"Yes? Spit it out, Skye." Ah there is the bastard I know.

I almost hang up the phone. What stops me is seeing Preston come out of the double doors openly crying as he walks into the men's restroom.

"Dad, I need your help." I'm pretty sure I sound pathetic.

"Go on." Not one smidge of compassion is in his voice.

"Preston's mom..." I can't seem to get all the words out.

"Yes, we saw her being taken out of the convention center. How is she doing?"

"Not good, Dad. She had a heart attack and they don't have health insurance."

"Oh? Is she at County then?"

"No, they brought her to Desert, but they are stabilizing her now to move her to County, because they can't pay." I keep watching the bathroom door to see if Preston is going to come out.

"That's a shame," he states flatly.

"I overheard the nurse saying she won't make it if they move her," I whisper into the phone.

"Why are you telling me this, Skye?"

The bastard knows damn well what I'm trying to ask for here, but he's going to make me say it. "Can we maybe help them?" I hold my breath once I say the words.

"Be very clear on what you're asking for," he states with his business tone.

"Can we pay for her medical care to stay here at Desert Hospital, is that clear enough?" I can barely contain my attitude.

"Watch your sass, girl. Remember it's you who needs me."

"Yes, Dad, can we help them, please?" I hate this bastard.

"You do know this will cost you, don't you?" he says smugly.

"Of course." There is always a high cost with him, but it

doesn't matter. For Preston I will pay it, no matter what it is. "I have the money... right?" I bite the inside of my lip to keep from running my mouth.

"Not until you're twenty-three, for now you are at my mercy. Want me to change my mind?" I can hear the steel in his voice.

"No. If you could make the call to the hospital, that would be great." I swallow. I just literally made a deal with the devil.

Just as I hang up the phone with my father, Preston comes walking out of the bathroom. I push myself off the floor as he turns and makes eye contact. I try to give him a small smile and he holds his hand out for me to take. We walk back in silence to the little room they gave us to wait in. The only sound that seems to filter into the room is the beeping from monitors up and down the hall. They punctuate our heartbeats as our anxiety fills the air. I can only pray one of them belongs to Liliya.

There's a knock on the door. "Come in," Preston is quick to answer.

Angel walks in the room. "Hi, we have her stabilized and we can give you a few minutes with her."

Preston kisses the back of my hand and jumps up looking to the nurse to follow her out.

"Is it ok if I wait here?" I ask. I don't want to go back to the waiting room to sit in the crowd of people.

She nods. "Yes, that will be fine. We'll need you nearby for the transfer papers."

"Okay, I'll be here. Give her my love," I tell Preston.

"I will," he says with a solemn tone.

I sit for a second, the reality of all that's happening not quite sinking in. I wish they could get someone to tell us what they could do to help her, more news or even an update. Instead it's a hurry up and wait game.

I should call Lea and let her know that Liliya is stable. I just don't want the questions that will follow. They all know I'm not much of a talker on the phone, so they will forgive a short text to Lea, she can pass the news along. Pulling out my phone I text her two words, "She's stable." I turn off my phone and shove it in my bag.

Three

"Is she awake?" My palms feel sweaty, so I wipe them on my shorts. I don't know what to expect when I see her.

"I'm sorry, no, they're keeping her sedated to keep her heart rate regulated," Angel replies softly.

We walk past lines of beds all shielded by curtains, it's a full house today. As we head to the end of the hall, two rooms actually have doors and glass windows. The entrance to the first is open, and I can see in. A sheet has been pulled over the patient's head, and the family is around the bed crying.

"What happened?" I can't help the curious whisper that comes out.

"Car accident," Angel says solemnly.

Losing a patient must be hard. I feel for the doctor that delivers the bad news. We stop in front of the second door and my heart starts pounding. These must be the trauma rooms. Not only is my heart racing, it's in my throat, choking me.

"Right here, Mr. Hart." Angel leads me into the room with beeping monitors and two nurses checking my mom's vitals.

They both check the machines one more time and then leave me alone with her.

Mama's lying so still. I inch closer to the bed. There's a chair at the side of the bed and I move it aside with my foot and stand over her. My shoulders slump, the color is gone from her face as well as the smile that always graces it. I notice the wrinkles around her eyes and how tired she looks.

I pick her hand up and gently squeeze it, noticing the wrinkles there too. This selfless woman, she doesn't deserve to be lying here. One of my tears drops onto the back of her hand. I quickly wipe the tears off my face, but more soon replace them.

"Mama, you have to fight. I need you. I need you so bad." I feel the desperation in my voice, making my muscles bunch and I feel as if a dam is about to break. "Don't leave me."

The door to her room opens and the nurse, Angel, looks in. She takes a look at me and bows her head. "I'll give you a few more minutes, Mr. Hart," she says quietly and backs out of the room.

I turn back to my mom and sit in the small space on the bed next to her, I have her fragile hand cradled between mine. I can't help but think I'm part of the problem. I haven't been able to provide for her well enough, and maybe it's the trailer park living that has her sick and worn out.

"Please, Mama, fight, and I'll make sure your life is easier. Just please...please fight."

I bow my head and bring her delicate hand to my lips and kiss it. I'm not sure how long I stay like this, but the beeping of the machines scares the shit out of me. I drop her hand and jump up, the door swings open and a small army of nurses comes in.

I back away from the bed as they swarm around her. "Mr. Hart? We are going to need you to wait outside while we work on her." I back out of the room, not taking my eyes off my mom.

"Fight, Mama, fight!" I can't help the gruff yell that I let out as they shut the door, so I can't see her any longer. Interlocking my hands behind my neck, I lean my forehead against the glass. I want to bust into the room and have them stop poking and prodding her.

I'm not sure if it's just been a few minutes or hours, the smell of the hospital burns through my nostrils. The beeping of the machines as my father struggles to breathe, I don't want to be back here. I sit silently beside the bed as my mama whispers loving words to him in Russian. My Mama is so strong, but she's telling him not to leave her, that we need him. She leans down and presses her forehead on his, it's at this moment I see the tears streaming down her face.

"Mama is Papa going to be okay?"

"I don't know, Preston. Come here and give your Papa a kiss. Maybe that will help him." *My mama opens her arms for me and sits me on the side of the bed.*

I place a kiss on my Papa's cheek and my mama squeezes me tight. I slide off the bed landing on my feet and sit back down in the chair, while my Mama pats Papa's hand.

Beep...beep...beep

The sound loud in the small room.

Beep...

This time the sound lingers, and my eyes go round in surprise.

"Mama?" *I move to the edge of the chair.*

"Nurse!" *my mama calls frantically rushing to the door.*

Three nurses come running in. "Can you please wait outside, Mrs. Hart?"

The beeping sound gets longer, it's not beeping anymore it's just a high-pitched noise now.

She nods her head. "Preston, come."

I stand up and feel a coldness spread through me, I don't want to leave my Papa.

"Papa?" *My voice sounds small over the noise in the room.*

My mama scoops me up with her arm around my waist. "We need to let them work, Preston," she says as she drags me out of the room.

"No! I want Papa. Papa wake up!" I wiggle trying to get out of her arms.

"Papa!!!"

"Mr. Hart?" a gentle voice says beside me.

I take a deep breath and turn to follow the voice. "Yes?"

"She's stable for now. If you want to go back to the private room, your friend is still in there," Angel says very softly.

I nod my head "Thanks" and start to walk down the hall; at least Skye will be there to wait with me. I'm about fifty feet away when I hear a voice I would never expect to hear here.

"Preston?"

"Bob... I mean Mr. Divine?"

"Yes, I heard what happened and came right over. I wanted to show my support for you and your mother."

His tone sounds sincere, and he looks it, but I can't help but be suspicious of his motives. "Yes, they are getting my Mom stabilized and then well..." My voice trails off.

"Does your mother have insurance, boy?"

"No." I can't help but feel ashamed, what kind of provider am I?

"Have you thought any more about my proposal?"

I swallow. I was so proud I told the bastard to go fuck himself, but now... "I already told you, I can't," I reply meekly and curse myself for sounding so weak.

"Things change though, don't they, boy? You have bigger concerns now, what with your mother's health so fragile and no money for her care. I wonder if you might be wise to reconsider?"

"I..." I falter. I was only ballsy enough to turn him down once, I don't know if I can do it again. Not now that I know Mama's life might depend on money, or the lack of it.

"I don't usually give second chances, Preston. I wouldn't think too hard. You have a lot riding on this choice, be smart. A month away from home and then you'll have enough money to make my daughter happy and pull your mama out of that hell hole of a trailer. Agree now and you can consider your mom's medical bills a signing bonus. Gotta have you focused on the job, not worrying about your mother." He studies me, his beady little eyes always calculating. "What's it to be?" he demands.

I hesitate for a moment, but then surrender. "I accept, sir." I need to save my Mom, and this is the only way. "Only, I can't leave right away."

"One week then," he states. "I'll give you that courtesy under the circumstances." He has a slimy smile on his face and I figure that courtesy will end up costing me somewhere along the line, but I have no options left.

"And the other parameters you set?" I ask, hoping he's changed his mind about me telling them I'm leaving.

"Everything is the same." He claps me on the back and laughs dryly.

"A week? But what if..." I can't even let the words come out of my mouth; I can't bear the thought of what if.

"We will cross that bridge if we come to it. For now, if she's out of the hospital, it goes down like I laid it out in our initial meeting. Just in case you forgot, boy, you leave and do it when I say without a word to anyone."

"I need to tell my mom something, Bob. I can't let her worry about me while she's recovering from this."

"I'll compromise there and let you tell her you will be out of town for work."

I look over at the door that I know Skye is behind; my heart hurts at the thought of leaving her for a month without telling her why, but when I look back to where I just walked from I know I have no choice. If this will give my mama a chance, I have to do it.

I know it will be the best thing for the three of us in the long run. I just hope Skye will forgive me.

"It's a deal, Bob." I extend my hand to further seal the deal.

He takes it and firmly shakes it. As soon as he releases it he starts barking orders. "Who's in charge? We need the best doctors in the Coachella Valley to come in and examine Liliya Hart."

Bob Divine has a high standing in the community, people know his name and the color of his money. It doesn't matter if the guy is a dick or not, this town values money, and he's got that.

"Hello, Mr. Divine, is there something I can assist with?" Jasmine, the lady that was helping us with paperwork, is now behind the counter.

"Jasmine? Correct?" he states. I'm not entirely sure how he knew her name.

"Yes, sir, that's me. Can I help with anything?"

"Jasmine, Liliya Hart is a patient of yours. I want you to keep her here and direct all bills to me."

"Mr. Divine, we would need to have a credit card or check on file before we can start treatment. That's hospital policy."

"Yes, I am aware of the policy. This should do it." He sets a black American Express card on the counter.

"Let me get a copy of this so we can go ahead and stop her transfer." She rushes off with the card.

"Thank you, Bob, I don't know how I can ever repay you." I know more words should be said, but that is all I have right now.

"Don't worry, you'll pay me back."

"Here's your card, sir. Will there be anything else I can help with?" she asks as she slides the card over.

"Yes, make sure the doctors move their asses and find out what the problem is." He almost growls this at the girl.

"Yes, sir!" she replies and rushes off. I see her stop Angel, the nurse that was helping us, and update her. She looks toward us with a smile, then starts off at a quick pace to my mother's room.

Things are already happening. Bob smacks me on my back chuckling. "You see, kid, money talks."

"So I see," I reply, trying to ignore his hand sitting on my shoulder. He gives it a squeeze and then thankfully removes it.

"I'll leave you to care for your mom. We'll talk before next week, yes?"

An answer isn't needed, he turns and is gone just as fast as he came. I stand and watch all the movement at the end of the hall where people are going in and out of Mama's room. My feet start moving on their own, following my steps back to where a barrage of people are working around her bed. Their talking doesn't even register in my brain, I focus on watching the heart rate monitor and see that regular beat that gives me a glimmer of hope.

"Mr. Hart?"

"Yes?"

"If you want to go wait in the private waiting room, we have a cardiac specialist on the way to evaluate her after we get her moved into ICU."

"Okay, thank you." I walk back to the waiting room. Skye's head pops up as I open the door, she's sitting on the floor hugging her knees.

"Hey, how's she doing?"

I don't answer right away because I don't know what to say, I can't tell her about her father. I take a seat on the floor beside her and put my arm around her shoulders. She turns and leans into me. She cups my face and looks into my eyes searching for answers. I hope she doesn't see the guilt I feel. I squeeze her tighter. Just being near her makes my thoughts more grounded.

"They are keeping her here," I blurt, still in shock that all her medical expenses are now taken care of.

"That's awesome!"

"Yeah, they have a specialist in with her now to see what's

wrong." I'm relieved when she doesn't ask me why they changed their mind about transferring her.

She puts her arms around my neck, and we sit in silence, waiting for someone to come in to give us the news. She gently runs her fingers through the hair at the back of my head, it's very calming.

A firm knock sounds and not waiting for an answer, in walks a doctor with a clipboard in his hand and his glasses slipping low on his nose.

"Hello, I'm Doctor Ross, your mother's cardiologist."

Skye and I both shuffle to our feet while he introduces himself.

"Thank you for seeing her so quickly doctor." I shake his hand. "Do you have any idea what's wrong?"

"As you know, your mother suffered a heart attack. We are still in the process of running tests, but based on her ECG, we see she has an obstruction of the left main coronary artery."

I interrupt him while he's talking. "Can you fix it?"

"I'm going to go in and place a stent into the artery to open up the blood flow. That is the best case scenario. If that isn't possible, then we will perform bypass surgery." Just as I open my mouth to interrupt him again, he holds up a finger and then continues on. "We are taking her down now, and I will do everything within my power to help your mother."

"Okay," I say with some relief. Skye is behind me with her hand resting on my back.

"How long before we know anything?" Skye chimes in.

"We are prepping her for surgery right now, and that can last anywhere from two to six hours, longer if we run into any complications."

"Thank you, doctor," I manage to whisper.

The next four hours pass at a snail's pace. Skye called and updated our friends and one by one they all showed up to wait with us. We're family to each other and I'm glad they're here, but thankfully none of them are trying to engage me in conversation. Skye and I sit silently with our fingers entwined, every now and again she squeezes my hand to remind me she's still here with me.

"Mr. Hart?" a confident voice cuts through the stifling silence.

My head lifts up. "Right here," I call as I stand and move toward Doctor Ross.

The doctor looks at all the faces in the room and then back to me. "Would you like to go somewhere more private?"

"No, everyone is family here." Skye steps up to my side and slides her arm around my waist. The rest of our friends are silent, waiting to hear but giving us enough space for the doctor to talk to us.

"Your mother came through the surgery successfully. The artery was too clogged for a stent, but I was able to perform bypass surgery. She is resting now in our cardiac care unit. Do you have any questions?"

I'm silent for a few seconds. "When can I see her? When can I take her home? Will she be ok?" I shoot off all three questions without taking a breath in between.

"Because of the lateness of the hour, we would rather let her rest tonight. She is currently sedated anyway. You can visit first thing in the morning. I suggest you go home and get some rest. If she does well she can go home within a week. I've seen some patients go home after three days but this is a case by case basis, so we will keep our eye on her."

"Oh, thank you, doctor. Thank you so much."

"You're welcome, now I'm going to check on your mom. We'll be in touch." He turns and walks out of the room.

I turn to my group of friends with a relieved smile on my face. "Thanks guys for being here."

Skye is the first one to hug me and one by one our small group of friends connects in one big bear hug. The last time we had a circle hug like this was when my father passed away. I let myself cry tears of relief and find comfort in the warmth of this band of friends.

Four

SKYE

Finishing up a music set on the Hollywood Walk of Fame, I cringe on the inside at the irony. *Fame my ass.* I try to ignore the cramp in my belly, but it's been a full day since I've eaten anything. Looking inside my guitar case, I see I have about twenty bucks and some change, just enough to eat or sleep somewhere.

I'm desperate, broke, and alone, just like every other bright-eyed girl trying to make it in Hollywood. So much for thinking I was special. Turns out, there are more people out there with talent than I thought. I don't stand out. Sure, I can sing, that's what my scholarship was for, but so can the thousand other wannabes that are scavenging the streets looking for some sort of gig.

Every audition is the same: change this, sing that. For a country that values individualism, they sure try hard to make us all the same. The same voice, the same look, and if you don't conform, well, you're on the streets. For a man it's easy, they can do manual labor and manage to get by, but us women? The laborers don't want us either because we're not what they're looking for. They're no better than the entertainment business in this town, I shouldn't have expected any less. So, when I say that if you don't conform then you're on the streets, it's literal for me and for thousands of other women.

If they can stay off the streets, their dream of stardom is sadistically twisted into nothing but a stage name, scant clothing, and silky promises. No one dreams of getting paid in ones, which I realize with a sinking feeling in my stomach is the road I'm heading down...or worse.

Days like today, I wonder if it's worth spitting out my pride to swallow just one decent meal. I stare down at my tattered shoes, a far cry from the kind I wore before I left. Back then, I had everything I could possibly want and nothing that I actually needed. So I left it all. Now look at me. When I left home I left my name and who I was. I didn't want anyone to find me, so I became invisible.

A car honking its horn startles me from my thoughts and I glance around. It's getting late. I need to move on before the light fades. I reach into my case and grab the money. There's a ten-dollar bill and a mixture of singles and quarters. I've got the ten tight in my fist when someone shoves me to the ground from behind. The concrete bites into my knees, the slight burn and wetness a sure sign that I've torn skin.

"What the fuck?" I spit the words out with a nasty glare over my shoulder. A big dude, more fat than muscle, pushes me again. I open my hand to catch myself when the ten falls to the ground. He reaches out and grabs my guitar and the fragile strap breaks. It's the last thing of value that I own and this thug just snatches it. I scream as loud as I can, "Stop! Someone help me, please!" Right behind him, another guy appears to be running after him to stop him. I look at him with pleading eyes, but he scoops up the ten-dollar bill off the ground. *What the fuck is happening?* The ass even has the nerve to say, "Thanks, Chica!" as he passes me with my money.

There's a crowd gathered around me watching this play out like it's some scene from a movie. "Uhhh HEELLOOOO? A little help here?"

They snap out of their daze and son-of-a-bitch, they all turn and go about their business. *Just my luck.* What the hell is wrong with people? Then again, no one has ever helped me before when I needed it, I don't see why that would change now. Everyone wants to put in their two cents worth, but they all turn a blind eye when you ask for help.

Biting my lip, I fight past the negative thoughts. I might not be able to get my money back since that guy is long gone, but I can still see my guitar. He's just strolling down the street as if I won't chase him. I grab the now empty case and take off at a run. It doesn't take me long to catch up to him and I swing the case, hitting him in the side. Catching him off guard, I then jab him in the kidneys with the case. The guitar drops to the ground and he turns around with a shocked look on his face. He opens his mouth and his eyes go round, he shuts his mouth and turns off at a run.

"That's right big boy, run! You don't want to mess with this!" I scream at him, suddenly braver.

I hurry and put the guitar into the case, noticing the broken string and a dent. I'll examine it fully later. Right now, I just snap the case shut. I sit on the sidewalk and lean back against a building, watching everyone go about their day just as mine has come to an end. It's time I face the reality that I only have two options left: trade my dignity for a roof over my head and some food on the table or sell what I refuse to, myself. It's time I pawn my guitar and use the money for a meal and a bus ticket back home. Things have to get better, they certainly couldn't get any worse.

The sun is starting to set, I must have lost track of time. This is not a place I want to be alone after dark. I need to find shelter for the night, and besides that, I will get a better price for my guitar during the day when the pawn shops don't think I'm desperate for a night's sleep. A couple of blocks over there's a soup kitchen. I used to visit there all the time, until they hung my picture up letting people know I wasn't welcome there. I've seen Lea in there and that's when I stopped using the free food banks. Life's rough for a girl who's not used to going hungry. You'd think after five years of being on the streets I would be used to it.

It's getting darker by the second and I'm very apprehensive as I start to cross the darkened alley. I could trade more than my dignity for a longer-term fix and that pimp is always there, waiting for the day that I'm so hungry I'll give in. My heart's beating in my throat, the urge to run strong.

"Well hello, Skye, it's a nice surprise to see you out so late. You hungry, doll?" The scratchy voice of the neighborhood pimp startles me. He's in his polyester suit, muscles bulging out, his dark hair greased back and a cigarette hanging out of his mouth.

"Sid." I gulp.

I'm caught like a deer in headlights, trying to steady my racing heart because he knows exactly where to push. At our initial meeting years ago, I thought I was ready for his type of desperation. I wasn't and since then my response to him is 'fuck off' and I run along, never showing just how close to the edge I am. Today is different. Deciding I need to go home has me off guard. His beady little rat eyes appraise me, not missing a detail as he looks at the disarray of my clothes which are ripped and dirty from the fall. He pushes himself off the wall and with every slow step he takes forward, I take one backward. A lamppost stops my movement, but he continues to stalk me as if I'm his prey.

He steps right up to me, not touching me but invading my personal space. I can smell the tobacco on his breath and it disgusts me, so I turn my face away from him and look down at the sidewalk. I flinch as he brings his hand up and fingers one of my curls, pulling it then watching it bounce back up.

"It's okay, doll, Sid will take real good care of you." He chuckles deeply. "Has your hunger finally knocked the fight out of you, doll?" He really isn't expecting an answer and the battle within me is keeping me silent. He moves in closer and smells my hair. I may be broke, but the one thing I won't go without is being clean. He starts talking to me low. "Come on, Skye, let me buy you dinner. Work for me tonight so I can show you how easy it is to live better." My silence encourages him more. "I won't have you on the streets, doll, the first night is always with me." My mind begins to race. I'm starving and a good three hour drive from where I once called home, but I've already decided I am going back.

I can only imagine the look on my mother's face if I showed up at their door now. Maybe she would be glad to see me after all this time? Oh, who am I kidding? She despises me just as much as my father does, she just shows it differently.

Sid's still whispering in my ear all the dirty things he would love to do to me. He really is a twatwaffle. He mistakes my shivers as pleasure, but it's the rage that is making my body quake. Turning my face away from him was a mistake, he's now placing featherlight, wet kisses on the sensitive spot on my neck. My hands ball into tight fists, my nails breaking the skin on my palms, but fear has me keeping still.

My body is stiff, and Sid starts kissing my neck. I'm so hungry I don't fight back. I start thinking maybe he can just take what he wants and give me some money. I try to concentrate on the cars passing by, which doesn't really help since I see the pathetic looks being tossed my way. He leans in, pressing his body flush to mine, the weight of him making my skin crawl. His muscles jump in excitement, and I can feel his erection pushing into my hip. The thought of him nauseates me.

Fear roots me to the spot. I never thought I would be in this position again, not since I first turned him down. I can't even manage to tell him no, only a small whimper escapes. He crowds me, but I don't push him away just yet. My stomach takes this moment of silence to growl loudly.

In my head I'm screaming at him to get the fuck off me, but I can't make myself react. I can't get the words out... I don't feel anything but disgust. I close my eyes so I don't have to see how people are judging me. Tears silently fall, but Sid doesn't notice, he's now grinding himself on me, making disgusting noises. I press myself further back into the lamppost, the metal digging into my back. My body is trying to get away from his onslaught of unwanted advances, my hands fisted in his suit, my mind on the few bucks I might make if I...I feel sick.

The honking of a horn makes me snap my eyes open and it takes a few seconds to focus due to the tears still filling them. Right beside us is a sleek, storm black Aston Martin. I can't see the driver's face, but from the way his hands are moving I can tell he is saying something.

Sid bends down, looks into the car and proceeds to yell, "Fuck off, dude. This one's mine tonight!" His hand squeezing one of my arms, he doesn't realize how tight his grasp is. I let out a small cry of pain, and he turns his head to me. "Shut the fuck up, Skye, let me get rid of this asshole so I can finish what I started." He emphasizes this by giving me a shake, making my head hit the lamppost.

I see the stars first then panic really takes hold. The hunger and desperation had me almost considering it for a second, but this is a done deal as far as he is concerned. He's dead serious and he won't let go now that he has ahold of me, he is going to take it no matter what. *This can't happen, I won't allow it ever again.*

I try to jerk my arm free, but my strength is no match for his. "Let me go, Sid, I don't want this." I'm shocked at how strong my voice sounds considering how weak I feel. The slamming of a car door grabs our attention, the sight that is before me is astonishing. He's 6'1. His hair reminds me of a cup of espresso, rich and dark. His jawline is more defined than I remember and he has a trimmed beard. He's in a designer suit, looks like an Armani to me, perfectly tailored to fit his broad frame and holy shit does he fill it out. My mouth drops open and I'm robbed of speech.

It can't be. He was the love of my life, my everything.

He gestures toward me but before he opens his mouth Sid starts yelling at him. "Listen, dude, this little whore is mine. I suggest you get the fuck back in your car and leave us to our business."

His inky blue eyes snap to me, they're deep pools of darkness that I used to know so well. I loved those eyes. I feel them burn into me, taking in my tears and how I was trying to pull away. I'm not sure of the message I convey to him, but he starts approaching us and counters back to Sid.

"Could have fooled me, looks like the lady wants to take her business elsewhere."

I take in a quick breath as I hear his warm rich voice. "Preston?"

It's been a long time since I've let myself think about him. Five years to be exact.

Sid drags my attention back to him. "Shut your mouth, not another fucking word, Skye. You won't like the consequences," he tells me in a low harsh tone as his beefy hand grips harder. *What the hell was I thinking? Oh, that's right, I wasn't.*

"Why don't you let the lady go?" Preston firmly suggests.

Sid puffs his chest out like a peacock. *You've got to be kidding me.* He turns his back to me. "Dude, I'll give you one more warning. Get back in your fancy car and leave this whore to me."

I see Preston press his lips together, does he think I'm a hooker? This is the second time Sid has called me a whore and whether Preston believes him or not, I've had enough. I swiftly raise my hand and pop Sid in the back of his head. He loses his hold on me and I give him a little shove.

"I'm no one's whore, you hear me? You both can fuck right off with your 'business' because I'm out of here." I'm furious that Preston could believe that I would be doing business here. I try to pass Sid, but he grabs my arm and I turn on him, ready to rip him a new asshole. What I'm not prepared for is the sight of him raising his hand ready to slap me.

"You'll learn some respect!" he roars at me as he punches me in the stomach. This makes me drop to my knees, gasping for air. He grabs a fistful of my hair and drags me back to my bed. With calculated intent he lifts me by my hair. I refuse to scream and give him the satisfaction of knowing he hurt me.

I shake myself so past memories of my father can't cripple me. I flinch out of habit.

Before the blow can make contact, Preston's hand catches Sid's wrist. Sid is bug-eyed. He can't believe someone would have the nerve to touch him. Preston's face is expressionless. He glances at me, and I flinch from the rage that flashes in his eyes. The pimp is a bit dense and doesn't seem to see the controlled rage Preston has as he keeps running his mouth. It's a look I don't recall Preston having...ever.

"Dude, you're going to regret touching me over one of my whores."

Preston's nose flairs and then he artfully places an uppercut to Sid's jaw, effectively knocking him out cold.

He straightens his cuffs and turns his eyes back to me and

narrows them slightly. "Are you all right? Do you need medical attention?" His eyes scan me from top to bottom and he stops at my scraped up knees. His eyes now hold concern, or is it pity? I can't stand people looking at me with pity.

Nervously shuffling my feet, I don't know what to say. I mean, what do you say to someone that was once your everything? I lower my gaze and look at the sidewalk. "Just another day in Hollywood," I mumble with a bitter laugh. He takes a step closer and places a single finger under my chin raising my face to look at him. Looking up at him with incredulity, I try to ignore the heat from just his one finger on my face. It pisses me off because I'm used to feeling nothing but disdain when touched. Except his touch. He's always had the power to make me feel. My jaw clenches as he studies my face, he has a look I remember well. One that says he knows what I'm thinking. I'm struggling to hold back my own anger. He lost that privilege of feeling anything for me or about me when he left me.

"Get your fucking hands off me," I snap, very low.

His eyes flash a sad look before they go guarded and hard. "What? No hi, Preston, how are you? You don't look happy to see me." Then, slowly, he moves his hand from my face. I have to hold back my whimper as his comforting touch leaves me. I wonder when he got so damn sure of himself.

"I'm a little surprised to see you again, you know... after *you* left," I sneer.

We stand there for a few moments, just staring at each other, his eyes calling to me with something I can't decipher as my heart begs for him. I hate that after all this time it's still him.

My stomach breaks the silence with a powerful growl, and my hand moves immediately to cover the offending noisemaker. He barks out a loud laugh. "Hungry, Skye?" As if the sound of my belly isn't an answer. There's one thing I can't stand, and that's being laughed at, and he *knows* this.

My stubborn pride will be the death of me because I look at him straight in the face and reply, "No."

He raises a brow as my belly roars with hunger again. A moan from the ground catches our attention. I do not want to be anywhere near here when Sid wakes. "Listen, Preston, I'd love to catch up, but I've got somewhere to be." The lie slips out easily. I kick the pimp in the side making him grunt.

Preston inclines his head and smirks at me. "Still just as stubborn, I see. We better get out of here before he comes round."

A small smirk plays about my mouth. He has no idea just how stubborn I can be these days. I purposely ignore the 'we'. "I should indeed. I've taken up enough of your evening, so I'll just wish you a good night." I collect my guitar and start to walk away, not asking him what he's doing three hours from home in Armani and a two-hundred-thousand-dollar car. The best part is, I know it will annoy the hell out of him that I didn't ask.

"Do you need a ride, Skye?" he calls out after me.

"Nope!"

It's fully dark now. I glance back behind me and see him leaning against the car. I pause, I'm tempted to go back to him. He takes a step toward me and it scares me how tempting it is to go to him, so I turn in the opposite direction.

"Skye, wait!" His yell has me walking faster to try to chase away the feelings of despair I have. *I will not cry. I will not cry.*

Five

SKYE

I keep my brisk pace up on Hollywood Blvd. until I reach North La Brea, and take a quick left, the signs and shops all a blur as I try to outrun my stupid heart.

My thoughts are racing. Preston Hart...even thinking his name has a devastating effect on me. We were friends since pre-school. He was my best friend, my lover, my heart, but he left without a word.

I left the desert once he was gone, I had to. Without him there my father would have killed me, if not physically then emotionally. Was this meeting by chance, or did he come looking for me? I mentally shake myself. *Stop it, Skye, you can't afford to let him break you again.*

The clawing in my belly is starting to hurt. Telling myself being hungry is a state of mind can only last so long, my nerves will soon make the feeling go away soon. Why couldn't I have just stayed with Preston, he seems to be doing rather well for himself. But deep down I know the Preston I just saw isn't the boy I fell in love with. That boy would have never left me.

The need to flee the area makes my chest tighten even more,

the last thing I need is to have a panic attack on the streets of Hollywood. Foregoing the soup kitchen, I walk five or six blocks, stopping at the bus station and digging out the last of my change from my pocket. Right now, I'm the poor one and it seems he's the one with the money. I try not to dwell on how the time has changed us so much.

The Metro bus is running to my advantage this time...late. Stepping on the bus and putting in my last dollar fifty in change, I know what this means.

At this time of night there is a line of people getting on the bus, everyone is getting out of work and wanting to get out of the city. Public transportation is always an assault on all my senses, the press of the bodies around me and the stench of cologne mixed with body odor. The sweat of the working class is sickening. I can picture the look of contempt on my mother's face at the thought of using this means of getting around, a small half smile plays upon my lips.

I turn to the sea of faces, it looks like finding a seat isn't in the cards tonight. I have the choice between two spots. Taking the one with the easiest exit off the bus, I hold onto the pole as the bus takes off.

I keep my eyes on the route we're taking away from Hollywood and into Beverly Hills, heading down Wilshire Blvd. I've been in this part of Beverly Hills more times than I can count. There's a distinct class difference here, it's a very wealthy part of town. Where I've been on the poor side of town, I've seen people surviving on a couple of hundred dollars a month. Here people wouldn't dream of spending less than that on a pair of jeans.

In the last five years I've been out on my own, I've never once had to resort to using my family name to find somewhere to rest, but finally it has come to me going back and using my connections. I'm upset with myself that I'm going to do it, but it's mine, it's time to claim it. My father was right when he told me I would never amount to anything without him, that I'd need him to get anywhere in life. Time to show him he's nothing without me.

I powerwalk the last few blocks, feeling both relief and defeat as I get nearer to an end to my discomfort. It's time to put the past five years where they belong, in the past. Finally, I come to a stop at the corner of Rodeo and Wilshire. The lights of the Four Seasons bring back so many childhood memories. I feel a pang of sadness because not many of them are good. But the first time I came here at night as a child, I was in awe. It was lit up just like this. It looked larger than life, it still does actually.

The light changes showing me the walk signal, the sparkle of the hotel beckoning me over. The window displays show off the latest and greatest shoes and clothes from the exclusive stores inside and they always catch my eye. The first thing I see are the shoes, they are something that I would have bought without a second thought when I was a kept rich girl. It sickens me now, how I used to spend.

I keep walking past the hotel entrance. I just can't bring myself to walk in.

A flash of white in the window catches my eye. There's a petite waitress, her hair pulled back into a sleek bun. She has a warm smile that lights up her whole face, completely out of the ordinary in a town filled with Botox and silicone.

I see the plate she sets down and groan at the thought of tasting the steak. It's what I used to order, filet mignon with three cheese-mashed potatoes. My stomach growls and cramps, this hunger has me in physical pain. The meal holds my attention as she cracks some fresh pepper on the steak. I imagine it's cooked the way I like it, medium rare.

So entranced with watching the meal that the small voice startles me, I turn my head around and find that I'm looking down at the waitress that I just saw in the window. I'm five four; she must be about five foot. She's curvy with a sweet face that you automatically want to trust. She has a welcoming smile on her face and stands up a bit straighter, clearing her throat.

"Excuse me, Miss? Uh, hi, my name is Marie." She looks back over her shoulder at the restaurant then back at me.

"Uhhh, hi." *Great*, I think to myself. She has come out to run me off, a guest must have said something. "Please tell me no one was complaining about me standing here."

Her eyes go wide. "Oh, no. It's not that at all."

Seems my stomach wants to have conversations with anyone that will listen tonight. As if on cue it makes a loud grumble.

She tilts her head then says, "Oh, good, you're hungry. I was afraid to ask you."

I'm at a loss for words which in itself is amazing.

She takes over, not waiting for a response, gently reaching out and touching my hand. I flinch.

"I won't hurt you," she says and reaches out again and pulls me by my wrist, and I follow her into the restaurant. I'm so confused, that I am just following her, although, this is better than going to the front desk and using my father's name.

As we walk across the patio and through the glass doors into the restaurant, I'm conscious of my less than stellar appearance. I'm a lot thinner than I used to be, almost stick thin, and my clothes are a bit raggedy. She guides me into a secluded booth. Sliding in the seat, my mouth waters at the sight of the steak sitting on the table. My eyes transfixed on the plate of food, I'm so confused. "I, er... thank you," I mutter. It's all I can muster after the night I've had.

She clears her throat and I look up at her. She looks nervous all of a sudden and that's when I hear his baritone voice. "Yes. Thank you, Marie."

My eyes immediately snap to the face across the table. Holy

shit, it's Preston! Marie's voice breaks the silence as I glare at him. "This is Preston, he asked me to invite you in."

I can feel my face filling with rage, a red flush covering me. My heart is pounding in my ears keeping me from hearing what he's just told her. She glances at me, nods her head and rushes off.

As he watches her walk away, I stand and start moving out of the booth, but those dark chocolate eyes turn to me. "Sit," he commands in a low voice. So startled by the command, I instantly sit. Placing both hands on the table I frown at him. He gets up slowly and comes to my side of the table, tenderly touching my hand. The shock that goes through me has me jerking my hand back. I can see the perplexed look on his face as he sits himself firmly next to me in the booth, blocking my way out.

Preston pulls his plate over to this side of the table and starts to cut his food up. Unaware of what I'm doing I lean toward the food, watching his skillful hands working. The meat is cooked to perfection, juicy and rare. As he lifts his fork, I notice a platinum Rolex decorating his wrist. How in the hell did he afford that? I wonder if he is on the up and up or shady as hell like my father.

He turns his attention to me. "Relax, want a bite?" he asks with a charming grin.

"No," I say and then press my lips together in a firm line.

"Liar," he whispers and takes the succulent bite into his mouth. He chews slowly, his strong jaw moving with intent, exaggerating his enjoyment for my benefit.

I let out an un-ladylike snort and mumble, "Donkey."

He raises a brow and gives me a crooked grin, then turns back to his plate of food. "You never used to be this angry."

I'm almost tempted to pinch under his arm. "Yeah well, I'm a product of my environment."

Marie returns, stopping him from responding. She sets down a plate of food in front of me. I look down at the same meal he has. She asks Preston, "Is there anything else I can get for you?"

"No, thank you, Marie, that will be all." He's always had impeccable manners, his mother raised him well. She gives me a soft smile and leaves us to eat.

I watch as she walks away. "Eat," he says softly so my attention is drawn back to him.

Turning to face Preston in the booth, I have a standoffish tilt to my chin. "Quit telling me what to do," I somehow manage to say calmly, not letting him know how eager I am to eat. Hell, the food is the only thing keeping me here. I will just ignore the fact that he's also blocking me in.

He barks out a laugh and points at my plate. "From the noise your stomach is making I think it agrees with me."

Narrowing my eyes at him, he takes a forkful of potatoes while I study him. His suit is a charcoal gray, tailored perfectly. A moment of sorrow passes through me as I think about how far he's come. I bet his mama is so proud of him. I need to sock those old feelings away.

He's stopped moving, I pull my eyes away from his large hands and look up. A confident smile is playing about his full lips, and I recall how they felt on my skin in an unexpected flush of arousal. I continue to examine all of him when I pause, captured by his gaze.

I blush, knowing he was watching me drink him in.

"You done?"

"Done what?"

"Done appraising my charms." He has a tilt playing on his lips.

I don't bother answering him. I just nod my head indicating that yes, I'm done.

"Good, now eat."

I don't recall him being this demanding. Instead of following his order, I reach over and grab the white wine, giving him a smug look. "Cheers!" I bring the glass to my lips and the crisp taste of apples hits my palate followed by a hint of peach. Mmm, Pinot Grigio, one of my favorites. I've been hungry for so long that the finer things like wine hadn't even crossed my mind, but oh how I've missed the crisp taste. I tip the glass up with all intentions of finishing it, but just as the first gulp goes down, the glass is lifted away from my mouth and out of my hands. "Hey!"

Again, he laughs and cuts up the steak calmly, then pushes the plate in front of me. He then passes me a fork that I automatically take. I don't start eating but I press my lips together to keep myself from telling him to go fuck himself. All the hurt I felt when he left is overwhelming me right now.

His clipped words break the silence. "Where did all this rage come from, Skye?"

"It's always been there. I just don't keep it restrained anymore. Anyway, where did all this bossiness come from, Preston?"

"It's always been there. I just don't keep it restrained anymore," he returns, giving me a sarcastic smile

"Look at me, *Detka*, I know you're fighting me. It's ok."

That name, his name for me, had the ability to bring me to my knees. Then I remember, and a bitter laugh comes out. "What the fuck do you know? You left."

His eyes slightly narrow and his jaw is set in a firm line. "More than you think. Don't forget how well I know you."

"Correction, how well you used to know me," I can't help but quip.

You can feel the tension in the air as I gear up to push him firmly away. Marie's perfectly timed appearance stops the internal battle I am having. "How was everything?"

"Can I get you any dessert, or perhaps a coffee?"

Preston gives her a polite, "No, thank you," while I finally find my voice.

I've never been one to shy away from food and the pastry

chef here used to do an amazing job. "Yes, I'll have the Peruvian warm chocolate soufflé please."

She smiles. "Certainly." She turns and is off like a bubble of energy.

Preston's eyebrows raise. "You really think your stomach can handle that?"

I shrug. "Maybe."

He turns to me with concern on his face. "I don't think the dessert is a good idea. The way your stomach was making a racket, I think that will be overkill."

"I want it, are you telling me no?" I challenge him.

"No, I am telling you it isn't a good idea because it will make you sick. It's very rich. When was the last time you ate heavy like this?"

I know he's right, but I am stubborn. "I'll be ok, it's just a bit of sugar." I ignore his second question, it's been years.

"You're so stubborn, you know I'm right." He shakes his head. "I won't sit here and watch you make yourself sick"

I point to the door. "You can always see yourself out, no one is asking you to stay." I know it's rude of me since he invited me to eat, but I can't stop myself.

He clenches his jaw. "I happen to be staying here. If you find yourself in need of a bed or bathroom..."

I scoot back in the booth, so my back is now touching the wall. "Is that it? You fed the poor street girl, so now she has to pay up?" I can't keep the venom out of my tone.

He gives me an astonished look. "Absolutely not! I'm worried about you. I just want to know you'll be ok, that's all."

I just roll my eyes at him, no one is ever worried about me. I watch him pull out something from an inner jacket pocket and set it before me, it's his hotel key.

"Here, don't be a fool, Skye. The room number is on the key, use it if you need to, no strings attached." With that he places his hands on the table and pushes his way out of the booth standing and adjusting his suit. He stops Marie on his way out.

I pick up his room key and run my fingers across it, my options are pretty simple. On one hand I can name-drop and my father will foot the bill for it all. On the other hand, I can use Preston for a meal and a place to sleep. I notice the room, the presidential suite? I drop the key on the table and rub my temples, already knowing I am going to go there after I am done. I only hope he can keep the smug look off his face.

After I scarf down the dessert my stomach cramps. I clutch the key and leave the comfort of the booth, my belly overfull.

The opulent lobby never fails to amaze me, so elegant but at the same time these halls are filled with bad memories. The tiled floors are so glossy I can see my reflection in them. For a moment I see myself as I was as a girl with my parents, my mother holding my hand as we walk through, my little shoes clicking with each step. My other arm was in a cast from one of my father's lessons, our trip was supposed to make up for the 'accident'. Shaking my head, I bring myself out of the pain of the past and continue on. Passing the front desk, I recognize someone who is in my father's pocket. He looks at me and gives me a slimey smile and crooks a finger at me to come closer like he's been expecting me to show up. I'm sure the minute I am out of sight he will be picking up the phone to call my father. I keep walking past and flip him the bird, stepping into the elevator.

Six

PRESTON

I could kick myself. I found her. I found her! That private agent, Jeb, I hired kept sending me on a goose chase. Every lead he passed on was a dead-end. Five years of dead-ends and I was about to give up.

And what's the first thing I do? I leave her in the restaurant. Crap, it was only blind luck that got her here to this hotel and I freaking leave her. I walk through the lobby of the hotel mumbling *idiot* under my breath. I promised myself if I ever found her I'd never let her out of my sight again, but here I am walking away.

It was by chance that I saw her. Thank goodness I did. Jeb had narrowed the search on the Hollywood area, but there were very few potential leads. I wasn't even in town to search. I had business, but once it was over, I couldn't resist the old habit to comb the streets for just a little while. It was fate that took me to that particular street and it was just in time from the looks of things.

The strength and stiffness in her stance with that jackass on the street suggested she still had some fight left in her, but I'd say she was close to the edge. It was quite shocking to see her in that situation. All the times I imagined finding her as I drove the streets, I never thought it would be like that. Or rather, I hoped it wouldn't.

I knew it was her from the top of the street. I'll never forget how lush she is...or was. Her curvaceous body is always on my mind. She's thinned out the years she's been away, but I'd know her anywhere. I can't help but think about how well we used to fit together, how she feels beneath me. Her eyes glazed with pleasure, her full lips parted with a sigh. Her curls could wrap around my hand and fingers like a lover's caress.

And now, after all these years without her, searching for her, I leave her. Walking away was hard, I just couldn't sit there and watch her make herself sick.

I'll never forget the devastation I felt when Bob, her father, told me with a smug smile that she ran away when he told her I was gone. I thought for certain he was hiding her somewhere. I promised myself I would never give up looking, and now I've given her another way to run. What am I doing?

I slide the key card into the door to the presidential suite. They couldn't accommodate me in my usual suite and I could have taken a regular room, but the manager insisted on this room. I do try to enjoy the finer things that were always out of my reach. I grew up with nothing after all.

This kind of luxury should never be taken for granted. But this is too much, and now Skye is going to think I'm a flashy asshole if she comes up here.

I know I should be proud of what I have achieved, but the price I had to pay was too high. I lost her...and parts of myself too. But it did teach me self-preservation and has given me a ruthless drive to succeed. My thoughts turn to the night I left...

I have a bored expression on my face as Bob continues to

explain that when I get off the plane, someone will be waiting for me. They will have more detailed instructions on what work I'll be doing there. He has covered most of this more than once. He has been unbendable about most of his rules; but it's time to press again.

"I want to tell my mother and Skye that I'll only be gone for a month."

"No."

"I can't be so vague with my mother when she just had heart surgery, be smart Bob."

He nods once. "Alright, you can tell your mother you'll be away for a month, but there are conditions."

"What conditions?" I give him a puzzled look.

"You can't tell her who you work for, or why."

"Is that it?" I say angrily.

"No," he says with a cruel smile.

"What else?"

"You can only tell her on the condition that she promises not to tell Skye a thing."

There it is. "Why are you so against Skye knowing where I'm going?" I manage to sound calmer than I feel.

"It's for your protection, she won't approve of you working for me."

"Bullshit, Bob. She trusts me." I grip the arms of the chair to keep me from doing something dumb.

"You want the truth?"

"I think you owe me that much."

"Let's get this straight, I owe you nothing but the money I'm paying you."

"So you say. I still want to know why I can't tell her. You know, Bob, I'm going to come back and marry her." I don't know where the words came from, but they just slip out. It's always been my plan, but I didn't need that ass to know.

He lets out a mirthless laugh. "Is that what you think, boy? By the time you come back she'll have moved on to something better."

"We'll see, Bob, what else do I need to know?" I won't give him the pleasure of acting like a lowlife.

After I have listened to him drone on for another fifteen minutes, I'm dismissed. The suitcase that he provided me with suitable clothes for the trip in hand and a backpack on my back, I walk out the front door, not looking back at him to say anything more. As I make it to the end of the driveway, I pause, a sickening feeling in my stomach and turn and stare at Skye's window.

I hope she understands and knows deep within her heart that I would never just leave like this for no reason, even if that's what it looks like. It's for us, for the life I want us to have.

"Detka, wait for me..." I whisper the words in the language of my people, then I turn and walk away, vowing to return and be the man she needs.

I head home one last time to pack a few personal things and break the news to my mama about my trip, before I am collected by a car bound for the airport.

The past haunts me and no matter how many times I go over it in my head, I still don't know if I would make a different decision, knowing what I know now. All I know is that at the time I felt I had no choice. It breaks my heart to recall my Mama's tears when I told her I had to leave, and not being able to stand to see her so emotional, I caved and told her more than Bob agreed I could. I told her I was going to Russia. A decision which might have changed the course of my life.

Once she had composed herself, she asked me to sit with her and she placed a small bag in the palm of my hand. "If you get into trouble in my homeland, you show these," she told me.

I opened the bag and shook out what was inside. I gasped with shock when two heart shaped diamonds fell into my hand. Confused, I asked her where she got them from. She never talked about Russia, just taught me the language and some foods she would make. Never let on that she had these magnificent diamonds. Maybe she was afraid I'd sell them so we could have a better life.

"That's the way where I come from. People know the families by the diamonds they mine. If you are in trouble, these will help you. I hope you'll never need to use them." She had told me.

Thinking about the family diamonds reminds me to check the hotel safe. Who would have thought those gems that my Mama gave me to keep me safe, would in fact put me at the top of the diamond trading business worldwide?

I go straight to the safe to check on the extra gems I brought with me on this trip. They are all safe and accounted for. I had a good day today, struck a huge deal. It was well worth the drive out from Palm Springs just for that. But this trip has been worth far more than the gems I sold ever could be. If I'd passed it up, I wouldn't have found her, I've been looking across the country for her for five years.

She's never left my thoughts, I've worried about her constantly. Not knowing if she's safe. Wondering if she moved on, met someone new, started a family. I'd wonder if I ever found her how she would fit into my lifestyle. Would she be proud of me? Forgive me? All these questions eat me up inside. I couldn't stand thinking that she had a new life when I missed her so badly in mine, but I had to know she was okay. The thought of never seeing her again was killing me slowly. The thought of never again looking into her beautiful hazel eyes that flash green when she's annoyed...*fuck* I've missed her.

She is the other half of me, and now that I've finally found her I want to keep her with me and not let her out of my sight. It took everything I had not to chase her when she walked away from me in the street. I calmly got in my car and got my guy on the phone as I watched her go. I couldn't follow her, she would have heard the Aston's roar, so I had him track her, but it was a risk. One that almost cost me dearly. When he called to say he had lost her, I thought I had blown my only chance. Then I looked up and saw her through the restaurant window. I couldn't believe my luck. I was meant to find her today.

I'm worried she's making herself sick right now, devouring that dessert, but if I go back down there, she'll shovel it in with a grin just to prove me wrong. I'm even more worried that she won't come up though.

I take my suit jacket off and put it on the back of the chair at the desk. Not able to stand the confinement of my shoes any longer, I slip them off too. I'm so much more comfortable barefoot.

I pour some brandy into a glass. Taking a small sip, the fire trail it leaves in its wake is an acquired taste, but I enjoy it. Swirling the liquid in the glass and setting it down on the desk, I turn and walk out onto the balcony that overlooks Rodeo. The traffic is still bad at this time of night. I nervously check my watch; it's been thirty minutes.

I can't afford to lose her again.

I can't leave it to chance, she might be slipping away. I step back inside and dial the restaurant, asking the hostess for Marie.

"Hello, this is Marie, how may I help you?"

"It's Preston Hart, is Skye still there?" My tone is all business but inside I'm afraid she's already gone.

"Skye? Oh! Your lady friend, yes she's still here."

I release a breath I didn't realize I was holding. "Thank you, will you call me when she leaves?"

"Sure."

"Thanks, Marie." I hang up the phone and rub my temples.

It's been a long day and I'm going back home early tomorrow, with her in tow. I vow this to myself. I really should text Lea or Craig to let them know I found her, but I'm going to be selfish for a while. Now that I've found her, I won't let her go. I need her.

I have everything a man could ever want: money, cars, gems that could pay for it all twice over. I could retire tomorrow. But I don't have the one person I did it all for. I lost her five years ago, and I won't make that mistake again.

I pace the room, my heart in turmoil. I haven't felt this way about anyone but her, that's why I haven't been in a real relationship since I left. She is the only one for me. I failed her in the worst possible way with leaving without a word, but if she gives me the chance to prove it, I will never fail her again. I'd show her I work hard for every penny and I've become something she can be proud of.

Picking up the glass, I toss back the rest of the brandy and unclasp my watch, setting it on the desk. I take off my custom black diamond cufflinks and pull off the matching tie bar. My bracelet never comes off, sometimes it's the only thing I wear; it was my father's. It's a simple solid soviet gold bracelet. He would never take it off and I wear it the same way.

I pull off my tie, laying it across the foot of the bed. My belt is tossed on the chair and I deftly remove my pants, folding them and placing them next to my growing pile of clothes.

The room is completely silent. Silence is rare for me and usually drives me up the wall, but I am feeling far too lazy to dig out my iPod to blast my favorite rock music. My thoughts are too loud in my head, I need to find some balance. I walk to the bathroom. My shaving kit is already on the sink and I consider using it, but the view of my face in the mirror isn't too bad. A bit scruffy, but I can last another day. Taking off my shirt and letting my boxer briefs fall to the floor, I turn the shower on. I turn up the hot water and change the pulse setting on the shower to soothe the ache in my muscles. Stepping into the stream and closing my eyes, I let the water relax me.

I soap up my body for a quick wash, but as I slide my hand down my stomach and rub the soap lower, Skye's face flashes through my head. Memories of her are never far from my mind, but this particular one jumps into my head as my slick hand skims over that sensitive skin on my dick. It's one of my favorite memories of us, on the golf course on prom night. I can still recall the way she felt sliding down onto me for the first time. I try to force my mind to shift back to the present and the fact that she is here. My body has a different agenda, my thoughts drifting back to the image of her in the restaurant and the way she took the first bite of filet off the fork. That small glimpse of her tongue as she welcomed that bite into her mouth had me imagining what it would feel like if she welcomed me there.

Turning into the spray, I duck my head under the water and try to wash away these thoughts. Now is not the time. She is here, and I can't blow it by letting myself think this way. As I wash my hair, I realize I feel more relaxed than I have in a long time, it must be because I finally know where she is. That makes up my mind. I get out of the shower. I am going to go get her- enough is enough.

Seven

SKYE

I have both hands on the table and am staring down at the key to his room. I know I'm going to use it, but I still need to get up the nerve to do it. I have to encase my heart in a safe, I can't let him break me like he did before. It's taken me five years to come this far and the pain I feel is still real.

Marie slides into the booth across from me.

"You know he isn't a bad guy." She nervously plucks an imaginary piece of lint off her uniform.

"You sound like you've known him for a while."

"I've known him for a few years now. He's been a good friend."

"I knew him once..."

"He's been looking for you for as long as I've known him."

My eyes widen slightly. "Really?" I always thought it was Lea and Shaina that were on the lookout for me and maybe Craig, but I couldn't get past the idea that they might all know where Preston was. That they were somehow in on him leaving.

She nods her head. "He's paid countless people to keep

watch for you. Only you don't look like the picture he shows everyone."

I wonder what picture he's showing people. I could ask but I don't want the walls that I'm building around myself to fall. "How did you meet him?"

"He got me fired from a diner a few blocks over." She chuckles.

"What? That's an ass move!"

"Really it was all my fault. I dropped his dinner in his lap. The owner saw it happen and immediately fired me."

"Oh, I see."

"It turned out for the best, he's the one that got me the job here. It's been a blessing."

"Does he know the management here?" This interests me since my father has his hand in the management team here.

"He used to be friends with the former food and beverage director."

"So, tell me more about your friendship. Do you guys hang out outside of work?"

"Not really. He's been over to the house once or twice, Peter and Preston will have a pint and chat."

"Peter, is that your husband?" She has a kind face and usually I don't get a chance to know people and well, I am sick of being alone.

"Yes, we've been married now for four years. Preston met me when I was expecting our son." She looks around the room. The restaurant isn't full tonight, but I know how unprofessional it is for a server to sit with a customer.

"It's good that he found you a job. That would have been horrible."

"He more than got me a job. He also paid for my Peter to finish his accounting degree. We wouldn't be where we are today without Preston." She reaches across the table and gently squeezes my hand. "Just give him a chance, Skye. I'd love to sit and talk to you, but I have to get back to work now. Maybe we will see each other again."

"It was nice meeting you, Marie." I smile. "Thank you for everything."

I stand outside the door to the presidential suite for a few moments, still in shock at how far he has come from the trailer park. I'm a bit sad that I wasn't there to see him succeed in his dreams. When did this all happen? Have I really been gone that long?

I hear the phone ringing and wait. I don't want to walk in while he's taking a call. Listening for his voice when the ringing stops, I hear nothing. Trying to get up the nerve to walk in is getting the better of me. This is silly, I can't stand here all night. Either I go in like I intended, or I go back down to the slime ball at the front desk and admit defeat.

I straighten my spine, lift my chin and slip the card into the slot. The green light on the door flashes, and I hear a click. Opening it slowly, I peek my head in and don't see him, so I slip in and shut the door harder than I normally would so that the sound echoes through the suite and he will know he isn't alone. I walk in and see his bag still by the door. The room opens into a sitting area and off to the left is what must be the bathroom. This must be their smaller suite because I have been in the family suite.

I notice that the shower is on in the bathroom as I walk past the open door. One bed...hmmm, I hope the donkey doesn't think I'm going to sleep with him. He has no chance. I notice a lounge chair that will be the perfect place for me to catch a few hours of sleep; I've slept in worse. The years I've been on my own, there been plenty of shelters and nights on the streets. I walk over to the desk, trailing my fingers along the polished mahogany wood, picking up one of his cufflinks and twirling it between my fingers, watching the little crystals catch the light.

"I knew you'd like those," he says in a teasing tone.

"Jesus Christ!" I jump, dropping the cufflink, but I manage to not go off on him for scaring me. After all, I'm taking advantage of his generous hospitality. "Jackass," I mumble as I turn to face him and catch my breath at the sight that greets my eyes.

Hot Fuck!

Preston's standing there with just a towel slung low on his hips, his skin still dewy from the shower. He always had a six pack, but fuck it's impressive now. I could see my fingers using those abs like a ladder, perhaps even falling a step or two along the way. The very defined V that disappears into his towel just begs to have teeth sunk into it. I can feel the fire slowly starting to burn within me as I imagine doing just that. *Come on, Skye, pull it together*, I think as my eyes travel down his body. The towel isn't doing much to cover him up. He has muscular legs and skin that looks as if the sun gods kissed him everywhere. He always had a nice body but damn were the years kind to him.

"Like what you see?" he asks and leans against the wall crossing his arms.

I bring my eyes up to meet his. I should know better than to be caught gawking like a schoolgirl at a damn man. The problem is he's like a shot of whiskey, a rich, smoky shot with many layers to it. Something so divine that once you taste it you crave it and will do anything to get it. I raise a sarcastic brow. "It isn't anything to write home to Mama about." The outright lie comes easy. I guess I've hardened a lot over the past few years.

I watch as his eyes narrow and form a hardness about them. That's a new look, he didn't like that.

He moves forward and stands in front of me. "Evil," he says with a smirk and what I think is a hint of admiration.

I lift my chin a bit higher and incline my head in agreement. "Always have been deep down."

He lowers his face to mine, so we are almost nose-to-nose; he smells like fresh linen on a summer's day. I find myself caught in the fantasy of tasting his freshly showered skin. What the hell is wrong with me?

He taps under my chin with a finger to grab my attention. The look on his face makes me think he knows exactly where my thoughts are.

My heartbeat is racing through my chest, and as I nervously shift a curl falls directly in front of my face.

He lifts his hand up toward my face, and I flinch just a little. He takes the curl and wraps it around a finger then tucks it behind my ear. The intimate gesture has a blush creeping up my cheeks and a shiver of delight rolling through my body. I've never gotten over him, but that doesn't mean I won't fight him. I'll think with my brain, because my heart is stupid as shit.

I see a flash of fire in his eyes before we break eye contact, and he walks over to the side of the bed where I now see a small suitcase. He bends down, and I swear he must be able to feel the heat of my stare as I wish for the towel to fall.

"You might want to cover your eyes," he states, barely containing his laugh. He rummages through the bag on the floor and pulls out a pair of black board shorts and a white t-shirt. I'm unable to take my eyes off him. He's always had this kind of hold over me, but now he screams power, strength, and control; things that attract me and attributes I wish I had. He stands with fluid grace, his muscles flexing down his back as he moves. I have never seen a more enticing specimen of a man; it's hard to believe he's the same boy I used to watch skate empty pools in high school. The lighting in the room isn't the best but it looks as though he has some markings on his back. I reach out but stop my hand in mid-reach. I want to touch him.

Then the towel drops. *Sweet baby Jesus* he dropped the towel!

My eyes snap right to his rear; it's muscular, round, and there's not a single sign of a tan line. He's bronzed a golden brown all over...Damn. He's changed, he went from Quicksilver hot to Tom Ford sophisticated. He bends over and steps one foot into the pant leg quickly followed by the other and pulls them up. I can't stop noting all the changes to his body and have to curl my hands into themselves because I want to trace my fingers over every defined muscle.

His deep chuckle makes me flush red, shaking me out of my lustful daze. He's standing before me with his shirt in his hand. My mouth feels as if I've been walking through the hot desert without a sip of water. My breath hitches. My reaction to him pisses me off. He's always been able to make me flush red as well as act like a school girl with her first crush. Well, he was my first everything. Something about his carefree smile and the way he flipped his hat backwards had me every time. He smirks at me before tossing his shirt on the bed. Crossing the room to the desk, he pours himself a tumbler full of amber liquid and turns to watch me silently with his brow raised.

I move back a few feet to the chair. All of this has made me weak at the knees and I need to sit. What the hell is wrong with me? It's not like I'm a virgin or some inexperienced woman, hell it isn't like I've never been with him. He comes back over to me and holds the glass out to me. My first reaction is to smack that glass out of his hand, and I see his hand grip it tighter, seemingly reading my thoughts.

"Drink. It will help relax you." There's no mistaking the command in his tone, but this will be done on my terms. I grab the glass out of his hand and give him a sneer and chug back the small amount of liquid.

It takes a split second for the liquid heat to start burning. I jump up and make a big show of putting the glass on the side table. I try to cover the wheeze and know I failed when he laughs again. "You sip brandy, Skye. You don't toss it back like a cheap shot."

I narrow my eyes in annoyance. "No shit! That would have been nice to know before you were a drill sergeant and ordered me to drink." The heat of the brandy is now mixing with all the food I ate. A small groan escapes, and I clutch my belly. I can see the concern on Preston's face. He steps forward and I hold up a hand stopping him, not sure if I'm going to throw up yet and not wanting to do it on him if I do.

Preston turns and grabs his shirt off the bed and as he's putting it on he says, "I'm going to run to the boutique in the lobby and pick you up something to sleep in." He takes an appraising look at me. It's clear he's giving me some space since it's obvious I don't feel well. If my stomach weren't hurting so badly I would have some smart comment for him. I don't like that he is going to put me even more in his debt.

"You don't have to, I can make do. Plus, it's eight o'clock at night. Are they even open this late?" I won't mention that he more than likely wouldn't get my size correct. After being on my own for so long it's hard for me to imagine the luck I am having in the last day. When I woke up this morning in the women's shelter my backpack was gone; the only reason my guitar wasn't taken is because I slept spooned with it.

"They're open until nine. I'll be back." He grabs his wallet and heads out the door. Who the hell does he think he is, The Terminator?

My body isn't used to this much food or any alcohol, and I'm feeling sick as a dog. I go into the bathroom and wet a washcloth and press it to my face. The nausea slowly calms down. I straighten myself and mentally give myself a pep talk. I've gotten through worse, I can get through this. I need to relax. After my day, a hot shower is just what I need.

I swiftly peel off my clothes and discard them on the floor. I hope he can find something in my size because I don't think I can stand to put those dirty rags back on, after all they were torn to hell today and dragged across the sidewalk. I really wish I had my backpack at this point. I only had a few things, but they were clean and mine. I turn toward the shower and make it as hot as I can take it. Stepping in, I quickly wash my hair and body with the soap the hotel has provided.

I'm starting to feel better as I step out, my body and mind not on high alert for once. The suite is clean and has no lingering scent of stale cigarettes or sex. It's reassuring to know that I won't have to worry about someone breaking in to do me harm. I look in the bathroom mirror and run my fingers through my hair, trying to untangle my curls.

I don't have the energy to wash my clothes in the sink, so I scoop them up and dump them in the shower. Picking up the liquid body soap, I squeeze some on the heap and turn the spray on high. The powerful spray rapidly washes away the soap and takes with it some of the Hollywood grime. I'm on autopilot as I wring out the few items and hang them on the towel bars. If he can find me something else to wear, I won't have to worry about whether they will be dry in the morning.

I wrap a towel around my body and listen to see if Preston is back. I hear only silence, so I go out into the room. I notice his dress shirt is still on the bedroom floor, so I decide not to stand here in a towel waiting for him to get back and grab it. The crisp white shirt engulfs me to my mid-thigh, so at least I won't have to put my dirty panties back on. I feel exhausted as I button it up, it could be the fact that I feel safe. I seldom feel safe. My home was not a safe place for me, and the life I have had since I left has put me even more on my guard. The only times I can ever remember feeling safe were with Preston. His scent wraps itself around me, it's comforting and smells like home.

He was my safe place, he was my home. I take a deep breath and open the door to walk back into the room. He still isn't back, which gives me time to get cozy on the chair so he can't argue, perfect. I pause in the middle of the room, taking stock, then head to the closet and find just what I'm looking for, an extra blanket and pillow. An expensive looking garment bag is hanging in there, but I'm so tired physically and mentally that my curiosity has left me. I have so many questions for him. But I won't ask, at least not tonight.

I take my bedding and go over to the chair, pushing the smaller ottoman flush with it to make my makeshift bed. I step back once I have made up my bed and smile. I'm very pleased with my little setup and I give myself a small hug. For the first time in a long time I'm relaxed. I close my eyes and breathe in deeply, feeling that same safe feeling of being with him again, then mentally shake myself because he left. He isn't my safe place any more. It's terrifying how just his scent can affect me.

I hear fumbling at the door and hurry into my little bed. I know this is so ungrateful, but I want to avoid any conversation. I face myself toward the door out of habit and relax my face, closing my eyes. My heart is pounding so loudly as he opens the door, I swear he must be able to hear it.

Preston is very quiet as he walks in. I can just see enough of him through my thick lashes to know that his eyes briskly scan the room then settle on me. He stares for a moment at me, but I can't read his expression. I slow down my breathing and relax my face and body. I've had plenty of practice doing this, from all those times my father would storm through the house looking for me. My pulse picks up at the thought of being in that situation again. I will *not* let my mind take me there now.

He quietly walks over to the desk and drops his purchases,

then moves toward me. He stands right in front me and leans down. Crap. I'm screaming in my head and chanting *don't move, just breathe!* His hand moves toward my face and I fight the urge to react. It's a physical art to be panicking on the inside and not flinching as I feel his knuckles caress my cheek.

"I've missed you so much, *Detka*," he murmurs to himself.

I almost didn't catch what he said because my heart is beating so fast.

He walks over to the bed and I see him insert his thumbs into the band of his shorts and pause. He looks over at me and removes his hands, then shuts the light off next to the bed and climbs in. The room is in complete silence and it only takes a few minutes for his soft snores to fill the air. It takes me a little longer to relax into my makeshift bed.

I'm woken out of a dead sleep being dragged out of bed by my hair. "NO!" I scream and start my struggle to get free from him. I'm quickly backhanded across the face; I can taste the metallic blood from a split lip. The pain from these types of beatings no longer has the ability to shock me. I kick with the heel of my foot, feeling it connect and a curse soon follows. The only word I am able to form is 'no' and it's being screamed at the top of my lungs, "NO, NO, NO, NO, NO!!" The tears are flowing down my face as I try to beat him off me. I feel my face being firmly grasped into his hands as I try to break free. I'm in a full-blown panic. This will not happen again without my putting up a fight, I don't know if I can live through this again.

A heart-wrenching sob escapes me and with all my strength I kick out again, then a new voice breaks in. "For fuck's sake, Skye... WAKE THE FUCK UP!"

I can't escape, his strength overwhelms me...but that new voice...it's home and I let the tears run free.

"Skye!" My face is given a little shake. "Skye, open your eyes.

Fuck...Open your eyes NOW, Skye!" At this command my eyes pop open.

I look at my surroundings through my tears. It takes me a moment to realize where I am. I look up into his face and whisper, "Preston?" He moves into action and scoops me up into his strong arms and takes me to the bed. I immediately start fighting him but he sits on the side of the bed not letting me go from his arms. "Stop!" he barks at me. "I'm not going to hurt you."

He lets his grip on me loosen and pulls the sheets back so I can get in. When I move all the way to the other side of the bed, he climbs in beside me. I'm still whimpering, trying to control the tears that continue to fall. He curses and reaches over, curling an arm around my waist and pulling me flush to his front. I start to kick my legs again, I'm half asleep but unable to control the fight reflex even though I know its Preston. He throws one of his legs over mine to keep me still, then wraps his arms around me firmly, holding me tight. I jerk a few times.

"Stop, Skye! Sleep. Just sleep." He moves one of his arms to cradle my head and moves my hair back from my face. "Relax now, it'll be alright. Just like old times."

I swallow hard as memories from the past flash through my head. Memories of how he would hold me when I slept, and how he would drive the demons of my mind away. The scent of him surrounds me and his gentle touch on my temples relaxes me. He has me firmly secured next to him, and I find the restraint of his arms so comforting. I'm so damn tired, it's not long before I'm drifting off to sleep.

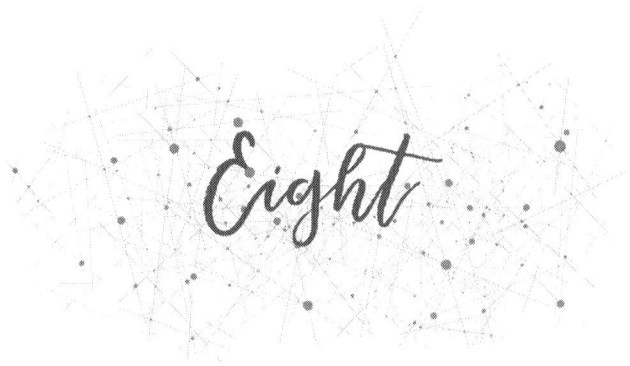

Eight

PRESTON

Her tiny moans have woken me up from one of the most peaceful sleeps I've had in a long time. My arms are still secure around her, but the comforter has fallen off us during the night. Her soft body is pushing back into my morning erection and though I have tried so hard to be a gentleman and not make her feel uncomfortable, right now I want to forget my manners, pin her down, and fuck her into tomorrow. But I have enough control not to ravish her on the spot; my mind knows she was having a dream and not inviting me to take advantage of her.

Her moans quiet down and she starts snoring, it's rather cute. While she's asleep in my arms, the previous night plays back in my head. I had hoped she wouldn't still suffer from the nightmares, but it's worse than I feared. She was a little hellcat, blindly fighting me off when I'm twice her size. I've always admired her spirit and the fire she possesses, but she was terrified last night. I've spent the past few years fantasizing about having her in my bed again, I can't let her go.

The California sun is in full effect this morning, lighting up the room. She starts fussing in my arms like she has been doing on and off all night. But when I gently stroke her hair, she settles back down. I glance at the clock, it's only 8:30 am. I'm reluctant to leave the bed just yet, her soft form fills my arms perfectly. I have missed this so much.

My shirt that she's wearing, hugs her curves the way it has twisted in her sleep. It has ridden up, leaving her bare from her waist down. The roundness of her hips has my attention. My dick jumps in anticipation, and I have to mentally give him a 'down boy.' It might be time for me to leave the comfort of the bed and make use of the shower.

After my shower, I pull out an old T-shirt I had packed. When I unfold it, I see the fates are working in my favor. It's my Guns N' Roses shirt that she bought me at a concert. It holds such good memories and has always made it feel like she wasn't so far away. Now she's here, and I don't want that to change, so my task is to convince her to drive back with me.

When I walk back into the room she is still sleeping, and I wonder when the last time she had a full night's rest was. Seeing her laying there, a punch of guilt slams into me. She doesn't understand that I had to leave. I just have to find the right time to explain it all to her, if she will let me.

I move over to the side of the bed, tempted to caress her face and run my fingers through those caramel strands. Fuck I've missed her so bad.

"Skye." I keep my voice soft so I don't startle her. "Wake up, *Detka*."

Her eyes slowly peek open and the glazed green looks like the moss after a summer's rain at home. Fucking stunning. The soft look on her face changes, her eyes narrow, and I swallow because I know that look.

"Don't call me that." She scrambles and sits up pulling the blankets up to cover her.

"What, Skye? That's your name."

"Detka... don't ever call me that again." She gives me a stony glare.

I hold my hands up. "I'm sorry, it slipped out."

"Is that the same shirt from when we were in high school?" she blurts out.

She's always been good at changing the subject when she doesn't want to talk about something. For now I won't press too hard. I know she has the ability to shut me out completely and I can't risk that, not now.

"Yeah, it is." I take pity on myself and break eye contact, walking to the window to watch the cars going by while I gather my thoughts. Out of the corner of my eye I see her scanning my body. Maybe there is some hope. I turn back to her and she quickly looks away.

"These are for you." I point to the few bags on the table.

"You didn't have to do that, but thanks."

"It was nothing. Do you want me to drive you anywhere? Back home maybe?"

Her eyes are filled with expression. She doesn't even have to speak, and I can see her mind working. She has a look of what looks like resignation on her face. She visibly swallows then clears her throat. "Palm Springs? You moved back home?"

Both my eyebrows raise at her question. "I never moved away, Skye, I was only gone for three months."

"Oh, well I didn't know, you know... cause I wasn't told," she says in a dry tone.

Ahhh yes, there's her spirit. She stiffens her spine and sits up a bit straighter, turning toward me. Now the buttons on the shirt are giving me the perfect view of her cleavage. Damnit, now is not the time to start thinking with my smaller brain.

"Eyes up here, buddy," she snaps as she waves her hands and points to her eyes. I make eye contact and give her a small smirk waiting for her to speak. "Yes, it's time I went back. I haven't been able to find work here, obviously."

Well, well, well... my little firecracker is willing to go back. I don't think she would take it well if I did a happy dance. "Okay, I'd like to head out shortly to beat traffic." I'm so damn elated that she has agreed. I thought I would have more of a battle on my hands when I finally found her. Play it cool, buddy, if she thinks you want her back, she will do the opposite.

It's evident she is relieved and relaxes slightly, murmuring, "Thanks, I'll make sure I get gas money for you when I get home."

I bark out a laugh and shake my head. "I don't need your money."

She gives me a nonchalant shrug. "I don't like being in anyone's debt."

"Well, whatever the case, I won't take your money." She must forget I've been in her debt for years, all the things she's bought and given my family.

"I'll go and get dressed then so we can be on our way." She rolls out of bed and rushes over to the desk, grabbing the bag and slipping into the bathroom.

When she comes back into the room, I find myself giving her the same treatment she gave me. Eyeing her up and down, I break my intense stare and try to focus on the TV. After last night I'm sure she feels a little vulnerable, and I can't help the urge to protect her, my past failure always on my mind.

"Enjoying the view?" she mimics my tone and has a sarcastic smirk on her face.

My face twitches by the corners of my mouth. "Yes, I am."

She grits her teeth, and I can tell she's fighting back a scathing remark. My eyes follow her across the room as she paces back and forth. It's nice to see some of her habits haven't changed.

I slowly rise from the bed and grab my bag. "Ready to hit the road?"

"Yep, let's get this over with."

As we walk through the hotel, I'm aware of the looks we are getting. I wouldn't be surprised if Bob has already been notified that she's been found. Well, it won't be by me, I haven't done his dirty work for years. Those days are long gone. We wait at the valet podium as they pull the car up, and I watch her face as she takes a good look at my baby. I love this car.

I check the mirrors and set the radio station, an 80's tune softly plays through the speakers. We have the same taste in music, it's another thing that made us close. I glance at her before I set off. "Ready?"

She turns in her seat and gives me a long look then plants a fake smile on her face. "Yep, overjoyed to get back."

I ignore her sarcastic response, just glad that I'm getting her to come home. I pull the car out onto the street and weave in and out of traffic until we are finally on the highway. The way she and by she, I mean my car, handles the turns and drives so smooth lets me forget about my passenger for a little while.

The radio softly plays, and we are completely silent. This would make most people uncomfortable, but not us. We drive for a couple of hours just listening to music, her softly singing a couple of the songs. I forgot how the sound of her voice could send shivers down my spine.

As we are pulling off the 110, I feel my hands start to go clammy. Now that I've got her this far, I don't know how things will go. Will she want to see me again? Will I have to beg? Will she run again? I hate not knowing, not having control. In no time we are driving down Vista Chino. I turn down Monte Vista, knowing the route to her house better than my own. Glancing at her a few times, I see that she keeps her face forward. She portrays herself as calm and cool, but I suspect underneath there is a torrent of emotions.

"Your mom is going to be so happy to see you." I doubt the words as soon as they are out of my mouth. I'm just trying to make conversation to break up the thoughts in my head.

"Yeah..." She nervously bounces her foot.

Turning on Las Palmas, dread consumes me. Soon I will deliver her home and have to drive away. I don't want her to leave yet. As we turn onto her street, Ladera Circle, the car hugs the sharp turns, climbing up the mountainside.

Her foot is still bouncing, and it concerns me that she's nervous. "Are you alright?" I look quickly over at her.

"Yeah, I'm fine," she replies as her foot keeps going.

"You don't look so well, you sure?" I don't believe her. I let the silence continue for a minute then clear my throat waiting for an answer.

She turns a fake sunny smile my way. "Just another day in paradise." I know she's being sarcastic, we used to hate it when the tourists said that.

As we pull further up her street the road is all torn up and there are construction signs everywhere.

"You can stop here," she says suddenly. We are literally three houses away, but she seems adamant. "You don't need to get the tar and rocks on your car."

I pull the car into the next drive. "You sure? I can take you up, I don't mind."

"I'm sure, thanks for the ride."

"I can walk you up, part of me wants to see your parents' faces when they see you." I give her a small grin.

"No, thank you, this is something I need to do on my own."

She opens the door and I feel panic. "Skye! Wait!" I blurt it out before I have time to think what I'm doing.

"Yes?" She has a raised brow and a tightness about her lips.

I look into her face and give her my boyish smile. "Maybe we can meet up for coffee sometime?"

"Hmmm coffee, maybe. I'll call you." She doesn't smile, she just walks off down the street to her house. I know damn well she doesn't have my number. I sigh and reluctantly pull out of the drive and head back to my house.

"Take care of yourself," I mutter to myself as I watch her get smaller in the rearview mirror.

Nine

SKYE

I stand at the end of our driveway and stare. Some things never change, and the house I grew up in hasn't changed at all. I try to summon the nerve to walk up, I must have been staring at the house long enough to be noticed. I see the blinds move and I feel my mother's stare. She'll be watching from the shadows for sure, and I know I haven't changed so much in the last few years that she doesn't know who she's looking at.

The few people I got to know on the streets couldn't understand why a rich girl would choose to live like I was, that nothing could be that bad at home. I mean yeah, I had all the fine dining and shopping I could handle, but it was all the other stuff. Stuff that no one should *ever* put another person through.

Eleven pm rolls around and still not a sound to alert me that he's waiting. I get up from where I'm sitting in the corner, watching my door and look out the window. I don't see him out by the palm tree where he usually waits until the house lights go off.

I do see my father though, standing in the driveway with one of his slimeball friends. They both look toward my window talking and my father points toward me. I move back into the shadows where I won't be seen. My father nods his head and they both laugh and walk back toward the house.

My breathing becomes heavy and I try to calm it.

Breathe... one, two, three... breathe...

I can't panic, not now... oh please not now. My father wouldn't go that far, would he?

Standing in the corner of my room, frozen with fear, I hear the handle to my door shake and then cursing.

"Preston, now would be a really good time to show up," I plead softly into my empty room.

I hear a key put into the door and it slowly opens, the light from the hallway reveals my father. He looks toward my bed. Stupidly I didn't even think of trying to make it look like I was in it. He switches the light on and scans the room.

I try and give myself a mental pep talk, "Don't let him see you're afraid, he wants that. Be brave! Be a warrior!"

"Why are you awake?" he barks when his eyes land on me.

He expected me to be passed out, that confirms he tried to drug me. "Because your wife drank the glass you gave me." I start feeling a little braver. Preston will be here any minute. He will save me.

"Ungrateful little bitch!" he sneers at me.

"You can leave my room now," I say, calmer than I feel.

"It's payback time. I thought I would be nice and take the fight out of you." He moves fully into the room and shuts the door behind him.

"You'll never take the fight out of me, not even if I'm dead." I'm seething but so scared and I take a step back and the wall stops me from moving any further. My hands fist at my sides.

That doesn't stop him from moving forward. "You'll do as you're told, you made a deal."

"The fuck I did, it's my money! You just want people to think it's yours while you still can!" I shout. I can't keep the anger from my voice.

I didn't realize he was close enough to strike me until he backhands me and I feel the sharp pain followed by the metallic taste of my blood that starts filling my mouth.

"You'll learn some respect!" he roars at me as he punches me in the stomach. This makes me drop to my knees, gasping for air. Grabbing a fistful of my hair, he drags me back to my bed, then lifts me by my hair like a ragdoll. I refuse to scream and give him the satisfaction of knowing he hurt me.

"I paid for your desert rat's mother to live, now it's time to pay me back. My friend John will be coming, and he'll have his way with you. Go ahead and fight him, you'll lose. He'll love it. I'll surely get a bonus." He smacks my face again.

This feels different than the other times. He's usually careful about my face; he wouldn't want anyone seeing my face bruised up. What does he mean his friend is going to have his way with me? I should be quiet but I'm not going down without a fight.

"Preston will be here any minute," I snap, praying he will get here right now

He gives me a cocky know-it-all look and lets out a sinister laugh. "Your little boyfriend can't help you anymore. He's gone, and he won't be back."

I always kept a stony silence about that part of my life. Who wants to admit how the people who gave you life treated you?

The front door opens, and my mother stands there with her mouth hanging open. She isn't happy to see me, just like I had expected. I didn't expect a warm welcome, but it still stings. The years haven't been kind to her at all. The last time I saw her she was drugged and lying in bed. I suppose that was my fault since it should have been me, but then everything was always my fault. I walk toward her and not one damn ounce of affection enters the woman's eyes as she looks me up and down.

"Hello, Mother." I force myself to say.

She greets me with silence and opens the door a little further for me to come in. She wouldn't dare deny me entry to *my* home, but that doesn't make me welcome. I pause midstride as my father's voice bellows through the door, "Victoria, who is it?" Ahh, finally some emotion in my mother's eyes. Fear. She's afraid to let him know I'm here. I wonder who she's afraid of more right now? I could wish that she would sneak me in and give me time to prepare to face him, but she never was on my side.

They knew when I left I would come back one day and claim what's mine. I'm the enemy.

"It's Skye, Bob. She's back." My heart sinks as I hear his footsteps coming down the hall. I should be prepared, but how can you prepare for this? I may be stronger, but I must face my fears to try and banish them.

My mother opens the door wider and his big beefy hand reaches out and pulls me in by my hair. My mother doesn't have time to close it behind me before he starts. He's 6'0" and rounder than Santa Claus, with a bald shiny head. I open my mouth to greet him, but I'm not able to get one word out before he backhands me right across the face.

"BOB! HER FACE!" my mother screams.

The damage has already been done. The metallic taste of blood fills my mouth and this time it is not a nightmare Preston can wake me from. I use the back of my hand to swipe at my mouth. "Slacking off at the gym while I was away?"

His face turns beet red, and I know this is just the start of my welcome home. I'm sure he will keep this pace up until he is worn out or until he has to call one of his doctor cronies to come and stitch me up.

"Fucking whore!" The venom is clear in his voice as he uses his favorite name for me. Then instead of another smack, his big beefy fist comes flying at my face. I try to move out of the way, but this only makes his fist clip me right under my chin.

My head flies back and hits the wall behind me, and he catches me by my shirt before I hit the floor.

"Why did you come back?" he spits in my face.

"You know why, it's only a month until by law I can claim what's mine." Not the smartest thing to say but it's the truth.

"If you make it until then," he sneers, then slams me back against the wall, knocking the breath from me.

I'm numb, I don't feel a thing. I've gotten really good at blocking out pain and feelings. It's one of the few things he taught me - to conceal the pain, because showing him any reaction just makes him happy.

I'm not sure how long he takes his anger out on me, I just know it needs to end soon. He kicks my feet out from under me. I know I am falling, it's as if this is playing in slow motion. Then my face bounces off the cool Spanish tile in the foyer and my world goes dark.

I wake in my own bed and can barely move. I don't know how long I was out. I'm still in the same clothes, and I can feel the blood dried on my cracked lips. I see water on the nightstand but can't face sitting up to drink. Some welcome home party! Actually, if I'm honest, this wasn't as bad as I was expecting. I mean hell, I'm alive.

Ten

PRESTON

From the car I sit and look at my house, the house I got for my Mama and Skye. For us. The character of the desert is alive in this house. It sits on the last road up the mountain. These houses almost never go on the market, but I was lucky and scooped it up quickly. The house doesn't look like much from the driveway. You pull into a small courtyard, filled with desert lilies that are a light orangish red in color, then you see the beauty of the house.

As soon as I walk in the door my mother comes to greet me. "Hello, Mama." I kiss her cheeks and step back to grin at her.

"Mama? What did you do wrong?" Her piercing gaze studies me.

Crap she knows me too well. I couldn't hide it from her even if I wanted to, but I can't seem to contain my joy. "I found her."

"Skye?" She pushes past me and looks out of the still open door. "Where is she?"

"I dropped her off at her house, but she's back." I sound like a kid who's just met his favorite superhero.

She turns on me. "Why on earth would you take her there?

We've plenty of room here." Her rare show of anger has me taking a step back.

"One step at a time, Mama."

"Preston, you need to think about this. Is her parents' home the best place for her? Sometimes, my son, you don't think. Remember what I told you about the night you left?" She slams the front door and shakes her head at me.

My mama's recalling of that night flashes into my head.

"Where is Preston?" Skye had asked my mom, panting and out of breath.

"What in the world happened to your face?" Mama asked her.

Skye's hand went to her puffy lip. "I fell. Where is he, Liliya?

"He's not here," Mama told her, keeping her promise to me.

"Where is he? I have to find him, now."

Mama said she had never seen Skye so panicked. "I don't know, Skye. I'm sorry. All I know is he is gone and will return."

"Return tomorrow?"

"No, he'll be gone a while. You can stay here of you are in trouble."

"This can't be happening, he'd tell me if he was leaving." Mama said she saw tears in her eyes.

"I'm sorry, Skye. Come in, let's talk about your face." Mama took her hand and squeezed it.

Skye said nothing, just rushed past her with a gasp, the need to see for herself that I was gone. She walked into my room and opened my drawers, seeing them all cleared out.

"He left me...and said nothing?"

"He'll be back, I promise you that."

Skye had looked at my mama with tears rolling down her face and had seemed defeated. "Take care of yourself, Liliya," she said softly, then kissed Mama on the cheek.

"Don't leave, stay with me," Mama begged her.

"I can't Liliya, I need to go. If my father comes looking for me, it's best to say you didn't see me."

Mama shook me out of the recollection. "If it was them that did that to her, she shouldn't be back there now." She looks disappointed in me. I know she enjoys the nice things we have, but she also thinks the price I paid was too high and she has no idea of the real cost. To this day she doesn't know Bob paid all her medical bills. I've kept her from the sordid details and the price I really had to pay.

"Point taken, mom. The drive was long, I'm going to go for a swim." I just want to be alone with my thoughts.

"Okay, Preston, but think about what I said."

The swim wasn't as calming as I hoped it would be. Climbing out of the pool and drying myself off, I head for my room.

There, in a frame beside my bed, is our prom picture. I trace her smile with my finger and think back to the night this was taken.

Wham is blasting, matching the eighties theme, and we both have stupid grins on our faces. I know how much she loves George Michael. We get to the dance floor just as the song ends and I can see the disappointment on her face. Trying to look around for anything that will make her happy, I see couples getting their photos taken in the far corner of the room. I grab her hand and tug.

"Come on, over here." I weave through the crowd.

"Where are we going?" she yells behind me.

We break through the crowd and I pull her into line. "Let's get our picture taken."

"Really?" She raises an eyebrow at me.

"Yeah, this night is forever." I put my arm around her and hold her close while we wait for our turn.

When it's our turn we hand the order form over and the photographer places us in the customary prom position, the one

*with my arms around her waist. After he takes our picture, I take
her hand in mine and "Eternal Flame" starts playing.*

"Would you like to dance?" I ask her.

Her eyes widen slightly. "You'll dance to this?"

*The corners of my mouth tilt up into a sly grin. "With you,
Detka, I'll dance to anything."*

She was so happy that night, that wasn't the case last night.
Her nightmare was pretty bad, and I wonder how she'll be
tonight. She wouldn't go back there if it was dangerous for her...
would she? I am going to drive myself insane, I need to take my
mind off her. I'm going to go to my office and do some work.

A soft knock on my office door sometime later pulls my head
out of my thoughts. I look up to see my mom peek her head in.
"Preston, I made us dinner."

I look over at the clock and realize a few hours have passed.
"I'll be right there."

I organize my papers on my desk. I haven't really been giving
the gem deals enough attention, so I set them aside. Walking
through the house, I look around and picture Skye here with me.
I think she would love this house.

I sit down at our long rustic table just as my mom gets to the
table with two plates. "Chicken and dumplings, it looks fantastic,
Mom."

"Mmmhmmm, your favorite." She sits down and dives
right in.

I glance at her occasionally as I move things around on
my plate.

She looks up at me with a frown on her face. "Hurry up and
eat, it will get cold."

"Yes, ma'am." We both eat in silence. There is no mistaking
her disappointment in me, unless I am just reading too much into
her facial expressions.

She finishes eating and quietly starts clearing away the dishes.

I silently follow her into the kitchen and work side by side with her in silence cleaning the dishes. After we are done I bend down and kiss her forehead. "Goodnight, Mama," I tell her, then wearily walk to my bedroom.

As I lay in bed my mind starts racing back to Skye and the look on her face when I dropped her off. I can't get her parents out of my head. I think back to all the times she talked about her parents, mostly her father. She kept me pretty far away from him when she could. She didn't hold any affection for him, she acted like he was just another person and not a good one at that. I switch on my bedside lamp and turn on my side, punching my pillow, trying to get comfortable.

I think back to that first time I snuck into her room to watch movies and accidentally fell asleep. She scared the crap out of me, waking me with her screams. We laughed later about it, or she did, but that night, in my arms, she slept soundly, and I knew I needed to be there for her always.

But I failed.

Now that I'm older and I am really playing back history in my head, I can see that maybe she's suffered for a long time and thought I couldn't help her. Damn it. I've been a fool. Why did she go back? I throw the covers off. I have to go and check on her.

Not wanting to disturb the silence of the neighborhood with my car, I walk the darkened street like I used to. Only this time, rather than coming from the trailer park, I am only two blocks away. The crickets are screaming in the night's silence. In no time I'm standing outside her house; all the lights are off. This used to be my sign that it was ok to come in, so I walk to her side of the house and try the window. Locked, *damn*. I turn to leave, but as I get back to the sidewalk I stop myself. A locked window would never stop me before.

I go back to her window and use a credit card to slip the lock open. *Cheap ass, Bob.* He hasn't changed the locks since the house was built, they're no match for me; not in high school and definitely not now. As I climb through her window, the memories jolt through me. I can see the outline of her on her bed. She is lying perfectly still but I hear the hitch her in breathing that lets me know she's awake. I don't want to frighten her, so I whisper to her.

"Skye? It's me...Preston."

Her voice is so soft. "You shouldn't be here."

I'm slightly disheartened. "Would you like me to leave?"

"Yes." As soft as she says it, it's loud in my head.

I can't give up hope. "Are you sure?" I stay still until she answers, studying the outline of her in bed.

"Yes, no..." her voice trails off.

Oh thank fuck. I stand by the side of the bed, unsure of what to do. What I really want to do is get into bed with her. "Skye?"

"Yes?"

"Can I hold you? I promise I— uhh. I just need to hold you."

"I'd like that," she says very softly.

I kick off my shoes but leave all my clothes on, unlike how I used to get into her bed, but I just made a promise. In my excitement, I bounce in and she gasps.

"Sorry," I whisper and then pull her closer to me. I hear her suck in a breath again as I settle behind her. "Is everything alright?"

She stills completely. "Yes, I'm just used to being alone now."

Guilt washes over me. I push her hair back and out of my face. I refrain from telling her I hope to change that. She makes my heart ache, she sounds small right now. She must be exhausted from living like that for so long. She stays silent. I think I hear her sniffle, but it was so light I could be mistaken. I squeeze her, just so she knows words aren't necessary.

She yelps in pain which scares the living shit out of me and I let go. "What the fuck? Are you alright? I didn't squeeze you that tight."

"I'm okay," she says with a barely audible sniffle.

"You're crying." I move away from her and turn to flick on the light beside the bed.

"Preston, NO!"

The light brightens the room and she hurriedly pulls the blanket over her head. "Let me see you," I gently say. I don't want her temper to flare.

"No, turn the light off. Better yet, Preston, just go home." She sighs.

I narrow my eyes and press my lips together. She's hiding something from me and the boy I used to be might have listened to her. But the man I have become wastes no time grabbing the comforter and with a quick yank, the blankets all come off the bed. My shock makes me drop them to the floor.

"Oh my God, D... Skye. What the hell happened?" I feel as if I've been punched in the gut.

"I fell?" She moves her face into the pillow.

I march into her bathroom and get a washcloth, putting cool water on it. When I come back into the room I walk around the bed, so I can finally face her. The sight that greets me is one nightmares are made of. One of her eyes is swollen shut, her lips are split, and a slow burn of rage starts within my soul.

"Bullshit, tell me." I sit down on the side of the bed and press the cloth to her eye. She hisses out a breath.

"I'd rather not talk about it, ok?"

"No, it's not ok. Where else are you hurt?" I stare into her face and use all of my self-restraint not to start searching her body. I push the curls off her face as I study the areas where she's injured. These bruises were not made by a fall.

"I'm fine." She tries to give me a reassuring smile but as she does her lip cracks open and starts to bleed.

"Talk to me." I press the cloth now to her lip.

She takes the rag from me and holds it to her mouth. "I'm fine, I'll be okay. I always am."

"Damn it, Skye, just fucking tell me." I grit my teeth, holding on to my temper by a thread, a very thin thread.

"Why the hell do you even care!?" The venom in her voice burns me.

"Everything I've ever done was with you in my mind." She doesn't realize she's treading on thin ice right now. The calmness in my voice is a sure tell sign I am very close to losing my composure. I'm not the boy she once knew. Russia changed me.

"Ugh...yeah...right!

"Oh, we will talk about this later. Now tell me what the fuck happened."

"It doesn't matter," she says in a dejected voice.

I can't stand it anymore, she's hurting, and I need to assess the damage. I lean over her and look into her eyes. I softly caress her face, tracing her bruises. "It does matter, you matter. I'm so freaking sorry for everything."

She closes her eyes, the swollen one an ugly shade of purple. She silently cries, and I use my thumb to gently swipe away her tears. "Don't cry, *Detka*. Please don't cry." Fresh tears gather at the corner of her eyes; it feels so natural to lean down and kiss them away. I'm surprised that she has allowed my touch. I ache for her. My fingers gently examine her face, and I start giving light massaging squeezes down her arms. I watch her and note each area she tenses after my touch.

"Please don't call me that...please." She hiccups.

"I'm sorry, I'll do my best not to." As I gently touch her ribs, she stiffens and bites her lower lip. "Show me." I say it low but firm. I expect a fight from her, but to my surprise, she looks at me through swollen eyes, grits her teeth and adjusts herself in my lap so that she can pull up her T-shirt to expose her ribs.

"*Shit!* Who did this to you? I know you didn't fall." I bring my hand back to her face and cup it, staring deep into her eyes. Since she has only been home for a few hours, I know deep down, my mother was right. I can't believe how stupid I've been all these years, how I failed her. It's worse than I imagined.

"My father."

"I'm going to kill him." My blood starts racing through my veins feeding my rage when she confirms it.

"No, don't risk yourself."

I set her gently on the bed. "We need to get some pain relief into you."

I've taken these steps into her bathroom so many times before. There is a bottle of ibuprofen sitting on the counter, brand new in the box. Someone knew to drop this off. I think back on how many times at night she used to have aches and pains. *Jesus*, how long has this been going on? I'm such a fool.

When I enter her room again she is sitting there watching me with expressionless eyes.

Rage...That's all I feel.

I feel as if a sledgehammer has just slammed me in my stomach. "How long has this been happening?"

She presses her lips together in a stubborn line.

"Please, Skye?" I move over to her and hand her two pills and some water. "Take this."

She takes her time, almost like she's stalling. I sit down on the edge of the bed and cradle her face as she swallows the pills. "Please tell me, please?" I beg her.

"A long time," she says very softly.

"Can you remember when it started? I'm sorry, D...Skye, I just have to know." My plea sounds desperate and it is. I don't think she understands how I am feeling right now, not like a man at all.

"Remember when my Grams died?"

I nod my head. "Yeah, wasn't it like kindergarten or pre-school?"

"Yeah, you have a good memory."

"I remember everything about us, all of it, Skye. Even my mistakes, shit especially my mistakes." I know that's currently an elephant in the room, but she needs to know.

"It started the night her will was read."

I get up from the bed, shocked by this bombshell, and start pacing back and forth by the side of her bed. I stop midstride and look at her. "Are you kidding me? You were a baby!" I have no words. My fists, however, want to have a few words with Bob.

"Not exactly. Just forget I said anything."

"Oh no, I won't forget a single word. I repeat...I'm going to kill him. I've been so freaking dumb." I make another turn around the room, seeing red.

"Don't worry, it'll all be over soon."

I keep pacing back and forth, barely hearing her. All these years, all this time. I've let down the very best thing in my life. While she was being my sunshine, I was too stupid to notice she was living in complete Hell.

"I'm taking you home." I stop walking the room and look down at her.

"I'm already home."

"The hell you are, you *never* belonged here." I sit back down beside her and as she opens her mouth to reply, I hold a finger up to my lips. "Shhh, don't say anything but yes...let me take care of you. My mother would be so happy to have you around, please?"

She sighs. "Okay, for now. I'll find somewhere else to go later." I don't like the circumstances that have made her say yes, but I can't help but be elated that at least she'll be under my roof and my protection.

"Need to pack a bag?"

She looks around her room for a moment, then shrugs. "No, it looks like they threw out all my stuff. There's nothing here I need, let's just go."

I glance around and all of Skye's personal touches are gone. I can't change the past, but what's within my power is the future and I can protect her from these people moving forward. I scoop her into my arms, ignoring her squeal. I know I didn't hurt her, I was gentle and mindful of her injuries as I picked her up, she's just resisting me.

"I can walk, Preston," she hisses.

"I'm going to help you out of the window, that's all. If we go through the house I can't be held responsible for my actions and right now I just want to get you far away from here."

She watches me for a second and then she nods.

I walk her over to the window and she opens it silently so that I can pass her through it. I lower her gently so that she can stand for herself and then I hop through after her. I hold out my hand for her in the darkness, not knowing if she will take it, but she slips her small hand into mine and squeezes.

We set off quietly and I resist the urge to look over my shoulder. Skye must have also been thinking about her father possibly watching us from the house, because she clenches my hand a little tighter as we walk away from the house.

The walk to my house takes about fifteen minutes in the dark. She doesn't complain about her aches.

"I can carry you the rest of the way," I offer after she limps over a curb.

"I can make it, thank you though."

There is a comfortable silence as we round the corner to my home. Skye gasps as she takes in the reality of who I have become, but she doesn't question me. I know that conversation will come, but for now it is pushed aside. Silently, I let us into the house and I take her straight to my bedroom. I look down at her, her eyes fighting to stay open.

"Get in bed, you look like you're going to collapse."

She gingerly lays down on the bed, taking her time settling down. Sitting on the side of the bed, I examine her face. She's silent as she watches me through hooded eyes. I should have hurt the bastard.

I gather some cool cloths from the bathroom then come back to her. I'm only gone a few minutes, but when I return I find her sound asleep, the feeling of safety obviously relaxing her enough to succumb to sleep.

I gently lift her ankle to move it onto the bed, but her foot is jerked out of my grasp and she swiftly kicks at my hands. I look up to find she still has her eyes closed but her lips are pressed together in a firm line.

I hold her foot a little bit tighter just to protect myself from getting kicked, and the sound that she makes is a heart-wrenching anguished wail, only it's small and childlike. "No...no...no... Please not that." She starts pulling her feet up toward her. I'm completely shocked, realizing I'm possibly dealing with more than just the beatings. How the hell did she hide this for so long?

"Skye!" I say sharply, hoping she snaps out of it. Nothing. I think back to all the times she's had nightmares, and the only thing that helped was me holding her. I move closer, gently grasping her shoulders and leaning in close to say her name softly in her ear, "Skye, wake up!" giving her shoulders a little shake.

Her eyes pop open, scared. I can see the confusion in them. We have time for questions later, right now I'm worried about the bruise on her face and the state of her ribs. I pick up the cold compress and apply it to her swollen face. She doesn't make a sound, words aren't necessary right now. I can see it in her eyes, she is tired and shaken up. "Hold this," I instruct her, waiting for her to lift her hand and hold the cloth to her eye. "I'll be right back." I leave the room for a brief moment; she needs ice not just cool cloths. I return with a bag of frozen peas and a small glass of whiskey.

Leaning over her, I lift the amber liquid to her lips. She shakes her head.

"Drink, it will make you feel better," I gently encourage her.

"It will burn."

"Shit, you're right." I set the class aside and run out of the room for a straw. The bar is in my study in a room next door, so it only takes me seconds.

When I put the straw in she takes the glass and sucks the liquid dry. After she swallows, she lets out a small hiss as she feels the burn of the whiskey.

I pull the covers over her and press the peas on her face. "Get some rest, you're safe here. I'll take care of you, my mom's here too, so rest." She nods her head and hunkers down in the covers. The day has taken a heavy toll on her and I can't blame her, a weaker woman would be in hysterics right now.

She doesn't take long to fall asleep. I get into bed next to her, moving close so she knows I am here for her, but sleep won't come to me for a long time. I lay back staring at the ceiling, thinking how in the hell am I going to fix this.

Eleven

SKYE

When I wake, the room is fairly dark, and I can only make out the outline of furniture. There is a moment where I don't know where I am, and I tense. Instantly I feel a strong arm around me and a hand brushing my skin in comfort. *Preston.* I relax slightly, I'm safe. It takes another second for me to realize that I'm not only laying on his chest, but next to my cheek it's a bit damp. I drooled all over him in my sleep. I want to slide out of bed and hide, but this house is unfamiliar to me. I gently pull myself away and put some distance between us. I'm not ready for all of this.

His sleepy voice startles me. "Morning, Skye." He withdraws his hand and slides out of bed. The room is getting brighter by the second. He must not have blackout blinds that cut the desert's rising sun. When he stands, I can't take my eyes off him.

His back muscles are defined. I frown as I see what looks like scars on his back.

"What happened to your back?" I squint trying to get a better view.

He pulls on a t-shirt covering his back. "I'll tell you the story another time."

"Why not now?"

"To be blunt? I don't think I have it in me today to tell you the story. My nerves are already shot from yesterday. Damn, I sound like a pussy."

"We can talk later about it, but a pussy? Honestly, Preston, vaginas birth babies and go back to normal. I'd say you were being more of a penis. Soft and tender." I crack a small smile, mindful of my lip.

It's amazing that after the last few years of feeling nothing romantic at all that the one person that hurt me is making me feel those feelings again. Preston's the only one I have ever wanted more than a passing glance at. With him I wanted everything.

I shift myself higher on the pillow, and bite back a moan. It must be time for some more pain medicine.

"Are you okay?"

"I think I need some Advil or something."

"I'll get it, you stay put." He walks off to what I assume is the bathroom in the master suite.

His thighs are so thick and muscular. Un-freaking-believable...even better than I remember. I can't keep my eyes off him. I have to remind myself not to get too attached; everything with him comes so easy and effortless, but he left me. I can't forget that.

As he comes back toward the bed, I quickly move my eyes off him. I don't want him thinking I've been watching him. I can't let him think I'm interested. I intended on just plopping back into my pillows, but my head smacks into the headboard with a loud thump. "Ow! Motherfucker," I yell as I reach up to rub my head.

Preston rushes over to my side. "You alright?" He reaches a hand out, touching the back of my head.

I just shake my head and mumble, "All good."

"How are your ribs?" He reaches for my shirt.

I smack his hand away. "Fine," I hiss in pain.

"I think you need to see a doctor," he says as he brings his knuckles to trail down the bruised side of my face.

"Naw, I've gotten through worse without one."

"Christ, *Detka*." He looks pained. "I can get one to come to the house. Do it for me," he pleads.

"Stop calling me that. I don't do doctors."

"Damn, I'm sorry. I'm really trying to not call you that. But I really think you need one."

"Try a lot harder. I don't, end of story."

He narrows his eyes in defeat and moves away from the bed, stopping once he gets to the doorway. "I'll be in the kitchen, it's straight down this hall." He points in the direction I'll need to go.

"Okay." Just as he begins to say something else his mother pushes past him with a huge smile on her face.

"Liliya!" I can't contain the pleasure in my voice at seeing her again.

"Mama, what're you doing?

"I've come to see Skye," she says all business like.

"How'd you know she was here?"

"You are about as quiet as a stampede of elephants." She looks over smiling at me.

"Your room isn't even in the main house, Mom." Seeing she's not listening, he gives up. "I'll leave you ladies to it." He shakes his head and walks out of the room. As he turns into the hall I catch a glimpse of the small smirk he has on his face.

I look back to Liliya and her kind, weathered face breaks out into a genuine smile. "Hello, Skye." She's aged since the last time I saw her, still fairly tan and her hair done in a French twist. Her hair is now mostly silver, her cornflower blue eyes still bright.

"It's *so* good to see you." I let the smile come naturally, trying not to wince when I feel the tightness of the bruises on my face and my lip crack open.

She laughs softly then tuts. "You look a little worse than the last time I saw you." I search her face for pity, finding none.

"My father can get happy with his hands." I'm honest, no use trying to hide it from her any longer.

"He should be skinned alive, the *mudak*," she says with a rare show of anger in her voice.

I just stare at her with my mouth open. It's very unlike her, but I kinda like it.

She looks at me then quickly at the door, then quickly back at me again. She walks across the room and opens a drawer. Liliya glances at the door again then pulls out a few clothing items. She turns back to me with a crooked smile. "Here's a few things for you."

"You just happen to have clothes for me?" I have to wonder how many women he's brought home that he keeps spare clothes in his bedroom.

"These are your things." She smiles. "He kept them all this time, close to him. Silly boy, thinks his mother doesn't know these things," she says with an upbeat tone, then sets the pile next to me. "I'll just leave you alone to freshen up, we can chat over breakfast." She turns on her heels and leaves me alone.

I push the blankets off and look at the pile of clothes, my old Guns N' Roses T-shirt and a pair of leggings is on top. This used to be one of my favorite outfits.

The bedroom has a master bathroom attached to it, so I scoop up the bundle and move in there to get dressed. I get a first glimpse of my face and wince at the bruising. I've had worse, he just used to take care not to put the evidence on my face. I take a chance and open the drawer and find some ointment I can use on my split lip. I'm thankful Liliya didn't look at me with pity. I look a sorry state that's for sure.

I shake out the leggings and shirt and wish I had some panties. I think about wearing the ones I have on for a second day, but I just can't bring myself to do it. I stare at the shower and decide a quick one won't hurt. Turning on the faucet, I step inside. The cool water feels good against my bruised body. Using Preston's soap and shampoo, I wash away the essence of my assault. I hesitate leaving the shower so quick, but I know they are waiting for me. I turn off the water and dry myself gently, feeling slightly better despite my image in the mirror. I pull on the clothes and throw my hair up in a bun with a rubber band I find in the drawer.

The clothes don't fit me like they used to, I'm at least a size or two smaller. Living on the streets will do that I guess. I see the clothes Preston bought me yesterday laying on the floor and out of habit, I almost throw them in the shower to clean them, but I'm not in the gutter anymore so I don't need to live that way. I make a mental note to ask Liliya if it would be possible to use the washing machine. Looking back in the mirror, I'm pleased with how I cleaned up with little toiletries. Now it's time to see where I am, because this sure as shit isn't the trailer park.

When I come out of the bathroom the blinds are open and the room is bathed in sunlight. The room is very clean and neat with very few personal touches. My eyes stop on the side of his bed. My feet move on their own to his nightstand and the picture frame that's sitting there. In it is our prom picture. I feel a thickness in my throat as I look at how happy we were on that night. The picture looks a little worn, as if he has carried it with him. I shake myself, swallowing past the lump in my throat threatening to choke me. I don't know if I have it in me to dream, those all came crashing down before.

The bed itself is impressive. It's huge. Probably a California king. It's made from a rich coffee colored wood, carved in a detailed flowing pattern. There's no mistaking it's an antique, I'd guess French, but I'm no expert. The whole room is decorated in shades of brown with a splash of red here and there. It's very masculine and tasteful. I always knew Preston had great taste, now it seems he has the money to show it.

Curious to see what the rest of the house looks like, I make my way into the hallway. The floors are done in a classic terra-cotta tile. There are pieces of framed artwork but no personal photos on the walls. I know how hard his father's death was on them both, so this doesn't surprise me. When I reach the foyer area, I stop to take it in. It's an impressive space. I note the custom features and wonder if they were his choices or if they came with the house. I can't help but wonder again about where he got the money to live like this. The terra-cotta tile is done in a pattern and it leads to a koi pond with a fountain. There are a few fish and even some lily pads with flowers blooming on them. It's very tranquil, and I know just who was contracted to do this work. One of my father's companies. I really hope this came with the house.

I can hear Preston and his mom talking in hushed tones. Following the sound, I soon find myself in a huge open kitchen. One wall is lined with windows, and I see a pool out on the vast deck. There's a huge long rustic table with chairs on one side and benches on the other. The end chairs look like something fit for a king and queen. He isn't sitting at the table though, he is on a stool at the counter.

Liliya is watching me intently, and Preston has yet to turn around to take notice. She clears her throat and says, "Do you still drink coffee, Skye?"

I give her a polite smile. "Yes, please." She sets the Keurig and brews me a perfect cup. Then she hands me a plate of toast with butter and jam on the side without even asking. I used to have this before school at their house every morning. I never was much of an early morning eater.

"Thank you." Smiling as I walk over to the breakfast bar, I take a seat beside Preston.

Preston looks up from his paper. I give him a half smile in greeting and the look on his face is not one I understand. I feel some strain, but it might just be me. It's kind of weird to be in his home.

His eyes glance right at Liliya, and she gives him a knowing smile, patting his back as she leaves the kitchen. When he turns back to me, the odd look has left his face. "Sleep well?"

Before I answer him I mix some cream into the coffee and take a sip. Who can think without coffee? The hot coffee warms my soul for a brief moment. I tilt my head and look at him. "Yes, I slept really well. Thank you." I have to remind myself of my manners and not shove this piece of toast whole into my mouth. The room is silent while we both drink and I eat my toast. I'd say it's a comfortable silence, even though I have many questions, and I'm sure he does too.

I can't believe I'm back in the desert, at Preston's house; his new HUGE house! I grip my cup of coffee a little bit tighter as I stare into space. I should make other arrangements. I can't just stay here indefinitely, with no money, and no belongings. I don't even own two pairs of panties. I guess I could call my mother to see if my dad has cooled off yet, but I know he never will.

I don't even notice he's staring at me until he clears his throat. "Penny for your thoughts." He sets his paper down and gives me his full attention.

I take a deep breath. "I have been thinking...I think it might be best if I go back home." I set down my cup and look at him. "I don't know that *this* is a good idea." I wave my hand across the room to clarify that I mean being here.

His piercing gaze is unwavering. He goes to open his mouth once then snaps it shut. Then finally, he lets one word out. "No."

"No?" One of my eyebrows raises, curious as to how he thinks he has the right to tell me no. I can feel my defenses rise from just that one word. When I'm told what to do my first tendency is to do the opposite, something he very well knows.

He swings his chair around to get closer to me. His face is pretty scary, no emotion showing on it at all. "No."

I turn back to face my coffee cup, giving a mirthless laugh before I take a sip. I carefully swallow and simply state, "No one tells me what to do."

He stands. My chair is suddenly flipped around, his arms cage me in. He isn't touching me, but his face is very close to mine and his expression is one of fury. "You could barely move last night, and have you seen your face?" His tone is firm, but I can hear the barely contained rage. "The past two nights I've held you while you slept, you tossed and turned, even cried out a few times. Don't forget how many other times I've held you through the night terrors. What else did that bastard do to you?"

At this point his nose is flaring, and I can see his muscles tighten, controlling his temper when I'm sure he more than likely wants to shake me. I just press my lips together in a tight line. I *will not* answer that question.

He leans a touch closer, his nearness does funny things to my insides and drives his point home. "I see. My 'no' stands."

He pulls back and reaches across for his mug. It's so quick that I don't have time to control the flinch.

When his blue eyes connect with mine, there's hurt in them. "I would never hurt you, Skye." He finishes off his beverage and carefully sets his cup down.

The irritation boils up inside me and I can't stop it spilling out. "I can't just stay here! For fuck's sake, I don't even have a job!" *I don't even have fresh panties!* I think to myself. I close my mouth before that thought spills out.

He raises a brow and leans in. "You will stay here. I won't hear any more about it."

I can't contain my anger anymore. "You asshole! You left. You don't get to tell me what to do." I kick myself for my outburst. I don't want him to see how leaving hurt me even if I do know it's obvious.

He sits back down. "Ahhh... now we're getting to the heart of things. Do you want to talk about it? Because I'm ready whenever you are." He runs his fingers through his hair then casually rests his hand on the counter, leaving his hair a perfect mess that I would love to run my own fingers through.

"No."

He nods, not pushing the subject for now. "Mom's getting older," he says abruptly, changing the subject. "If you need work, you could help her with whatever needs to be done around here. You really would be doing me a favor. Mom needs the help. She insists on maintaining the place herself, but it's a struggle for her. I help out where I can, but she is old fashioned and likes to look after her family. You know as well as I do, a place this size should have a housekeeper, but she won't hear of me hiring anyone. I'm worried about her. If she thinks she's helping you, then she'll tolerate the assistance. This is a win/win situation for us both, plus she adores you, Skye."

Damn him, I want to say no, but what he is saying makes perfect sense. I'm very fond of her and this house is too much for her to deal with alone. I don't want to seem too eager, but I can't pass this up. "Ok, I'll help Liliya until I find somewhere else to go."

"Great, shall we discuss pay?" he asks.

I twirl and pull a curl, a nervous habit of mine. "No money, you're doing enough."

"You need to buy some clothes, don't you?"

Shit! He's got a point there. "I'll call my mother, maybe she kept my things in storage." I nod firmly, thinking I have won this round.

He stands quickly and puts his arms on the back of the chair, swinging me to face him again. He brings his face so close that I can feel his breath on my skin. Lifting his hand, he gently traces the outline of my bruise. "You. Will. Not. Go. Back. To. That. House," he says slowly, making sure to define each word. Nothing needs to be said about the marks on my face, he has made himself perfectly clear. Plus, my mother most likely tossed my stuff in the trash.

He takes a finger and raises my chin, so I can't help but look him. I feel as if I'm drowning in the deep dark pools of his eyes. He inhales deep through his nose, and his eyes narrow slightly.

"Do you understand me, Skye?"

I lick my lips. "Ok...ok...ok... I won't go back to the house."

"Or call," he demands.

"Or call." I sigh. I totally ignore anything about money, I won't agree to that.

He releases my face and stands up removing himself from my air space, finally allowing me to breathe. I don't move but to take a sip of my coffee as I watch him walk out of the kitchen. I have so many questions about what has transpired in the last five years. He makes me curious to get to know the man he's become.

Twelve

PRESTON

I leave Skye in the kitchen without a word; I have some things to take care of. I'm not even two feet out of the kitchen when my mother appears beside me, her hand on my elbow stops me.

"Yes, Mama?"

"Where're you going? Did you tell Skye where you're going? Do you think it's wise to leave her alone in her condition?" she peppers off the questions frowning at me.

"No, I didn't say anything. I've something I need to take care of." I can't make eye contact with her.

"I'll go to her then, I'm sure you have a good reason to leave her alone." She gives me a calculating look then rushes off to the kitchen.

I enter my office closing the door, leaning against it for a few seconds. This room has a calming effect on me, it's my place. There is a chocolate brown leather sofa that faces the backyard, I can look at the beautiful desert mountains. This is my chill spot to be alone with my thoughts. I take a deep breath and go to my desk.

The years of searching have finally paid off. I'll have to keep myself in check, go slow, win her back gradually, but Christ I need to know if she can forgive me.

I have to try and get some work done to keep my mind off of her for a little while and stop me going out there and begging her to take me back, but first I need to make a call.

Normally, I'd text Craig, but not today. He'd have my balls if he just got a text saying that I found her. I need to tell him, but I don't want the others to know yet.

His phone rings a few times. Just when I think I'll get his voicemail, he picks up. "Preston? Everything ok?"

"No, well yes...I found her."

Out of all our friends only Craig really knows how hard it hit me to come home to find her gone. I was completely devastated, and he helped me pull my shit together. He's the only one who understood why I left. We both came from the same trailer park and fought our way to the top. He knew what an offer of a better life meant for me, my mom, and Skye. So that I could be the man she deserved. In my shoes, he would have taken the job too.

"You there, Craig?" His silence is unnerving.

"Holy shit! Seriously, Preston?"

"Yes, she's here." I keep my voice soft. I don't want to be overheard, and I need him to come here.

"Want me to call the gang up? Dude, Lea is going to freak." He's rushed and excited.

"No, she's hurt. She needs to see a doctor but she's refusing."

"Shit, what's wrong?"

"Christ, Craig, I just need your help."

"Ok, man, let me call Shaina. Want me to see if she can meet us at the emergency room?"

"No, here's fine. She won't go to the E.R."

"Give me five minutes and I'll call you back."

Sitting in my office, I anxiously pass the time debating

whether to tell Skye or just spring it on her. I decide the less time she has to think about it the better.

My phone doesn't even finish the first ring before I snatch it up. "Hello?"

"I spoke with Shaina, she's already on her way to pick me up. We will be there soon, man."

"You don't both have to come over."

"We all missed her, Preston." Craig reminds me that I'm being selfish. He has searched almost as hard as I have over the years.

"Whatever," I huff, knowing he's entitled to come.

"See you in a few."

I can't think about work right now. I'm pacing back and forth across my office, even the view isn't doing anything for my nerves.

The chime of the doorbell brings me running to the door. "I'll get it!" I yell out. This is out of the ordinary for me, but I want to get Craig and Shaina inside before she freaks out. I hope she at least trusts that Craig and I will be here along with Shaina. Jesus, Preston, just freaking breathe. Great, now I'm talking to myself.

Fortunately, Skye and my mother are nowhere in sight. Mom must be showing her around. Sweet, I'll have a few minutes with Craig and Shaina before my Mama and Skye realize I called them here. I open the door for my friends and greet them quietly. I usher them straight into my study. As soon as I shut the door, I start to pace.

"Thanks, guys, for coming on such short notice."

"Where is she?" Craig asks, looking confused as to why I shut us in here.

"Skye's with my Mom, I'll call them in a minute," I reply, rubbing the back of my neck trying to relieve some tension.

"Dude, would you stop pacing. What's wrong with her? How's she hurt?" he asks, concerned.

I stop in the middle of the room and look at Shaina. "I'll let you take a look at her."

"Why are you being so secretive? Either you know, or you don't. Do you know how she got hurt?" he asks firmly, crossing his arms across his chest.

"It's not for me to say, and don't use your boss voice on me, buddy."

"Oy vey... will you two just shut your pieholes?" Shaina's raspy voice shuts our mouths. She's about 5'2" with auburn hair that's pin straight cut blunt just above her shoulders, she's looking at us like we're crazy. Her and Craig have gotten closer over the last few months but refuse to commit to being committed.

"Sorry, Shaina, I've just waited so long to find her and I'm fucking things up already, without having a chance to apologize for things I screwed up before."

"So...where did you find her?" Craig asks.

"I found her in Hollywood and brought her home." A smile crosses my face.

"Did she kick you in the balls for leaving? Does she know I'm here?" he asks.

"Before you two get caught up in patting Preston on the back for finding Skye, why don't we talk about why I have to make a house call," Shaina interrupts, with her hands on her hips.

"Ugh, I'm sorry. You'll have to ask her."

"You know I took an oath in the state of California. If she has been assaulted, I will need to report it."

"Yeah, I know." I sigh.

Craig and Shaina exchange a glance.

"Does she know you called us?" Craig asks.

"She has no clue at all, I didn't want to tell anyone yet that she was home. We have so much to talk about, and I'm not ready to share her." Craig stifles a laugh at my honesty. "But I think she needs medical attention. She says she won't see a doctor, this was the only way I could think of."

Craig looks skeptical. "You think she'll let Shaina take a look at her?"

"I think you should let me try woman to woman. It might go better that way." Shaina shakes her head at us.

"You're right." I hear my mom chatting with Skye as they come down the hallway, and I hold up a hand to silence Craig and Shaina. "Let me grab them." I pull open my office door right as they are passing and throw on a charming smile. "Ladies, mind if I talk to you for a minute?"

My mother gives me a frown but walks into the room first, sees Craig and smiles, then she focuses on Shaina. "Dr. Rae, how good to see you again!" She walks over to Craig and he takes both her hands in his, kissing her frail knuckles. She laughs. "Smooth devil!" she teases. Then she looks between Skye and myself and turns back toward the door. "I'll leave you kids alone to catch up."

My mom passes Skye and seeing the tension in her body, pats her arm in reassurance as she leaves. Skye looks ready to run. "Craig?" she asks quietly, almost to herself, her eyes narrowing as she assesses him. He has a shaved head these days and a beard which he keeps trimmed. But he's still the same old Craig.

"Hey, Skye." He offers her a warm smile.

Her face flushes red and her eyes connect with mine.

Craig moves to her and pulls her into a bear hug. "We've all missed you," he tells her, squeezing her tighter as if it will stop her running again. She hisses in pain, and he quickly pulls back and looks at her face. "What happened to you?"

I watch this interaction as calmly as I can. I was never the jealous type, but the past few years have changed me. Everything has been focused on getting her back. So now that I have her here, the possessiveness I feel is overwhelming. I don't like him touching her and knowing he hurt her, even by accident, has me grinding my teeth. Fuck I need to calm down.

She ignores his question. "Does everyone know I'm back?" She looks over at me with daggers in her eyes.

"Can I take a look at you, Skye?" Shaina's voice is gentle and soothing.

"You're looking at me now."

"What happened to your face, how does the other guy look? How do you feel?"

"I'm fine." She turns her accusing gaze my way. "What did you tell them?" she demands.

I hold my hands up. "I just said you were hurt and should probably get checked out."

She turns away from me. "Mmmmhmmm."

"Don't be angry with Preston. He's worried about you," Craig chimes in, always there to protect me.

"He should have warned me," Skye spits.

"She's right." Shaina narrows her eyes at Craig.

"I know, I'm sorry." I clasp my hands in front of me, watching them.

"Does anyone else know I'm back?" Skye's very quiet, the only way I can tell she is nervous is because she is ringing her hands.

"No." I decide to be honest in the hope it will help her trust me. "Because I'm selfish and don't want to share you with everyone yet. I only called these guys because I'm really worried about you."

She nods. "Good, I'm not ready yet to be bombarded with questions."

Shaina clears her throat. "Speaking of questions, do you mind if I take a look at you?"

Her shoulders stiffen. "I'm fine, Shaina, but thank you."

The room is silent for a second, and I take charge of the situation. "Skye, Shaina is a well-respected doctor."

"Congratulations, I still don't need a doctor."

"Skye, sorry hun, I'm glad you're back and everything, but you look like shit," Craig says gently.

"Please, Skye? Just a quick once over." It would be easy to accept her refusal, but that is not what is best for her.

"Did you put your little heads together and come up with this scheme? Huh? Let me make myself clear, you will not trick me into seeing a doctor. You can both go fuck yourselves!" With that she runs out of the room and seconds later we hear my bedroom door slam shut.

"What the actual fuck?" Craig's shocked voice whispers to me.

I don't look at him, I'm torn. I take one step in her direction and I feel a hand on my chest. When I look up Shaina has a stern look on her face.

"I don't think you should go after her. Let me try." She gives me a sympathetic look.

Maybe she's right. I nod. I watch as she walks down the hall with her bag, positioning myself near the entry so I can hear her as she talks to her through the door.

She speaks softly, "Let me help you, Skye...you can trust me," then she slips into the room.

I begin pacing again, can't help it. But thankfully you can't wear out the Spanish tile floors. Her voice stops me dead.

Skye's shrill yell bounces off the walls. "Don't you fucking touch me!"

What in the hell is going on? I don't think, I act. Sprinting across the hall I fling open the door to see Skye backed into the corner and Shaina standing back.

She glances over at me. "She doesn't want me to take her blood. If you give me a minute I can talk to her."

Her eyes are huge and frightened. "Preston, don't let her near me with that needle!" She's desperately looking for an escape from the room.

With determined strides I find myself right in front of Skye holding out my hand, she takes it and as I pull her in I can feel her body quake in fear.

"Why do you need her blood?" I ask Shaina while not taking my focus off Skye.

"She's had some trauma to the abdomen. I want to check her blood count for signs of internal bleeding. She also hasn't had a checkup in the last two years. It's fairly standard. Skye, it'll be quick, I promise."

"No! That's what they all say! Preston, please..."

I shush her and sit on the bed, pulling her onto my lap. She tries to fight for a moment. "Skye! Stop it right now!" I say softly, catching her eyes with my own. I bring my fingers up to gently stroke the side of her bruised face. "Please, Skye, just look at me. You're okay, I got you."

"I need her verbal consent." Shaina steps closer to Skye and me. "Skye, can I do this blood work? It's either this or end up in the hospital later where the choices will be out of your control."

"Do it, hurry please. I don't like needles." She breathes heavily but doesn't break eye contact with me at all. She stiffens slightly as the needle breaks her skin.

"I'm here, I'll protect you," I whisper. I'm not sure who I am reassuring, her or myself.

She whimpers, closing her eyes.

Shaina finishes up and releases her arm. "All set." She walks out of the room, leaving me with Skye.

I hold her for just a few minutes longer and let her catch her breath. "You're ok, it's all over now. Look at me."

She opens her eyes and that crazed look has left. "Preston?"

"I'm here, *Detka*, I'm right here." I wrap my arms around her and she doesn't fight me, instead she puts her head on my chest and slowly breathes.

"I told you not to call me that," she finally mumbles against my chest.

I can't help but smile kissing her forehead, then I pull back. "Do you want to go back with me and talk to Craig and Shaina?"

She shakes her head. "No," she whispers.

I nod my head. "Ok, want to go get a cup of coffee with my mom? I have to see them out."

She nods her head, and I give her a little shake so that she looks at me. "Yes, coffee," she mumbles. "I'll go get some."

"Here, let me help you." We walk into the next room, making eye contact with my mom. She takes one look at Skye and comes straight over.

"Can you get her some coffee, Mom? I need to see them out."

"Yes, go on. Come here, Skye." She grabs Skye's hand and waves me off.

I enter my office and find Craig and Shaina already sitting in the chairs across from mine. I sit down behind my desk and look into his questioning eyes. "What did she say?"

She is very still. That alone should be a warning. "She said nothing, Preston. She only told me it was ok to examine her. She has symptoms of P.T.S.D. and should really talk to someone."

"Yeah, I doubt that's going to happen."

"I would try again in a few days."

I rub my temples. "Did you get a chance to check her ribs?"

"Yes, I'm pretty sure they are just bruised, but without an x-ray I can't say for certain."

I nod my head, the treatment would be similar either way.

"What the fuck, Preston? Who did that to her?" Craig's calm, but the contained rage is clear on his face.

"It's for her to give you the full story." I sigh. I could really use a drink right now, but I won't go that route. "Shaina, apart from her injuries, is she okay?"

She looks at me carefully before she responds. I can't read her expression, but I sense suspicion. "Since she's now my patient, I'm not at liberty to discuss that with you."

She gets up and has her medical bag already in her hand. "I need to get back to the office, Preston. Call me if she gets any worse and I'll come right over. Craig, are you coming?"

"Yeah, I'll call you later, Preston."

"Thank you both for coming over. I'll call if anything changes."

I scrub a hand over my face. The look that he gave me was one of *I-hope-you-know-what-you're-doing-buddy*, but I'd rather have all eyes on me than have people questioning Skye. I will do what is necessary to protect her, even if that means scrutiny from my best friend.

Thirteen

SKYE

Preston left the bed early this morning; I should get up. I should fight him on slipping into the same bed as me, but it's been so long since I had peaceful sleep I'm reluctant to give that up just yet.

I'm very sore today, but I knew it would get worse before it gets better. Hearing the phone ring, I look at the clock on the side of the bed to check the time, it's ten am. Damn, I need to get my lazy ass moving.

Hearing someone walking down the hallway, I look up. Preston stops and leans on the doorframe. He has an annoyed look on his face as he speaks low into the phone.

"Shaina needs to speak with you," he says as he covers the phone. "Are you up for it?"

"Yes." I try to sit up but groan at the pain in my stomach and freeze.

"Jesus, sit still," he says as he walks across the room and hands me the phone.

"Hello?" I say, biting back another groan of pain.

"Hey, Skye, how you feeling today?"

"I'm ok, is that why you called?" My eyes narrow as I see Preston pacing the room and stopping every few feet to look at me.

"Yes and no, I have news on your bloodwork. Are you alone?"

"No, but you can tell me." I press my teeth into my top lip as I wait for the news.

"Is Preston pacing the room?" she asks, amusement in her voice.

"How'd you guess?" I laugh as I watch him take another turn about the room.

"He's pissed off because I wouldn't tell him why I was calling."

"Oh, well why didn't you?" I ask with some surprise.

"Because you're my patient now. Nothing about your health will ever be discussed with anyone but you."

Hmmm so this oath thing is real, who knew?

She clears her throat. "The results of your bloodwork show that your red blood cells are very low."

"Ok, what does that mean?" I notice Preston has stilled in his pacing and is now watching me.

"It probably means you're anemic, but given your injuries, it could also mean you have internal bleeding."

"I'm not going to a hospital," I tell her firmly, and Preston comes walking across the room. As soon as he opens his mouth, I hold up my hand for silence.

"I figured that," Shaina continues. "I have portable equipment. I want to come over and do a quick ultrasound. Will you allow that?"

"What happens if I don't?" I freeze at the thought of any doctor touching me.

"If you have internal bleeding and we don't treat it you could die. Please Skye, let me rule this out," she pleads.

My mind races for a moment. It's all well and good her

coming here, but if she finds what they did to me she's going to want to cart me off to hospital for treatment, and I won't allow that. I'd rather take my chances with death. But then I look up at the concerned look on Preston's face and I sigh. "Ok, but only you and no hospitals."

"I'll be right over, start downing as much water as you can." The line then goes silent as she hangs up.

I put the phone down by the side of the bed and struggle to sit up. Preston is quickly by my side helping me.

"What did she say?"

"She thinks I'm anemic but she's going to come over to make sure it's not something else."

"She had me so worried when she said she would only speak to you," he says as he runs his hands through his hair.

"It will be fine, I need to get up and start drinking some water."

He helps me up. "I, uh, was out this morning and picked you up a few things, so if you wanted to change into some fresh clothes."

"You did?" I'm a little shocked he would think about that.

"Yeah, nothing much. Just some shirts and shorts so you can be comfortable," he says nonchalantly as he ushers me down the hallway.

We stop by what I'm assuming is the guest bedroom. Glancing in I see multiple bags on the bed. "That's more than nothing much..." I frown.

"Not nearly as much as you deserve. I'll leave you to get dressed. Call out if you need help, I'll be near." He quickly moves down the hallway slipping into another room before I can argue.

Walking toward the bed, I lift the first bag. It has a stack of soft cotton T-shirts inside, the second bag has coordinating shorts. There is a third with a bunch of underwear and a fourth containing new white Converse just like a pair I used to own. I slowly shake my head and pull out an outfit to slip into. This is so like the Preston that I was in love with. The one I can't let back in.

Thankfully we didn't have long to wait for Shaina; it seemed like hours when in all actuality it was only thirty minutes. I'm waiting for her in Preston's office when she arrives. Preston wanted me to stay in bed but I didn't want to stay there. I'm not an invalid. Plus the silence in his office had him fidgeting in his seat, it was a win-win for me.

Preston shows Shaina into the room. "Hello, Skye," she says with a small smile.

"Hey." I can't come up with anything much to say because the minute she walks in I feel that nervous punch in my gut and my palms go sweaty.

She looks around the room. "We can do the test in here if that will make you more comfortable."

Preston looks right at me with worry. "Would you like me to stay?" he asks very softly.

I slowly shake my head. "No, it's ok. I'll be fine." I look over at Shaina who's staring at Preston with an odd look on her face.

Shaina just shrugs her shoulders and looks back to me.

"Call me if you need me, I won't be far." The look Preston gives me is a new one, he looks wounded.

I note that seems to be his line now. Does he not plan on leaving me alone ever again? We will see about that. I watch as he and Shaina exchange an odd look. Preston's eyes narrow and he gives her a flash of anger. Shaina doesn't break that eye contact but slightly inclines her head with some silent communication. Preston nods his head once and then he walks out of the room, closing the door softly behind him. I notice that I'm wringing my hands and cross my arms to keep myself from fidgeting. What the heck was that all about?

"I'm going to set up right here by the sofa, it will just take a moment."

I stand off to the side and watch in silence as she carefully sets her machine up and examines everything, making sure it's clean. I swallow hard and start to bite on my thumbnail. I take a deep calming breath and will myself to move closer to Shaina.

"You ready, Skye?" She sits back on a footstool she pulled over.

"Yeah, where should I sit?" I ask as I take a small step toward her.

"I need you to lay on your back, right here on the couch." She pats the space with her hand and doesn't make any move toward me. Good move making me come to her, putting me at ease.

I nod my head and then look at my feet. Slowly I lift one then the other and walk over to the sofa. As I sit across from her I look at my knees and breathe in as I lift my legs and lay down on my back.

"Relax, Skye, this won't hurt a bit," she says softly.

I turn my head to look at her and only see concern. I have to remind myself she is a good person and not here to hurt me, but old habits are hard to break. "What do you need me to do?" I manage, trying to make my voice sound strong.

She has a soft smile. "If you could just lift your shirt and make sure the band of your shorts is pulled down low by your pelvic bone." She pulls out a paper blanket, handing it to me. "You can use this to cover yourself, and I'll push it aside if I need to, ok?"

"Ok." I lift my hips up to pull my shorts down first and moan in pain as I stretch sore muscles.

"Do you need help?" she asks with a small frown.

"No, I'm ok." When I lift up my shirt the black and blue bruises are bright on my skin.

I look up at Shaina and see the concerned look on her face.

Glancing at the vivid bruising, she frowns. She looks down at her hands but then takes a deep breath and looks up into my eyes.

"Who did this to you, Skye?"

I freeze. The shame I feel at my situation prevents me from answering.

"You know whatever you tell me is completely confidential, right? You can trust me." She glances at the door, then looks back to me. "If you are in danger, I can help you."

All at once I realize what she is asking. "It wasn't Preston, he would never—"

Shaina releases a sigh of relief. "I know, it's just that he's being secretive. He wouldn't tell me anything, and I had to make sure for my own peace of mind. I need you to know you can trust me as your doctor and as your friend."

I give her a small smile. "Thank you."

"Do you want to tell me what happened?"

I take a deep breath. She may as well know now that she has seen me in this state. "My father," I state simply. "This was my welcome home."

"I see. And is this an isolated incident?"

A bitter laugh escapes. "Oh no, I've had worse over the years."

A deep crease forms on her forehead as she probably works through all the years she knew me and all the times something happened that I had an excuse for. I can see the guilt forming on her face.

"It's okay," I reassure her. "I covered it well, not even Preston knew."

She nods. "I just want you to know if you ever need to talk, I'm here to help."

Breaking the tension, I adjust the paper towel. "Thank you, I'm ready."

She gives me a small smile and turns back to her equipment.

There's a little wand object and a small TV monitor. She's very systematic as she turns everything on and squeezes some gel looking goop onto the wand.

"This is going to be cold, let me know if it hurts you when I'm near your bruises." She then reaches under the paper and sets the tool on my stomach. I hiss out a breath because it's cold, but it also feels good on the bruising.

The next few minutes pass in silence while she works. She concentrates on the screen, and I try not to panic about her touching me. I turn my head to look at the little monitor as she makes sweeping moves across my belly. I don't know how anyone can read the images on the screen, they look like a jumbled mess to me.

She keeps going back to the same two places on each side, and I'm starting to think I might have to go to the hospital. That's enough for me to break the silence. "Is everything okay?" My voice has more confidence than I feel.

She looks up confused. "Have you had any surgeries?" Her hand stills the wand on me.

My breath hitches. "Why?"

Her jaw tenses and she moves the wand back and points to the screen then she looks up. "Because you're sterile, you have coils implanted. Did you do this after you left?"

"No. I'd never..." I stop talking, I can't seem to find the words to finish.

"How then? Hmm...they're not fresh, this is something that's been here for a while, scar tissue has built up." She moves the wand back to the other side examining both areas.

"You don't want to know, Shaina. Let's just drop it," I say very softly.

"You are mistaken, I need to know." She pulls the ultrasound wand out from the paper and sets it down by the machine then sits back giving me a little bit of space.

I sigh. I knew the day would come when I would have to explain what happened to a doctor. I'm sick of keeping secrets, of covering for the piece of shit father I have.

"It happened one of the times we were on a family vacation to Mexico." I pause for a moment.

"But that was in high school, right? I believe it was in my senior year, so you were just a freshman the first time you went."

"Yes, you were getting ready to graduate," I confirm, surprised that she remembers that far back.

"I came home for spring break and you were gone, Preston was pissed because he wanted to spend spring break with you. I'm sorry for interrupting, keep going." She gives my hand a small pat.

"My father drugged me and when I woke, it was already done. He had his doctor friend sterilize me. He wanted to be sure I never had kids." My tone's flat as I recall the moment when I realized what depths my father would go to for money.

"Oh my God..." she says.

"That's why I don't trust doctors, they either cover for his abuse or do his dirty work," I spit angrily.

Shaina grabs my hands in hers and squeezes. "You can trust me, Skye, I won't ever betray you."

I nod my head and pull my hands back, eager to change the subject. "Do I have internal bleeding?"

She shakes her head. "No, thank God. I'll get some iron pills for you." She starts to pack away her portable machine.

"Do you hear from Lea?" I've been frightened to ask, because I know she's probably hurt and mad.

"Yes, I see her quite a bit. Do you have any idea how happy she's going to be to see you?"

"Happy?" I frown.

"Sure." She grins.

"I'm so afraid, Shaina," I whisper.

"Afraid, of what? She's going to shit herself." Her eyebrows are raised.

"I ran, I was a coward. She's going to be sickened by the sight of my face. What I've allowed to happen to me." I catch my breath, and I'm able to stop the tears from falling.

"Don't be silly!"

"I don't know if I'm ready, it's just...I thought she might have shown up here if she knew I was back, that's all." I press my teeth into my bottom lip. I've shared so much, and I have lived so long with these secrets I feel sort of relieved.

"She doesn't know yet, she's away for work right now." She pulls her phone out, looks down and swipes through the calendar. "She'll be back in a month."

"Oh..."

"She'll be happy, I promise." She squeezes my knee and there is a knock on the door. "He thinks I'm going to hurt you," she whispers and rolls her eyes. "Come in, Preston, we're done."

Preston peeks his head from around the door. "How's everything going?"

Shaina gives me a smile. "I'll let you tell him." She then turns toward Preston. "I'm just finishing up." She quickly folds the rest of her tools back up and closes the case, turns and says, "You need anything, Skye, you call me. Preston, make sure she rests and takes some ibuprofen. I'll check in with you both later."

As fast as she came, she shows herself out of the house.

"Well, what's the verdict?" Preston asks.

"Anemic, I need to take some iron." I slump my shoulders, emotionally drained from the morning.

"Perfect, I am going to get you some medicine and then you can rest. We need you better, Skye."

Fourteen

PRESTON

Skye hangs out with my Mama most days. Mama looks after her and I'm still trying to give her space, time to think, but we really need to sit down soon and talk about things.

I'm not the boy who left her anymore, I'm the man who spends every night with her in my arms. That's when I don't have to give her space. That's when she is *mine*. It's an unspoken agreement, we sleep wrapped in each other and there are no bad dreams. It's complete hell, she feels so right there but I hold myself back. Over the last month she has physically healed, but there is a long way to go on the inside, she has so many invisible scars. And there are things I need to know, questions that still need to be answered. I am too chicken shit to ask them though.

She's still quiet, but she is generally at ease here which pleases me. More often now, I'll find her working alone, whereas she was my mama's shadow when she first came. She has taken to the role of my mama's assistant which is a relief because I'd been worried about the workload Mama insisted on carrying alone. Mama knows I can hire someone to come in and take care of the house. I had to negotiate with her just keeping the inside in order. They're both very stubborn but I'm happy they get along well.

Mama and Skye have been out all day, shopping and doing a little pampering at the spa. I told Mom what I had planned and she agreed to occupy Skye and bring her back all done up.

Skye has been very stubborn about accepting the things I want to provide for her, but Mom is very smooth about buying clothes and such for her in a way Skye can't refuse. Today is no exception. She made up some nonsense about having a spa gift card that was due to expire and how none of her friends are into that kind of thing, so Skye would really be doing her a favor if she came with her. The woman is devious, but I love her.

I noticed that her clothes were starting to hang off her. I had felt the odd poke at night from her hipbones and thought it might be in my head. But it looks as though she's getting even smaller. I want to have a closer look, but I can hardly march up to her, lift her shirt, and demand her to present herself for me to examine. That would be a dick move. So instead I had my mom 'notice' while they were at the spa and true to her ever persuasive nature, she managed to convince Skye they needed to go buy some better fitting clothes.

Craig has been on my ass about having a party to welcome Skye back. But Lea had been away on business and in truth, I wanted to keep her to myself. I'm a selfish bastard I know. So, the plan was to have her return from her day out to a surprise dinner with Craig, Shaina, and Lea. No way is she ready for a party, but this I think she can handle.

The doorbell chimes and I jump up and walk briskly to the door while it chimes again and again, Lea's way of letting me know how excited she is. She just about barges in, giving me no time to berate her about it. "Where is she?" Her crystal blue eyes search the room.

"Nice to see you too, Lea, she isn't back yet." I shake my head and give Craig a questioning look.

Craig holds up his hands. "Don't look at me, I can't control her."

Lea turns around and has a stubborn tilt to her chin. "That's right, I'm the boss of me." She points her finger at the both of us.

"Don't get too mouthy, Lea, it's not too late to cancel this whole night." My voice is firm. She knows how stubborn I've become and is wise enough to not poke further.

She presses her lips together in a pout. "How's she been? Have you told her why you left yet?"

"Lea, she doesn't know yet and I'm still not sure how she'll take it, so I'd appreciate it if you could keep it to yourself for tonight. I'll find a good time to tell her."

Lea's eyes widen slightly, she opens then closes her mouth. "You know what's best...or so you think."

"Wiseass. Craig, when's Shaina going to get here?"

"Sorry dude, she's going to be late. They had a trauma come in to the ER that she had to handle."

"It's cool, at least she's coming."

Skye should be home any minute. I am starting to have second thoughts about this, but it's a little too late to back out now. Craig and Lea are happy she's back, heck everyone is happy to have her back, they have no reason to think that she won't feel the same way. They don't blame me for her leaving, I blame me.

The front door shuts and the room goes absolutely silent. Skye walks in with my mom and stops, two things happen in quick succession. First, Lea screams and rushes over to Skye, grabbing her in a crushing hug. Second, Skye looks over Lea's shoulder at me with murder in her eyes. *Shit*.

I run a hand through my hair, yep it could have gone either way, but she does not like this surprise.

"I thought you weren't due back for another week?" Skye asks Lea.

Lea shrugs and wipes the tears from her face. "Job got done early, and I was sick of us catching up on the phone."

I didn't realize they have been chatting it up on the phone, now I look for an escape. I see Craig talking with my mom and notice how tired she looks, so I take the coward's way out.

"I'll see you home, Mama," I tell her as I reach her side. She just nods her head in acceptance. She says goodnight to Craig and Lea and pauses for a moment with Skye, thanking her for a lovely day and giving her a reassuring squeeze.

As I pass Craig he chuckles quietly. "Pussy," he whispers just loud enough for me to hear.

I flash him a grin. "Or a smart man," I mutter and usher my mom out of the house.

We walk out of the sliding glass doors onto the patio. The main reason I bought this house is because it had its own guest house. I wanted Mama with me, but she didn't want to impose. This was the best solution. Her house is set back into the side of the mountain and has its own entrance which we never use. We walk the path around the pool in silence and I open the door for her and usher her inside her cozy home. Waiting in her sitting area as she gets ready for bed, I begin to pace nervously. Coming out here removed me from the tension for a few minutes, but soon I'll have to go back in there and face Skye. I saw the look in her eyes, and I don't like my chances. Mama comes out into the living room in her flannel pajamas. Only my mama would wear flannel pajamas in the desert. I stop pacing and give her my warmest smile, her eyes sparkle. "Did you do something wrong, Preston?"

I chuckle, my smile has gotten me out of many situations. "Besides organize a surprise dinner?" I lean over and kiss her on the forehead.

She inclines her head at me and studies me for a moment then gives me a serious look. "Make sure Skye eats, the silly girl is wasting away."

Ahhh, so she has noticed too...She is always so astute. And although she has never been the matchmaker type, I get the impression she is trying to encourage me by the sunny smile she is giving me now. "I'll make sure she eats," I assure her, leaning over and giving her a kiss on the cheek. "Goodnight, Mama, sleep well."

As I walk back to the main house, I see Skye standing in the kitchen alone, waiting for me. "Hey," I say cautiously as I walk through the back door.

She grips the counter, her head hanging down. "You should have told me about this." She lifts her head up, and I can see the anger in her eyes.

"Why? So you could say no and keep hiding away?" I keep my tone level so I don't start a shouting match with her.

"Yes, you had no right!" she raises her voice slightly.

I move closer to her and lean down so I'm in her space. She doesn't step back. I have to clutch the counter to keep from touching her. "I'm sorry, Skye, but you can't hide forever, she's your best friend. She was dying to see you and I thought that this would be easier on you. Everyone at once and now it's over."

She presses her lips together and inclines her head. We stare at each other for a few seconds and she then breaks eye contact and turns her head away. She's so beautiful and she has no clue, that just makes her even more beautiful in my eyes.

"Don't be mad," I plead. "This will be good for you."

"They served the food already, and Shaina is here now too," she says, ignoring me. She turns without another word and walks into the dining room.

I sigh, this plan has totally backfired.

Craig, Lea, and Shaina are in deep conversation as we sit

down, the catering company I hired has set out dinner for the five of us. I had ordered enough for mom to take some home, but she was tired and declined.

The conversation flows around us as we eat, but Skye doesn't join in unless she is asked a question directly. It's beginning to irritate me. Craig makes eye contact with me and then leans in and says something in Shaina's ear. She blushes, then looks over at Skye and frowns. Skye has been pushing her food around, not really touching it.

"Skye?" I ask, drawing her attention.

"Yes?" she replies absently.

I look down at her plate and raise a brow. "Is the food not good?"

She just shrugs and takes a sip of the wine that was served with dinner. "It's ok."

Our guests fall silent and watch the exchange. All eyes are on us.

"Have you even tasted it yet?" I slowly set my fork down.

She shrugs and pushes another forkful around.

I pause for a moment then raise my eyebrow. "Would you like me to have them serve dessert now?" I offer, hoping to entice her to eat at least something. "It's your favorite."

"They? Oh, the caterers. I sent them away after they served dinner. I can go get it if you want, I had them leave it in the fridge."

She doesn't wait for me to answer but leaves the table and Lea follows her, taking our dishes.

I don't know why she's so worked up about company when it's our best friends, but she can't blame tonight for her appetite. She hasn't been eating properly for a while, and it is starting to piss me off.

"Christ, she needs to snap out of her funk," Craig mutters. He's right, but I choose to ignore him.

"Do you want me to talk to her again?" Shaina offers.

"You can try, I just don't know how to get her out of this mood."

"You should just give her space and try to find her someone to talk to."

"I've tried, she said she's fine." I sigh.

"That's usually the first sign that she's not. I'll see what I can do later."

Lea and Skye come back with plates. I ordered our favorite cheesecake and despite her sour mood, I notice she has served it on the plates just like the restaurant serves it, with dollops of whipped cream and strawberries. It makes me smile, perhaps she will actually eat this. She sets mine down in front of me without a word and moves to go back to the opposite end of the table to sit with Lea.

"No," I say abruptly.

She stops and turns to me with a bewildered look. "No?"

The tension builds for the next few seconds and the table is silent as she waits for me to answer. "No, sit here. I uhh... want you to sit by me."

"Umm ok." She looks bewildered. She sits in the seat beside mine, then looks right at me. "Happy now?"

"Yes." I nod, aware that I made it weird and hoping everyone will turn their attention back to their dessert. I take a forkful, ignoring our guests and groan as the smooth, creamy goodness tickles my taste buds. Even in these circumstances, the cheesecake wins.

I watch as Skye starts playing with her food again, damn it, I don't have the patience for this. This cheesecake is too damned good for her to just smear it on her plate. "Quit playing with your food and eat the damn thing!" I snap, forgetting for a moment that we have company.

I glance over guiltily at them and see Craig's amusement, not very smooth on my part.

She sets her fork down carefully, too carefully in fact. "Now that you mention it, I'm not hungry."

I drop my fork onto my plate, surprised that the fine bone china doesn't crack. "You didn't touch your dinner, Skye. So eat the cheesecake."

She pushes it a little further away. "No."

I grind my teeth so hard my jaw hurts. She's so damn stubborn. She's wasting away to nothing before my eyes. I turn in my seat to face her and try another approach. "Skye, please, eat the cheesecake, or..."

Craig's hiding a smirk behind his hand while Shaina and Lea are watching this with interest not knowing where the hell I'm going with this.

She lets out this deep husky laugh. "Or what?" she asks defiantly.

"Or I'll make you," I growl.

"Preston!" Lea says in shock.

Skye's laugh gets raspy and deep. "Make me? What are you going to do, tie me up and feed me?"

I bless her with the exact same smile that I gave my mama earlier and answer with a simple, "If I have to."

She laughs again, her laugh is really something. It's a sound I've missed terribly. She's being playful, it's a side of her that she rarely shows. She looks at me with a dazzling smile. This is the most relaxed I have seen her since she has been home, it's almost as if she needs something to push back against. I should have known.

"Do it then," she demands, sitting back in her chair with her arms folded. "Make me."

Lea gasps, reminding me they are there. I wish they would

just disappear. I want to see this thing through with Skye. I look around the room, first at Craig as he sits back with a smirk, then at Lea and Shaina, their surprised looks are hilarious. It's bad form to humiliate her with an audience, but she's asking for it and Craig nods subtly, letting me know he would go for it in my position.

I glance around to see if we have anything I can use to tie her, I don't trust her to stay put if I go in search of something. I'm about to ditch the plan and just drag her onto my lap when the ruby red table runner catches my eye. I grin and take my plate off the fabric which runs from one end of the table to the other, starting to pull it toward me slowly. Thankfully no other plates were in the way. I have her full attention, her gaze locked with mine, and I don't break it as I gather the material in my lap. The table centerpiece slides toward me and I pause to pick it up and put it aside, pulling the rest of the cloth with a snap. This makes her jump, but she doesn't break eye contact with me.

I rise as I gather the end, and she watches me with her moss green eyes. I move to stand behind her chair but she doesn't turn her head to follow me. She puts her hands on the table, she has a sassy tilt to her head. Behind her I shake out the runner and slip it through the back of the chair and then under her arms.

She sits patiently with the fabric in her lap. I move to her side and pick up the end, pulling it over her arm. I lean over and do the same to her other arm. I'm surprised she is allowing this, but there is an air of challenge that I feel she can't back down from, so I take advantage of the silent permission. I glance down and can see her pulse hammering where her neck and shoulder meet.

She looks up at me with a playful glint in her eye despite her resolute defiance. "Are you going to tie a little bow?" she goads.

I step back behind her and pull the fabric back. "Yes," I reply, securing her arms behind her. I hook my foot into the leg of my chair, pulling it close to hers and take a seat beside her, picking up her plate. "Now," I begin. "I can see that you haven't been eating properly, Skye." I take a small forkful and glance up at her.

She narrows her eyes at me. "I have been eating until I'm full. I don't eat a lot," she huffs.

"I know you better than that, now open up. This is your favorite." I bring the fork up to her lips. She presses them together in a firm line and shakes her head.

I set the plate back on the table and raise my hand slowly, so she can see I'm not going to hurt her, moving it in close to her face. She flinches as I pinch her nostrils shut. Her eyes pop open and a moment later, so does her mouth. Before she can close it again, I pop the cheesecake in and use a single finger to push her chin up, effectively closing her mouth.

She chews reluctantly, and I watch her closely as she swallows and then licks her lips. "Ok, you made your point." She sighs.

"I don't think I did."

She opens her mouth for a smart remark and I pop another bite in.

"I think we should give them some privacy." I hear Craig whisper to Shaina and Lea.

"I kinda want to watch this play out," Lea says in awe.

"Come on, ladies, let's go grab a beer or something." Craig quietly ushers them out of the room. I owe him one.

"Knock it off, Preston," Skye says with a mouth full of food.

"And just watch you starve yourself?"

"I—" Her argument is cut off by yet more cheesecake, which I watch her chew and swallow. Her tight jaw working reluctantly and her eyes set grimly on mine just serve to push me on. I have never wanted her more and yet my instinct is to care for her even as she fights me.

"You think I don't notice your clothes falling off you and your plate always full at the end of meals?" I challenge. "You're thinner now than when I found you on the street. Why?"

Skye rolls her eyes and parts her lips to answer, but finds only cheesecake on her tongue where she wanted words to form. I bite my lip to suppress my smile. I have a serious point, but her frustration with me is amusing. I can tell she is slightly amused too, except she is maintaining her annoyance.

"If there is a good reason you aren't eating, then tell me and I will help you. But if this is simply some misguided ambition to be as scrawny as the women on Rodeo Drive then let me tell you, bones aren't sexy." I deliver more cheesecake and I'm as surprised as she seems to be when she takes it willingly, distracted by my speech.

"What is sexy, Skye, is softness." I brush the backs of my fingers over her cheek as I withdraw my hand. Her eyes flutter closed at the sensation. "Sexy," I whisper, "is your empty plate and your full belly and the carefree smile on your lips." I can't stop myself as I lean in and press the smallest of kisses to the corner of her mouth. She gasps.

"Sexy," I murmur against her skin, "is your warm, curvy ass curled up against my body while you sleep peacefully."

My breathing hitches. I'm so aroused. Every cell in my body begs me to kiss her and make her mine again.

Her sigh is inviting and I imagine taking her now, right here on the table.

But I can't.

We have to talk first. I need to admit so many truths to her before I can do that. It would be unforgivable of me to give in to my desire before she knows the truth.

I pull back, breathing heavy from being so near her. She lifts her eyes to mine and they are shining with emotion. It would be so easy to give in, get lost in her and forget everything. I reach out a hand to…I don't know what. I just need her.

Damn it, Preston.

I suck in a breath, stand abruptly, reach around the back of her chair and give a tug on the end of the runner. The fabric comes loose and her arms fall free.

"I'm sorry," I whisper, then head quickly for the door. I have to get away from her for both our sakes. Pausing just beyond the doorway, I steady myself and then in the shadow cast by the dining room lighting against the doorframe, I steal a glance back into the room.

She stares dumbfounded at the empty doorway, unable to see me in the shadows. Then she snaps herself out of her trance and sets her lips into a grim line. She scowls down at the plate realizing she ate all but the last bite of the dessert I chose for her.

She grabs the plate and stands, then turns and pauses. She looks down at the red table runner hanging off the back of the chair. I can tell she isn't pleased by the slight flaring of her nose. She looks up at the doorway again and I draw back further into the shadow. She stares for a long moment, then shakes her head and walks toward the kitchen.

I hear the plate smash as I head down the hall, away from temptation. Away from her.

I let myself into my workout room, the tranquility of it surrounds me. The space is open, and I stop at the top step taking in the view. The far wall is smoked glass, overlooking the mountains, but the sun has already set so it's just darkness I see and that suits my mood. I have every kind of workout equipment in here, lined up against the walls, but I don't need any of it tonight. I step down into the room and go to my rack of custom boxing gloves. Right now would be an ideal time to spar with Craig, but the bastard left.

I strip to the waist and roll my shoulders back trying to loosen up my muscles. I haven't been working out in here as much as I should. I stretch my neck and take a moment to soak up my surroundings. I crave the peace I can find in this room and I already feel some of the tension leaving me.

I move toward the punching bag in the corner. I pull my arm back and let my first swing fly, the thump of the bag soothes me and I work my aim up and down the target. I'm not sure how much time passes, hours maybe? But I keep going, sweat pouring off me and my breaths searing my lungs, trying to forget. The burn in my upper torso and arms is a good indicator that I've had enough and eventually, I give in to it.

The moment I stop and set the room right again, thoughts of her come crashing back into my head. I need to tell her why I left, I yearn for her forgiveness. We have to talk.

Fifteen

SKYE

I'm stirred by soft kisses on the back of my neck, my favorite spot. I must be dreaming. I moan and arch back into him, feeling his breath at my ear and then teeth scraping down my neck ending in a gentle bite on my shoulder. I've missed this. Him. I've missed him. I turn slowly to face him, reluctant to open my eyes. I don't want this to be a dream.

I lift my head, my mouth seeking his. I don't have to wait, his mouth crashes on mine immediately. It's familiar yet different. He takes charge, starting a tango with our tongues, a dance we haven't done in over five years. He tastes like home.

I cup his face, still afraid to open my eyes. I press myself against him, wrapping my legs around his, feeling his hard length pressing into me. His hips thrust. I rise to meet them, cursing the clothes that separate us. Feverish need rolls through me. I wrap my arms around him and pull him closer. My heart is beating a thousand beats per minute.

He pulls one of my hands and then the other, entwining our fingers together and pressing them down into the pillow on either side of my head. He presses his body fully down on mine. I can't move, but I don't feel trapped. I trust him, I always have. He kisses me hard and then pulls back, my head lifting to follow him.

"I'm so sorry, Skye." The huskiness of his voice makes me shiver. "So sorry for everything."

I squeeze my eyes shut tighter, this isn't a dream. None of my dreams have ever been this perfect. Teeth pressing into my bottom lip, I sigh and my eyes flutter open, my senses on high alert. I fight back a whimper at the sight of him above me.

"I want you," he says so softly, then kisses my forehead before raising himself off me. "But we have so much to discuss first." He quickly rolls out of bed and walks to the bathroom. "I'm going to take a shower, then we can talk."

Ugh!!! Frustrated, I curl up on the bed with my back toward the bathroom door, my damn body betrayed me while my mind was still half asleep. He thinks he knows what I need, but maybe I just needed that closeness. I don't know? It felt so good.

Anxiety grips me at the thought of losing myself to him again and my breaths hitch in my chest. I can feel the panic attack building and my mind goes straight back to feeling this way last night.

The minute Preston left me alone with our friends to tuck his mama in, Lea fired off questions like I was in front of a firing squad. It's obvious that she'd missed me, I missed her too. But it was question after question. By the time she asked if Preston and I are back together, I had myself braced with my arms on the counter just trying to breathe. Thankfully Shaina showed up and saw the signs of the panic attack I was fighting off. She was able to get Lea to go back into the dining room. I just hugged myself and took deep calming breaths.

Shaina asked me how long I had been experiencing these symptoms and when I told her, at least since middle school, her concern grew. She offered me medication, begged me in fact to take it. She is certain it would help me, but I told her no. She knows why I don't trust medication. Not since...

She is right though, my anxiety isn't at a manageable level and her, I trust. I know she has my best interests at heart. At just the thought of an end to the crippling panic attacks I have dealt with for years, this latest anxiety eases. Before I lose my nerve and ignore the issue again, I grab my cell phone off the nightstand, opening up a new text.

'Morning Shaina, I've thought about it and I'm willing to take your suggestion about my anxiety. I'll try the medicine. What do I need to do?'

I hit send and put the phone back on the nightstand. I can do this.

I feel as if Preston and I have been growing closer, but we haven't talked about our past or the present. It feels as if we are moving forward and yet, getting nowhere. I shouldn't be wrapped in him every night and have no idea where we stand, but still, I haven't even tried finding somewhere else to stay. I feel at home here, comfortable and safe, those are my ideas of home. Something I have never had before now.

I try to read him, gauge him by his actions, and I come up empty. It's utterly frustrating. And after going to bed alone last night while he brooded somewhere in the house and then how he woke me this morning, only to walk out again...I'm even more confused. Not only by him but also by my feelings. I need the help that Shaina has offered. I'm closed off, confused, and need to start caring again.

I snap out of my brooding when I hear the bathroom door open.

"Will you meet me in the kitchen when you are ready?" he asks as he throws a towel in the laundry basket.

"Yeah, I'll be right out," I mutter absently.

I clean up quickly, dreading what I'll walk into. I know this conversation is long overdue, but I'm afraid of how it will go. I stand in the doorway of the kitchen and see Liliya walk in from the sliding glass door.

Preston notices me and floors me with a bright smile I rarely see from him. "Come on, ladies, we're going to go out for breakfast," he tells us enthusiastically. I'm completely thrown. I thought he wanted to have a serious talk and here he is almost bouncing with excitement and bringing his mom with us to breakfast. This should be interesting. We've never all gone out together, it's usually just Liliya and myself. Preston is always so busy. Liliya and I do everything together, she has brought a sense of normalcy into my life. They both have if I'm being honest with myself. Something I seriously needed, I dream of knowing what normal is really like.

Preston's in great spirits as we leave the house, and it's infectious. We're going to Liliya's favorite breakfast place, A Bit of Country. I haven't been there in years. We all order our favorite things and chat happily while we wait. I'm excited for the Eggs Benedict, it's been too long since I've had it. And after last night with the cheesecake, I want to show Preston that I do eat when I'm hungry. And yeah, okay, maybe I'm allowing myself to be a little more hungry than I have been since he told me that he finds soft, sexy. Maybe.

The food is delicious, and we're having a great time, until I look across the restaurant. The smile is wiped right off my face as I see my parents. I freeze in my seat and brace my hands on the table, as I see my father rise from his chair. Not once does he take his eyes off me, he just says something to my mother, probably an order not to move and then he begins to walk across the restaurant. I frantically look around, searching for the exit.

Run! My mind is screaming, *don't let him get near you.*

Liliya's hand squeezes mine and her soothing voice breaks into my panic, "Skye, what's the matter, *milaya?*"

I look briefly over at her and whisper, "It's my father." She's never really had any face to face dealings with him, so I fear she won't understand how dreadful this situation is.

My eyes snap back to him just as he reaches our table and before I can bolt, Preston stands.

"Is there something I can help you with, Bob?" he asks in a low firm tone.

My father has never been one to back down. "I want a word with my daughter," he demands, looking past Preston like he isn't even there.

"I don't think she has anything to say to you," Preston informs him. "Right, Skye?" he asks me over his shoulder without taking his eyes away from the man I detest.

I sit up a little straighter, somehow braver, knowing Preston is here to protect me. "Nope," I reply, attempting to sound confident.

"Don't be difficult, Skye." My father leans around Preston to level his best look of intimidation on me. "We have things to discuss."

"You heard her Bob, she said no," Preston says flatly.

"You can't stop me," he blurts, what I call his red rage face slowly emerging.

Preston gets the evilest smile and leans closer to him. I have to strain to make out what he says.

"Is that what you think, Bob? It would be such a pleasure to show you how wrong you are." He leans back slightly, the smile still plastered on his face.

My father's face is bright red with rage now. This is usually the time when I would be running to find a room to lock myself in. But I don't have to do that anymore. He pauses for a moment, calming himself down and gives me such a hateful look.

"I'll be in touch," my father growls at me. It's a threat, not a promise. Then he storms back to his table.

Preston's calm voice breaks through my thoughts. "You ladies ready to go?"

"I think we are," Liliya says and clasps my elbow as she stands. As Liliya leads the way out, I follow directly behind her, but can't help but glance over to my parents as we pass.

My father, usually a king manipulator, doesn't even look our way. My mother looks up at me with stone-cold, dead eyes. He whispers something to her ignoring us.

"Are you all right?" Preston asks just low enough so I can hear, and I nod my head. Does anyone ever say no when they are asked if they're ok?

Once we pull into the driveway, Liliya announces that the morning has been tiring for her and she is going to go and lay down. Preston gives me a worried look, she typically doesn't take naps. "Liliya, we will come and get you all settled in," I tell her, hoping that it will reassure Preston that everything is okay if we accompany her.

I follow Liliya into the bedroom in her cozy home and tuck her in, kissing her forehead. "Sleep well, Liliya."

She gives me a warm smile and pats my hands. "Can you send Preston in, *milaya*?"

"Sure, I'll go get him." I smile back.

Preston is pacing back and forth as I enter the living room. Pausing his stride, he shoots me a concerned glance. "Is she asleep?"

I tuck a curl behind my ear and shake my head. "No, she's asking for you."

I know this is a private conversation, but I'm concerned that she isn't feeling well and they might need me, so I follow him and stop at the door to her room. I can see her lying in bed and watch as Preston sits right next to her.

"What is it, Mama?" he says with concern.

"Preston, I want to talk to you about Skye."

At the mention of my name I move back out of sight but can still hear them. Me? Why does she want to talk about me?

"Okay, is something bothering you?"

"Yes!" she says emphatically, her voice has me pressing my back against the wall. Does she hate me?

"What is it?" Preston sounds concerned.

"Did you see her father? *Svinya,* I wanted to teach him some manners."

His mirthless laugh sounds through the air. "Mama!"

"I'm serious, Preston, he needs to be taught."

Preston's voice turns serious. "Don't worry about him. He won't get near her, I won't allow it, he'll get what is coming to him."

I peek around the corner to get a look at them. She claps his hands.

"Promise me, Preston, promise me you will look after her."

"Don't worry about Skye, she'll be okay."

She lets go of his hands, practically throwing them away from her. "She's like the daughter I never had, you must promise me!" she demands.

"I promise, Mama, I will look after her. Her family won't hurt her anymore, you know I'd do anything for her," he assures her softly. She nods and they exchange no more words as he kisses her forehead. He obviously doesn't need me for anything and I'm really intruding and feel horrible about it. I tiptoe back to the house, so he can have his privacy.

It's three in the afternoon and I just finished a swim. Preston comes in from his workout and sits at the table. "Where's Mama?"

I set my cup down. "She hasn't come back up yet, I figured the extra sleep would do her good."

"You're probably right." He picks up his paper to scan the local news. "We might want to wake her up by four though, or she won't sleep tonight."

I open my mouth, thinking it might be a good time to ask him about this morning. He told me we needed to talk then took us out for breakfast with his mother. I'd also like to know why he was talking to my father privately, but I quickly lose my nerve and go into the kitchen.

When I have the dishes done, I glance up at the clock and see it's now three forty-five. I wipe my hands on the towel and set it on the counter, then I walk out of the sliding glass doors and around the pool, to go and wake Liliya.

I softly knock on her door and then let myself in. The house is silent and just the soft glow from the lamp illuminates the space. I walk around the living room first, as I have seen Liliya do countless times, opening up the curtains that block out the bright desert sun.

I don't want to startle her so I softly call out, "Liliya, it's Skye. It's almost four o'clock." It's strange though, usually when I let her know I'm in the house I can hear the rustle of her sheets as she starts to get up.

As I stand at her doorway I can see the outline of her in bed. "Liliya? Wake up." Still there is no movement. I don't really want to shake her awake, so I turn the light on in her room and I see the blankets are pulled up high. I sigh because I am going to have to wake her, and I don't want to disturb her peaceful sleep, but Preston is right, she'll be mad if she sleeps all day.

I sit down in the same spot Preston was perched earlier in the day and gently shake her shoulder.

"Liliya? Come on, time to get up."

I frown, concerned. I gently peel the blanket back and have to tug because she has them in her grip. "Liliya?" My heart starts to pound.

I pull her shoulder toward me, rolling her over. Her eyes are closed and she has a serene smile on her face. My brows furrow because things are off, her lips have a tinge of blue to them.

"SHIT!" I move into action and press the panic button next to her bed. That sends a request directly to the paramedics and also an alarm to the house so Preston knows he's needed here. I push her onto her back and take her tiny wrist into my hand. My lifeguard training never quite prepared me for this, but I know this is bad. Blue is bad.

I press into her wrist, noting how cool she is to the touch, *come on old girl be there for me.* No pulse, and I see her fingernail beds are black, she's not getting oxygen.

"No, no, no..." I mutter, adrenaline pushing me on. The bed is too soft for CPR, thankfully she doesn't weigh much so I move her to the floor.

I first take my knuckle and rub it hard against her sternum. "Liliya, wake up!" I yell at her loudly in the hopes that the pain will shock her system, it doesn't.

No response.

I go over my training in my head, C-A-B comes directly to mind: circulation, airway, and breathing. I kneel by her shoulders and then place a palm in the middle of her chest and put my other hand on top, going over in my head how I was trained to do this. I press down hard, making sure my elbows are straight and count to thirty.

I take my hands away and press a palm to her head and cradle her neck with the other, opening her airway. I check her chest for any movement then put my face close to hers to see if I feel any breath. When I see no signs, I hurry and pinch her nose and make a seal with my mouth over hers, breathing my life into her.

When I glance at her chest I see it rise. I give her another breath then go back to giving the chest compressions. I am unsure how many cycles of breaths and compressions I have done. I glance up and see Preston frozen in the doorway. "What are you doing?" he gasps.

"Go let the paramedics in," I say as calmly as I can, given the current situation. He doesn't move, he just stares horror stricken at the scene as I try and revive his beloved mama. "Preston, GO!" I demand. He takes one last look at his mother and vanishes. I turn back to Liliya. I have to keep going, this has to be done and help will arrive soon.

Before I know it, a young paramedic kneels on the other side of her head, and I quickly tell him that I haven't been able to find a pulse and that I started CPR as soon as the panic button was hit.

"Ma'am, can you move away so I can assess her?"

Is he kidding? I continue my CPR on her. "No, we need to keep going." Ignoring him, I keep counting in my head.

I feel an arm go around my waist and lift me off the floor. "No!" I yell. I have to keep Liliya's heart moving so they can save her.

"*Detka!*" Preston says urgently in my ear. "Let them do their job, you did what you could."

I try to jerk out of his arms, but he has me in a tight hold. As soon as I look down to where they are working on her, the fight leaves me. I lean back into him and he moves his head down to press his forehead into my shoulder. At this point I'm unsure who is holding up who.

I see both of them shake their heads and the one that was talking to me looks at his watch and writes something down on his paperwork. The other one gets up and walks over to us. "I'm sorry," he says gently. "She has been gone for a while."

I gasp. "No..." I whisper.

"Oh my God." Preston cries into my shoulder, squeezing me tighter. "What am I going to do?"

Numb, that's what I feel right now. I don't have an answer for him, so I just hold him tight as they take her out and have Preston sign some papers, telling him where she will be. I stand there staring at the bed and then the floor as I try to make sense of what just happened. She can't be gone, we were just laughing it up this morning.

The emergency crew clears out of the house, leaving traces of the work they were doing. I'm still standing in the same spot, and I can feel Preston not far behind me. I just don't know what to do at this point, the pain in my chest is so real that I know this isn't a nightmare. In my own shock I didn't think about him. I'm being so selfish, he needs me. I turn to see how he's taking this and find that he is just standing there staring at the floor where she last was, his hands fisted at his sides, his body tense.

I take a step toward him and stop when I notice his face is stained with his tears. My heart aches, and yet the tears don't fall for me. He needs me, hell I need him just as much right now. I stand before him and wrap my arms around him holding him as tight as I can. His mama was his everything.

He stands stiff for a moment as if I've shocked him but then his arms crash around me. He puts his head in the crook of my neck and I feel his tears on my skin. I stroke his hair as he silently cries on my shoulder.

I don't feel the need for words right now, and I assume he is feeling the same. Slowly, he pulls back and takes a look at my face, then abruptly, he turns on his heel, and with long strides, he leaves Liliya's house.

I don't know if he's mad because I couldn't save her. I feel so heartless. I wanted to tell him nothing ever comes from crying. Then again, I used to get a beating from my father if he caught me shedding a tear. In that situation, you learn to cry on the inside and not show your sorrow...*ever.* Now I only cry in my sleep when I have no control.

Sixteen

PRESTON

She's gone. The one thing that has always been solid in my life, just...gone.

I mindlessly walk back to the main house and into my office, silently closing the door. I look around the room and my eyes settle on a picture in the corner. It's my parents' wedding picture, and when I pick it up and study their young happy faces, the lump in my throat threatens to choke me. My mind flashes back to Skye performing CPR, the fierceness she had as she tried to breathe life back into her.

"Mama..." I whisper.

My eyes search the room and all I see is touches of her everywhere, all of this was for her to have a better life. My legs give out and I fall to my knees, looking up at the ceiling. "Why, God? Why her...why?"

I ball my hands and pound the rug as tears stream down my face, it was just the two of us for so long. She helped me deal with the loss of Skye, guided me to find her. She gave me the drive to want more, for her and for Skye.

"Mama..." I repeat desperately.

After a while passes, my knees begin to ache. I have no desire to move or pull myself together. I just want to curl up here and cry, but I know it's pointless. I can't afford to get lost in my mind right now. I slowly get to my feet and walk to my desk. Mama and I had spoken about what she wanted me to do when she passed away, and this gives me some purpose.

The only thing she wanted was exactly what we did for my father, we cremated him because we couldn't afford to bury him somewhere nice. I'll respect her wishes and cremate her, but then I will bury them together somewhere worthy. I use the sleeve of my shirt and wipe the tears from my eyes. I should call Craig, but I just can't bear to say the words out loud yet.

There is a soft knock on the door. "Come in," I answer, flatly.

Skye peeks her head into the room. "I brought you a sandwich," she says softly.

"I'm not really hungry." My tone is harsher than I meant it to be.

She steps in. "You need to eat," she demands. She marches right over and puts a plate with a sandwich and chips on the desk. "You need to keep up your strength. I'll come back in an hour, make sure it's gone." And she's gone just as fast as she came.

I look around at the empty room and remember I was about to do something. As I'm getting an email ready to send off to the funeral director, I glance at the sandwich and my stomach growls. She'll come back in an hour, I know she will. Slowly as I type the email I eat the sandwich to make her happy. I outline everything I want done for my parents' service. This will be my way of honoring them both. When my father passed, just a few people from his work came by to bring us casseroles and such. If it wasn't for Skye and Lea, the house wouldn't have had any flowers in at all. I write some other notes on a piece of paper, a to-do list for myself. I press my pen to the paper and pause, images of my mom filling my head. My teardrops stain the paper as they start to fall.

"Oh, Preston..." I hear Skye mutter.

I lift my head to see her rush in. She takes my handkerchief off the desk and wipes away the tears.

"She's all I had left, Skye." Emotion chokes me, and I can barely swallow. She's murmuring next to me, but I can't hear what she's saying because the comfort of her is all I know at the moment. She makes me feel as if I have more to work and live for. I grab her around the waist and pull her onto my lap.

"I loved her too," she says as her fingers gently run through my hair.

"I know you did." I pull her closer.

She doesn't say a word, we sit in silence and grieve together. She is all I have now. Like a knife to the heart, I realize my mother will never see what becomes of Skye and me. But I will make her proud.

She slips off my lap and takes the plate. "I'm going to head up to bed, it's getting pretty late. Are you okay? Do you need anything?"

You. I need you. I can't voice the thought though. I just don't know how to make those words come out the right way, so I shake my head. "I'll be there soon, I've a couple more things I need to take care of."

She silently leaves the room, leaving me alone again. I'm sure I could ask her to help with the arrangements, but this is something I need to do on my own. Putting my elbows on my desk I rub my temples, warding off a tension headache. I can't believe this is happening. She has been in such good health, I never expected this. My cell phone lights up on the desk next to me and I glance at the screen and see it's a text message from Craig.

"Dude, I'm so sorry, Shaina just let me know. Do you need to talk?"

I sigh. Craig's the older brother I never had, even if he's only older by a few months. He knows me too well, that's why he didn't call. I feel guilty that he had to hear it from his girlfriend, but I'm just relieved I didn't have to tell him myself.

"Not yet, arrangements will come shortly."

My response is short, but if I ignore him he would be knocking at my door. He's done it before when I came back and found out Skye was gone. I went a little crazy and my mom called him to come over to get me under control.

His response comes in a few seconds later.

"You sure?"

I reply, "I'm okay, Skye is here. I'll call if I need you."

I shut everything down and close up for the night, a wave of tiredness has finally washed over me.

When I enter the bedroom, I know she isn't asleep. She's laying on her back, and I can see the whites of her eyes as she stares at the ceiling. I head into the bathroom and get ready for bed. I only just promised myself I would make Mama proud and hold on to Skye, but already I fear what will happen to us when I tell her the truth about why I left. Steeling myself, I come out of the bathroom and slide into bed beside her, laying on my back, afraid to touch her, terrified she'll turn me away when I just need to hold her and forget about the pain for a little while.

"Are you okay?" she whispers.

"Yes," I reply. "And by that, I mean no." I chuckle mirthlessly.

She turns on her side in bed and faces me, her eyes luminous in the twilight of the room. She opens her arms. "Come here, let me hold you tonight."

"Are you sure?"

"More than ever, for years you've chased away my nightmares. Let me help you find some comfort with everything that has happened."

"I'd love that more than anything right now," I admit, not

feeling ashamed to need her. After everything with my mother is dealt with, I am going to do what my mother wanted. I'm going to make Skye see how much I love her. She's all I have left.

I move closer and her arms wrap gently around me. I'm not sure if either of us will sleep tonight. But at least we have the comfort of each other's arms.

Seventeen

SKYE

Today will bring some closure for us both. After the funeral, we can move on and start to heal ourselves. Preston decided that his parents will be laid to rest together. I didn't know his father well but I do know Liliya would be happy that they are being laid to rest together.

I'm nervous. Actually, that's putting it lightly. I'm terrified. I don't feel ready to stand at Preston's side and have all eyes on us. People in this town talk and today is not the day for us to be scrutinized. But I will do anything to show him my support, and if that means dealing with people, then so be it.

Dressed head to toe in black, we sit silently in the car as it pulls into the cemetery. I see the whole gang is already there as well as some of Liliya's friends. The last time I was here was when my grandmother passed away. I never wanted to come back, there are too many bad memories. Everything changed after that day.

Preston shuts his car door and it brings me out of my memories. I step out of the car, and I follow him to the graveside.

Under the awning it feels stark and cold, you wouldn't guess it's a hundred degrees outside. I slide my hand into his because I know he needs me to be strong and help him get through this in one piece. He squeezes my hand hard.

"Are you alright?" I whisper.

"I just need to get through today," he replies, loosening his grip on my hand a little.

We listen to the service and lean on each other, staring at the casket. It contains the cremated remains of his mom and dad, together at last. He squeezes my hand again as it's lowered into the ground. When they look to him to throw the first shovel of dirt on them, he releases my hand and steps forward. After tipping some of the dirt into the grave, he then takes something out of his pocket. It catches the light and sparkles as he tosses it into the grave and I wonder what it was that he sent with them to their resting place as he shovels more dirt over their casket.

Turning back, he takes my hand in his. I squeeze it hard as an unfamiliar lump forms in my throat. It's foreign, almost as if I might cry. Swallowing, I start to visualize Liliya reuniting with her husband and peacefulness surrounds me.

A number of guests have gathered and are waiting to offer their condolences to Preston. It makes me nervous to be around so many unfamiliar people and I make my excuses. "I'm going to go stand with Shaina and Lea," I tell him feebly. "I will send Craig over."

"Please stay with me," Preston pleads. "Mama would have wanted you to meet her friends."

"Okay, I'll stay." Even though I would rather not, I would do anything for him.

Preston tugs on my hand and keeps me by his side as he greets people and accepts their condolences. I tense beside him as I catch a glimpse of my mother. Why is she here? Did my father come with her? I brace myself for him to cause a scene, but my mom just makes eye contact and drops a rose into the grave then leaves without a word.

Preston planned a luncheon where he makes an effort to speak with all of his mother's friends. I stay by him for a few more minutes and then motion Craig over to stay with Preston while I make sure the manager of the restaurant knows to come to me with any problems. It's good for me to be strong for him like this. As I walk back to Preston, I slow, and my heart starts to pound. Dimitri and Evgeni Volkov are greeting Preston and hugging him. Then they stand back, as their father Vasily steps up to Preston. My chest tightens and my thoughts start racing. I first met the brothers one winter when they were here on vacation visiting my father. Their family is in the diamond business with hints of mafia connections. They are known for being brutal and I'm in shock that they are here. How on earth does Preston know them?

Vasily takes Preston's face into his hands and says something to him then kisses each cheek. He's the same height as Preston but seems so much larger than him in this moment. I stay where I am, not wanting to interact with any of them. I just stare in shock, watching as Vasily gives Preston a hug. When he pulls away I swear I see tears in his eyes. Preston turns toward me and our eyes lock. He inclines his head in question, noticing my demeanor. After a minute or two of polite conversation, something I didn't know the Volkovs were capable of, Preston excuses himself and crosses the room to me.

"What is the Volkov family doing here?" I demand. "I didn't realize you knew them." My voice is devoid of all emotion, I won't let him see the internal freak out I am having.

"You know the Volkovs?" He raises a brow, then catches himself. "Of course you do." He shakes his head as he realizes that they are most likely associates of my father's. "Fuck, Skye, we really need to sit down and have that talk. That is my Uncle Vasily and my cousins," he tells me and looks back at them. They are watching us.

"You're kidding me, right?" I choke.

"No. Come on, let's go find somewhere more private and I will tell you all about it." He takes hold of my hand.

I stiffen and gently slide my hand out of his. "There is a time and a place for a conversation like that, Preston. We just buried your parents. Let today be about paying respect to your Mama. I won't let this get in the way of what she deserves." Plus, the conversation we need to have has to be done in private. If the Volkovs are somehow involved I suspect it won't be pretty. I won't say that out loud though, because I don't want him to lose his nerve.

"You're right, but we will have this conversation soon, it's long past due," he says solemnly.

I stayed by his side the whole time, not really talking with everyone but listening and picking up on the conversations. This is how I found out more about the connection between Vasily and Liliya. She was born Liliya Rose Volkov...my mind was blown by this. All this time, through all their hardship, she was related to one of the wealthiest families in Russia. Vasily re-told stories of his sister and him growing up and I joined in with everyone laughing, despite myself at what a practical joker Liliya was. Even though I was near bursting with questions I saved them for another time. I was enjoying all the stories of Liliya, of hearing how kind she was, not only to me but everyone...except apparently Vasily. Eventually people slowly start to trickle out and once the last guests had gone, we rode home in silence.

Once back home, we change, and Preston tells me he has a little work to do. Part of me wants to tell him to leave work for today, but I know that he needs an escape and maybe I am delaying the inevitable too. I don't know if I'm ready to know what business Preston has involving associates of my father. But I trust him, so I let it go. Now is his time to grieve, everything else comes second.

Eighteen

SKYE

The awkward morning routine where I would move an inch and he would jump from the bed like he was on fire, is gone. Now we lay wrapped in each other. I open my eyes and watch him for a minute. The tightness in my chest that used to be present has gone, but the butterflies in my belly are there in full force. This is the good type of anxiety. I smile and lean forward, lightly kissing his full lips, then pull back.

Needing to go to the bathroom, I try to free myself from his arms, but he pulls me closer, locking me to his chest. His breathing steadies and he opens his eyes. "*Dobroe utro karasavica,*" he murmurs.

My brow furrows. "Morning. What does that mean?" I can't resist the urge to trace my fingers from his eyebrows down the side of his face.

"It means good morning beautiful." His arms fall slack and he just watches as I study his face with my fingertips.

"I like it," I admit.

"Get used to it." He smiles. "I will tell you every day," he says, stirring up the butterflies once again with his intense look that I have come to recognize as desire. I don't know when things shifted between us, but we are definitely more than simply two people with a history. It excites me and terrifies me in equal measure and while I enjoy the gentle touches and light kisses we share, I can't predict when and if he will want to turn it into more and that makes me nervous.

Catching him off guard, I jump out of bed to escape any possibility of him making a move right now, and make a mad dash to the bathroom, snatching some clothes from a drawer on my way.

"Skye, what the hell? Get back here," he says in a husky, sleepy voice.

"I'll be right back. I need to use the bathroom..." My voice has a nervous pitch to it. Ughh!

I want him. He's everywhere in my head, and I love the way he consumes me; my every thought, the simplest action. Through all the hell I've experienced and despite what we've put each other through, Preston has always been my calm. The way he makes me feel with a simple brush of his knuckles against my face. Just him saying my name... is simply A-MAZING.

I thought I'd never feel like this again. But no matter how good it feels to be close to him again, we have so much to talk through before we can take the next step and it makes me sick to think about opening up about my past to him. It's one thing to sleep side by side with him every night, but telling him everything brings my worst fears to the surface. Fears I cannot face, fears he has helped me through the years to get over, without knowing he was helping. I don't want to see him look at me with disgust, just as I view myself in the mirror. But I feel in order to put it in my past, I need to share it all with him. Just like he needs to share some things with me.

My mind veers back down memory lane. While my friends were having pool parties and going to the movies, I was learning to hide from my father's friends and dealing with how they would leer at me.

How sick and dirty they would make me feel. I sit down on the edge of the tub as the dark thoughts and horrors of the past try to grab onto me and pull me down. I can still see each of their faces, smiling or winking at me. The older I got, the more they made it seem like accidents, a brush here, or what they would pass off as a playful smack to my bottom there. I was unable to fight them off, because then I would feel the wrath of my father, trying to figure out what I did so wrong to deserve to be treated this way.

I never could understand why my mother allowed it to happen, she did nothing but drown herself in a bottle. Once upon a time I loved my parents, but they destroyed any emotion I felt for them as they destroyed any semblance of my childhood.

My mind continues to pull me deeper into the darkness of my past, of things I cannot change. All the love and happiness left my life the summer my beloved grandmother passed away. That was when the abuse began. It took years to figure out why my parents hated me so much.

Money, it always boils down to money. They acted like it was my fault Grams left all her money to me.

In the darkness of despair, although it's rare, I feel the anger slowly snake its way up my back. I want to scream, lash out, bring pain down on my parents for all the suffering they caused me. As my hands begin to sweat and my chest begins to shake, I inhale a deep breath, mentally chastising myself to keep it together.

And as quickly as the darkness encompasses me, it's shoved away as I hear my name being called. "Skye...Skye? *Detka*, you're scaring me, open the door!" That name snaps me out of my memory but I'm still frozen.

I try to reply, but I can't. The door bursts open, revealing Preston in the doorway. It's his concerned look that has me leaving the past right where it belongs, in the past. I choke back the fear and swallow.

"Yes?" I don't let any of the raging emotions pass through in my tone. Calm and cool, that's my motto.

"Are you alright?" he asks carefully, assessing me.

I want to scream about how broken I really am but chin up and all that. I won't let the past break me even further.

"Yeah, why wouldn't I be?" I reply.

He pauses for a moment, his eyes searching me. "I was calling you."

"Oh." I shrug, slightly. "Sorry, I didn't hear you. I must have been daydreaming." I give him a crooked smile.

Thankfully he seems to take this at face value and returns my smile. "Let's do something fun today," he suggests after a moment. "We both need to get out of the house for a while."

Nineteen

PRESTON

Judging by the look of horror etched on her face when I barged into the bathroom, I'd say she's anything but fine. I meant what I said, we both need to get out of here and do something fun. I've a special place in mind that I think will do us both some good.

"What do you want to do?" She tucks her hair behind her ear and gives me a smile that doesn't quite reach her eyes. I'd do anything to put that rare look of joy back into her eyes.

There's one place that we used to go and sit and talk for hours; I haven't been there in years. The last time I was there was when I first came back, and I thought maybe she could be hiding in the mountains. My mood suddenly lifts at the thought of taking her there; to our place.

I'm still as I watch her face, hoping she'll like my idea. "A hike sounds good, are you up for one?"

She perks up at this. "Yes! Where?"

"Taquitz?" I feel like that young boy again.

Ahh yeah...there's the smile of hers that reaches her eyes and makes them burn. "I'd love that! The last time I went there was with you," she finishes softly.

"Then it's perfect that you'll go back with me." The cocky smile is back on my face.

She looks down at herself, a towel wrapped around her. "Can I get dressed first?"

"I think that's a wise idea." I back out, giving her space as she dresses.

When she's in the bathroom I slip on a pair of board shorts and a t-shirt. Just as I finish putting my shoes on she opens the door and steps into the bedroom. She's in shorts and a tank top. I slowly smile at her.

She rushes over and throws her arms around my waist, hugging me tight, shocking the hell out of me. It's unlike her to display affection like this.

She pulls back slightly, and I squeeze to keep her by me. She looks up at me, and I study her face, brushing my knuckles down her cheek and then I tuck a curl behind her ear. "That's better, *Detka.*" I hesitate. "I know you've asked me not to call you that, but..." I place a soft kiss on the tip of her nose.

She cocks her head to the side and eyes me. "But you keep doing it anyway."

"I can't help it, it just slips out." I stroke her face again. "Would you let me call you that again?" I ask, hoping beyond hope we are in that place again.

She blushes perfectly and leans her head on my chest. "Yes, I'd like that."

The reality of her acceptance has warmth spreading through me, and I begin to really think we will be okay. No, I know we will be okay. After we talk, that is.

We get in the car and drive up the mountain road. I remember back to my first time up here, it was during our winter break from school. Skye and I walked up here because we didn't have a car. The day was beautiful, seventy and sunny.

We pull into the parking lot that overlooks the valley. I remember when it was illegal to come up here so we would sneak past the house at the end of the road.

"Looks different, doesn't it?" I say to Skye as I stop the car.

"Totally, when did they build this?" She points to the new outpost building.

"A couple years back, beats sneaking up. Ready?"

She looks at me and gives me a small smile. "Yeah, let's go."

We get out of the car and she takes a second to look at all the changes. There's a parking lot for one. All the big boulders we used to climb over now lead us to the building. We start walking to the new visitor's center. It's pretty cool, and you can learn all about the native Agua Caliente band from this area.

I smile at the girl behind the counter. I'm not sure she remembers me, but we both went to high school with her. I pay the park admission and strike up conversation. "Is the water flowing today?"

"Yes, just so you know, there have been signs of rattlers on the trail path."

"Thanks for the heads-up," I reply. Taking Skye's hand, we make our way outside to the trails. I take a moment to study the map and notice some of the rules on it...no swimming? Well, isn't that a load of shit. So really not much has changed since I was a kid and came here, but it's all about not getting caught.

I love it here so much, and although it hurt to be here without her, it became my place to come and reflect. I'm so excited that we get to come up here together today after the hours I have spent here alone with only her on my mind. We don't rush through the trail because at this time of the morning the rattlesnakes like to come out and either sit in the middle of the trail or find a nice warm rock to sunbathe on. The heat isn't that intense at this time of the year, so the rare treat of wild flowers adds splashes of colors throughout the path. I look over at Skye and she has a smile on her face as she takes everything in.

"It's as beautiful as I remember it." She smiles and squeezes my hand.

We take the right side up the mountain trail, probably not wise since this is where the sun is hitting, but I want to take the left side on the return, the two-mile hike does a loop through the canyon. Down the middle of the canyon is a wash, when the snow melts on the mountains the water flows through. The rush of the water gets louder as we hike. Up a rocky path and through the next set of trees, we walk out on to the flat peak. We stop at the edge of the water to watch the waterfall.

She's right behind me and gives me that smile. Damn she's beautiful when she smiles.

"This is so amazing, every time I see the falls it's like the first time," she says in awe.

I pull her across the fallen logs and down into the sandy area on the other side. She takes off her shoes and walks by the water's edge, standing toward the side watching the water rush over the shoals.

I move behind her and wrap my arms around her waist, locking her against my chest. I can feel her breath hitch. I kiss her right below her ear, noting the goose bumps that immediately rise. I lean down and rest my chin on her shoulder, watching the falls with her for a moment.

"I'm so glad we came here," she says on a breathy sigh.

"So am I. I think it's time we started going out in the real world again." It's been so long since we had this easy acceptance of each other. "I think we can do it, together."

Skye looks up at me. Hope fills me at the look of agreement on her face, but she still looks like she has reservations and I know the time for addressing them has come. We need to talk and we are going to do it here.

I know exactly where we can do it too, somewhere we won't be interrupted by other walkers. "Come on, let's keep going." I point across the stream where some kids are just now coming down the trail.

I take Skye's hand and we continue our hike. We go a bit slower. This side of the trail is steep with some narrow paths and rocky inclines that we'll need to be cautious in climbing.

I stop on the path as we turn a corner, a huge rock stands before us. We used to sit and talk for hours up there. On the map I grabbed at the visitor's center, I notice the rock is marked as Sacred Rock. It was or is known to most of the locals as Jesus Rock because it is so high that people think once you climb it you can talk to Jesus from the top.

I pull her along the pathway up to the top of the rock, making sure she gets to the top safely. The view of the desert from here is spectacular. From up here you have a view of the whole valley. Many late Saturday nights were spent lying on this rock, drinking beers while we wondered up at the stars. When the park rangers would patrol, we'd have to lay perfectly still so they wouldn't catch us trespassing.

I stand close to the edge and think of all the times I've been here alone, usually to clear my head.

"This is my favorite place," she says. "I thought about it a lot while I was away." Her voice pulls me back to the present. Having her here with me again, I feel as if everything between us is possible.

"It's so pretty," she muses.

"I know a view that's prettier." I look down beside me and see her smirk. I pull her back to sit down on the rock, positioning her between my legs so we can watch the city below. As the calming silence surrounds us, Skye relaxes into my chest releasing a gentle sigh. I decide this is the time to start our discussion. "Will you tell me about your childhood?" I ask gently, unsure how else to begin.

"I don't want to talk about it." She presses her lips together in a tight line.

"Skye, you have to talk about it."

"Preston, I shouldn't have to. I fucking lived it, that was bad enough."

"Don't hide it from me, okay? I want us to move forward, away from the pains of the past. Together."

I visibly see her swallow, she draws in a deep breath and answers very softly. "I can try."

"Thank you." I give her a gentle squeeze. "Was it awful?"

"Worse than awful."

"I need to know, did your father do more than beat you?" My voice is deathly calm.

Her demeanor changes abruptly. "Why?" she snaps. "Do you want to know if you were the first? So, you can know if I was his whore or not?

"No! Oh God no. Skye, I'd never see you that way. I need to understand why I didn't know. How was I so blind?"

"I hid it too well. I don't know what's worse, the mind games he played or the beatings I took. You've really got no clue of the shit they put me through."

I wrap my arms tighter around her and rest my head on her shoulder as she stares off into the desert sky. "Tell me," I plead, although I'm certain I really don't want to know.

She gives her head a small angry shake. "No, I can't. I'm sorry."

"You can't or you won't?" I sigh in frustration.

"Can't. If I voice it, it makes it real. It needs to stay in the dark. I can't let it into the light when I've tried too hard to keep it from destroying me." Her voice gets softer with each word.

"You should talk about it, it might make your nightmares go away." I squeeze her gently hoping to give her some courage.

"I can't."

"Tell me, *Detka*. Talk to me. I don't want this eating you up, I want to help you heal from it.

"I'm afraid," she says so softly I almost miss it. She turns back and leans against me.

"You don't have to be afraid, I won't let him get to you anymore." I squeeze my arms around her.

She laughs a humorless laugh. "I don't care about him," she says, venom lacing her voice.

"What is it then?"

"You. I don't want you to look at me differently." She tries to pull out of my arms, but I won't let her.

"I promise I won't, nothing could change the way I look at you."

"I trust you, Preston, but can I trust you with this? The burden is sometimes too much for me to bear."

I turn her chin to me and lean over her shoulder, so we are face to face. "You can, *Detka*, you can always trust me."

She turns back to look over the valley. "I want to, I really do."

"Whenever you're ready, I'm all ears."

She sighs. "Okay, where do you want me to start?"

"You start where you want to, I'd like to know everything. Share it all with me if you can."

She nods and takes a deep breath. "It started when my grandmother passed away, I told you before. From the fights that I heard my parents, it turned out my father obviously married my mom for her money. My grandmother must have seen this side of my father because when the will was read, she named me the sole heir to her estate." She pauses, gathering her thoughts.

I suck in a breath, but keep silent and she continues. "It

started with just the beatings, but quickly escalated into something more vile and sinister." Her voice starts to shake.

I squeeze her. "It's ok, you're safe here. Keep going."

She gives a little nod of her head. "Remember when we went to Mexico?"

"Yes, I missed you so bad. You came home sick too, I told you not to drink the water."

"My father must have drugged me. I woke in a doctor's office with cramping and overheard them talking about how I would never have children."

"What?"

"They explained to my father how they put implants in as he requested and that it's as good as me having my tubes tied."

If I wasn't being her strength in this moment, I'd slump over in shock. The onslaught of questions that are swirling my mind are overwhelming.

"I can't have children because of his greed, but that isn't even the worst of it." She brings her fist up to her mouth.

I can't stand the sight of trepidation clearly written on her face. I lift her and pull her sideways so she's sitting across my lap and press my lips to hers quickly, then pull away. "Look at me, *Detka*, don't get lost in the past. Tell me all of it."

She nods and breaks eye contact with me as she begins. "I didn't know how he did it, but I would wake up and not know what happened the night before." Her eyes find mine. "I couldn't stop them, Preston, I know they did bad things to my body but I can't remember. I know from waking up sore. I swear I didn't want it. You were...are the only one I ever wanted that way. But I don't know what happened and sometimes that paralyzes me."

Son of a fucking bitch! The fury that builds in my chest sends a blazing heat of fire through my veins. It takes everything in me not to let go of her go and find Bob to beat the fuck out of him. I don't let any of my rage show, I need her to get the whole story out.

"It wasn't your fault, they're sick. None of this is you. Look at me." I put a finger under her chin and her eyes meet mine. "You didn't do anything wrong. You hear me?"

"You're not disgusted with me?" she asks in a small voice.

"Oh my God, *Detka*, no. You're a fighter, you've fought a hard battle. I could never be disgusted with you."

"Are you sure? My...my father would taunt me...he'd say no one would want a little whore like me when they knew what I'd done."

"Your father doesn't know shit, I'd never..." I hug her tighter to me.

Relief washes over her face and a ton of bricks seems to be lifted off her shoulders. It's like she transferred all her pain and suffering to me in that moment. The past five years come crashing back down on me. This is not the time to share how her father deceived me, his deception can never compare to what he's taken from her.

"Preston, don't look at me like that." She bites her lower lip with worry, naturally assuming I'm judging her like her father always promised her I would. He is going to pay.

"I'm just so sorry, *Detka*. You need to know how sorry I am. I failed you. I left you alone with them when I should have been protecting you. I hate myself for that."

"You didn't know." She looks out over the valley.

"I should have known," I whisper.

Twenty

SKYE

"I should never have left you with them. I need to explain why. This ghost in the room has been with us long enough," he says gently, interrupting my turbulent thoughts.

I nod, unable to trust my voice. He's going to explain things to me I'm not sure I can forgive him for. We have settled down together so well that I almost don't think I want to drag this all up again, but he's right, it has to be done.

"When I left..." He pauses and takes a moment, and clearing his throat, starts over. "When I left, it was for work, Skye. I got a job that was going to pay me very well, but I was made to sign a non-disclosure agreement to not talk about where I was going, or why."

"I don't understand. I would have kept your secret." Breathe... just breathe, I tell myself. I can't let my emotions get me all worked up and black out on the conversation at hand.

"I know, I was a fool and I'm so fucking sorry for what I did to us," he continues.

I don't trust myself to speak, I stay silent waiting for him to continue on.

"I was asked to go to Russia to oversee a business deal."

"I'm confused. How did you get a job like that right after graduation?"

"They needed a Russian speaker on the ground, that was all. I needed the money, there were circumstances I couldn't control. I did what I had to for my mom and for us, Skye. To give us a future."

My silence stretches on. I have so much to say about what he is telling me, but I can't find the words, so I wait.

"I was sent to Russia to oversee a transaction. It was supposed to take a month. When I arrived, I expected to be met by my boss' associates, but no one came. I went to the hotel that had been arranged for me and waited. Days went by. I tried to contact my employer, but he was always out of the office, or didn't pick up. All I could do was wait.

During the second week I was getting tired of waiting. Spending my days and nights in the tiny hotel room, missing you, and for what? I regretted leaving you for nothing and with no contact from the boss back home and no way to get in touch with whoever was supposed to meet me, I gave up. I packed my things and left. I took a taxi to the airport and headed back home to you."

I relax at the idea of him coming back for me, but Preston's body language is the exact opposite. He tenses beneath me, reliving a memory.

"They were waiting," he says through clenched teeth. "As soon as the taxi left town and was on a deserted stretch of road, they made their move. It happened so quickly, we were slammed from the side and run off the road. When we rolled to a stop, they were there. They put a gun to my head, and took me to..." He sighs. "I don't know, Skye, some abandoned warehouse. It was dirty and desolate. A real 'no one can hear you scream' kind of place."

I gasp, thinking of Preston going through this horror.

"I was beaten, hung up, and lashed. They seemed to think I had stolen from them. They were under the impression I was bringing in a shipment of diamonds from the US and when I hadn't shown up as arranged, they watched the hotel. When I tried to leave, they moved in to get what was owed to them."

"W-why would they think that?" I stammer.

Preston rolls his shoulders without realizing, possibly reliving some of the pain that I'm now certain put the scars on his skin and in his soul. "Because they were misinformed," he replies tightly. "I was subjected to interrogation for days, but nothing I said made a difference. All my truths were lies to them. Their methods were..." He drifts of to another place. "Too horrible to tell you about, *Detka*. I think they began to realize that I was enduring more than any liar could stand and that maybe there was some truth to my story.

"I could hear them talking at night, wondering why I hadn't given up the gems by now. They didn't know what else to do with me. So they called in their bosses. 'The brothers' as they called them. The next day the brothers came."

"Dimitri and Evgeni?" I gasp, making the connection. My mind goes back to the Christmas they spent with my family. My grandmother had me stay with her while the boys ran rampant in our house, not wanting me near them because their reputation was ruthless.

Preston nods. "The Volkovs." He laughs but none of the humor reaches his eyes. "Not men you would wish to be on the wrong side of, I assure you." He shakes his head. "I was tired, starving, and beaten and yet they wanted to start at the beginning. Question after question and each one I answered truthfully. I didn't know about any diamonds. I was there to meet associates and they never showed. I tried to contact my boss but he had left me high and dry. I didn't know why. Again and again I was treated to some good old fashioned Volkov correction, but my answers remained the same.

In the end I was hoping for death. It couldn't be worse than living that way. Then I remembered something my mom had given me. The shock from my abduction and the constant beatings had caused me to forget my one hope of an end to the nightmare."

"What was it?" I plead, desperate to know that the torture ended there.

"Before I left, Skye. I told my mom I was going to Russia."

I snap my eyes to his and he immediately holds me tighter. "Don't hate her now, Skye, I told her she couldn't tell a soul. I should have told you as well, but there were factors stopping me. I only told her where I was going because I thought the worry might kill her so soon after the heart attack. She was protecting me by keeping my secret." He looks at me, pleading in his eyes. "Please, Skye. Don't hold it against her. It wasn't her fault.

"I don't," I whisper, finding it very hard not to hold it against him. He could have trusted me. But I need to know how the story ends and flying off the handle at him won't get me the information I want. I take a breath to steady my voice and ask, "What did she give you?"

"She gave me two diamonds. Apparently her family, my family, mined them and she thought they would get me out of trouble if I found myself in any."

"How?"

"She said they could tell who mined them and would know I belonged to her family. She said they would protect me. She was right. When I remembered, I begged to have my bag. I told them I did have diamonds, they were in a secret pocket in my backpack. They had already ripped my bags apart but had obviously missed the hiding place and thinking that I had willingly deceived them, they knocked me out."

I close my eyes, shaking from the fear of what more I'd have to hear of the terrible torture he endured and from my anger that he couldn't confide in me.

"When I came around I was in another place. A warm bed in a clean and luxurious room. At first I thought maybe I was dead, but I could hear voices in another room. I rose to try and get away and realized the pain I was in. It made me cry out. That's when the brothers came."

"Oh God," I groan fearing more.

"No, it's okay, things were different then. Very different. They came to check on me. I had been cleaned and dressed and put on pain medicine while I was out. They were relieved I was up. I was so confused. I noticed the brothers both showed signs of a beating themselves and were very concerned for my welfare. It was baffling, until Vasily arrived. That's when it all fell into place. He came to my bedside and placed the two diamonds they had retrieved from my bag along with our prom picture that I had been keeping safe.

"He asked me where I had gotten the diamonds and when I told him he wept. As you know, it turned out that Mama was his sister. She had run away so that she could marry my father. They had given up everything to be together because her father disapproved of the match. He never forgave her and forbid anyone to look for her. After their father had died, Vasily searched for her, but the trail was cold."

Preston sighed deeply. I could tell that it all weighed heavy on him still.

"What did your mom say? I'm surprised you even talk to those knuckleheads after what they did to you."

His brows furrow. "They didn't know, Skye. We were all deceived. I forgave them a long time ago for that dark time. Vasily went crazy when he found out his boys had been torturing someone who was carrying family diamonds. While I was unconscious, he whooped their asses pretty bad. After I woke up I realized the brothers had been taught a valuable lesson. I've never seen that sick side in them again. I think Vasily beat it out of them.

They took care of me, Skye. We bonded. I stayed in Russia until I was fully healed. I didn't want to return broken and cause even more worry. I spent some time with my family, learned about their business and came home a very different man."

"When I came back, I decided not to tell my mom about the trouble I'd had in Russia. I just made out that the job dragged on longer than it was supposed to. Besides, by then you were gone and I had bigger concerns. I did ask her about her family though and she freaked out, ended up in the hospital again. After speaking with my uncle, we decided the best course was to keep our relationship on the down low."

"Didn't your uncle want to see her?"

He sadly shakes his head. "Her health was more important to him. He just wanted to know that she was safe and happy, after years of not knowing, that was enough for him."

"How sad for them."

Preston nods. "They gave me her inheritance so that I could look after her the way she deserved, and they taught me how to capitalize on who we are and what we do. That's how I got into the gem business here in the US." I see his jaw clench.

"What aren't you telling me?" He has an odd look about him, which he quickly shakes off.

"Nothing. I was just brought back to that time and what I was feeling then that's all. Sometimes it just overwhelms me to think about it while other times I am okay with it. Does that make sense?"

"It makes perfect sense, post-traumatic stress syndrome. Have you ever talked with Shaina about it?" I want to help him the way he doesn't realize he's helping me.

"You're right, it probably is. I always just think of it as one of my demons. Maybe I do need to talk it out."

"It might help," I tell him, knowing I'll need to follow my own advice eventually too.

"Skye look at me," he says softly.

I bring my gaze back to him. He has a soft look on his face, a look that reminds me of that boy I fell in love with so long ago. I place my hand into his, his touch awakens all those feelings I've had locked away for five years. My eyes are wide as I look at him.

"I need you," he whispers.

"I'm right here," I reply.

He presses his forehead to mine and exhales deeply. "I've made so many mistakes. I'll never forgive myself. I had no clue your home life was *that* horrific. I could have—" I pause and look at her and sigh. "I *should* have stopped him."

"What were you going to do? Go up against the great Bob Divine? We were kids, Preston."

"I could have tried," he says, sounding defeated.

A bitter laugh escapes me. "But instead you left."

He nods somberly. "Will you ever forgive me?"

"I'm here, aren't I?" I tell him. "Sometimes you have to listen to your heart, even when it's stupid as shit." I offer a crooked smile.

Preston smiles softly back, then looks around us. "Come on," he says suddenly. "We need to get home before we fry in the sun."

It's a silent walk back to the car, but we hold hands all the way. It feels good to have told each other some of the things that have burdened us. Sharing has made our bond closer. Maybe now we can finally start to heal.

Twenty One

PRESTON

The last few days with Skye have been amazing. Since opening up about most of our secrets, she's more carefree, as if the burden has finally lifted. I feel guilty about not telling her the contracted job was for her father. But after she confided all the secrets of her past to me, I thought it would destroy her to know it was him I sacrificed us for.

I run my hands through my hair and rub my temples. I had a plan...all these goals that were made before she came back. I was always going to take down Bob for what he did to me. But now? Now I'm going to ruin him. Strip everything he holds dear from his grasp. When I'm finished with him, he'll have nothing...be nothing. Words can't even express what I am going to do to him.

As if on cue, my work phone rings and I look at the caller ID, perfect timing. I've been waiting for this call all week. "Harrison?" I bark, not sparing any pleasantries. "Give me good news!"

I can hear him pacing the floor, he has a heavy stomp. "I'm trying, Preston," he says without confidence.

"What's the hold up?"

"We have to be delicate, Preston, you know that. If we arouse his suspicion the game is up."

"Just tell me things are progressing at least. I want him finished."

"I thought you just wanted to dry up his supply?"

"Things have changed. By the time I'm finished with him, he will be grateful to even have an air supply." Even I can hear the malice in my tone, so Harrison's intake of breath doesn't surprise me.

"I'll see what I can do to get things moving faster. I have a meeting with..." As Harrison carries on, I see Skye peek her head around the door. The moment she sees I'm on the phone she starts to back out of the room. I wave my hand, motioning for her to come in.

She slowly walks toward me and I crook my finger, urging her closer. I give her my dazzling grin and hit mute on the phone. "Come here," I demand, smiling in the way she brings out of me.

She giggles. I can't remember the last time I heard that naughty giggle she has. She takes slow, calculated strides, accentuating each move with her hips. I'm so busy watching her that I don't hear what Harrison is saying. Once she's within reach, I move forward and snake my hand around her waist, pulling her toward me. She lands with a giggle on my lap. Harrison is still stammering, making excuses in my ear.

"Are you there, Preston?"

I take the phone off mute. "Harrison, just get it done and call me when you have news." Not waiting for a reply I hang up the phone and meet Skye's curious, wide eyes.

"Everything all right?"

"Everything is perfect with you here." I adjust her slightly so she's not so tempting sitting there. I have been finding her temptation harder and harder to resist. I need to let things heal between us some more before we take the next step. I don't want to push her.

"It sounded pretty serious."

"Nothing I can't handle."

"Maybe you need an assistant to field your calls," she suggests playfully.

I raise my eyebrows, imagining Skye as my assistant. "Are you applying for the job?"

She shrugs. "I might. Depends on the benefits."

"I can think of a number of benefits."

She giggles and squirms in my lap and I wince.

"Careful, *Detka*," I warn, squeezing her tighter. She makes me want to swipe my hand across the desk, clearing it of its contents and take her on it.

"Why?" She has a voice of sin and the look of the devil.

"Because I'm finding it more and more difficult to control myself around you."

She smirks. "Oh?"

I tip the chair back so it tilts all the way. She yelps, turning to grab onto my shoulders. We are chest to chest with each other, I smirk and push her hair out of her face. *Fuck.* Her smile is so damn beautiful. "Damn, *Detka*..."

Her brows furrow. "What's the matter, Preston?"

"Nothing." I stare into her eyes, swimming within the deep pools of green.

"You sure? You have a funny look on your face, are you going to be sick?"

I chuckle and then cup her face, momentarily at a loss for words as I soak in her beauty. "Are we gonna have a go at this?" I finally blurt.

"At what?" She smirks. "Me working for you?"

"No, I mean *us*."

"Us? What about us?" She furrows her brows with a perplexed look.

"You're making me feel like a teenager again asking you to go out with me. I've grown up too much to start acting like a boy now."

"I don't know, I kinda liked that boy a lot." Her eyes sparkle with mischief.

"Oh, *Detka*, you know what I mean, are you *mine*?"

"Ohhh, possessive..." She wiggles.

I playfully tap her nose. "You have no idea. Now what do you say?"

She puts her elbows on my chest and rests her chin in her hands. "Preston, are you asking me to be your girlfriend?" She breaks out with a sweet smile.

I know better than to think her smile is innocent, she is being devious. "Girlfriend is so high school, but yes, *Detka*, I am. That and so much more."

"More?" she asks so softly I almost miss it.

"Yes, *Detka*, more. I want you to be my partner, my lover, my best friend. My everything."

She doesn't have time to reply. I bring her down on top of me and pull her face to mine, kissing her tenderly on her soft lips and holding her tight.

"I've missed you too, Preston." She chuckles. "Now, let me go. I can't breathe." She starts to wiggle out of my arms.

"Okay, smarty pants." I let up on my squeeze a little. "It's just good to see you smile."

"It's easy when you're the one making me smile. I'm going to go for a swim, you finish up your work." She slides off my lap and blows me an air kiss as she walks out the door.

I watch her leave and thank whatever force is up there helping me make this happen. I can't quite believe it's real. She is mine, perhaps not fully yet, but it's coming. She's going to be mine from here on. Her birthday's coming up and the little witch hasn't said one word. I bet she hopes I forget. Not a chance. I can't help but smile thinking about how pissed she will be when I surprise her.

My office phone rings and I glance down at the ID. "Have something new for me, Harrison?"

"I have an update on the overseas operation."

Before I reply, I get up and look out my office door. I can see Skye's already in the pool swimming. I close the door so I'm not tempted to say fuck work and join her. "Tell me."

"We've had a result on his next shipment," Harrison informs me.

"Oh?"

"Let's just say, the goods missed their flight." I can hear the satisfaction in his tone and I smile.

"Well that's a shame," I declare with a heap of sarcasm. "Let's hope they make the next one or Bob is going to have some unhappy investors."

"That's just it though, they seem to have disappeared. It's the damnedest thing. No one knows anything. They're just...gone!"

I try not to laugh. "Hmm, weird. I hope Bob doesn't value his kneecaps. The Volkov brothers have put a lot of trust in him. They won't be happy if he doesn't deliver. How long before he knows he's screwed?"

"Couple of days, I'd say." Harrison chuckles.

"How are we coming along with the plans stateside?" Harrison is used to me firing off a round of questions. I pay him well, very well. He's been with me since I came back and started up on my own, so he's just as invested as I am.

"Baby steps, Preston, the plan is coming together. Have some patience."

"I don't have any more patience for this sick bastard. I want him ruined," I growl in a rare show of my temper. It doesn't faze Harrison, that's one of the reasons we get along so well.

"We'll get there, have you been able to talk to Skye about it?"

"No, we won't be bringing her into this mess," I growl. "No matter what happens she's off limits and not part of the plan. Understood?"

"Woah, Preston, I was just asking. I know what that bastard did to you personally. We'll get him."

The doorbell chimes in my office. I flip on my computer and view the surveillance cameras. I smile as I see Skye is now on a raft in the pool soaking up some sun. I'll join her in a minute and bring out some sunblock. She has a bad habit of not wearing any. The second camera has my blood boiling. "Speak of the devil. Bob is at my front door. I'll talk to you later."

"Pres..."

I end the call as he says my name. The last thing I want to hear is him trying to talk some sort of sense into me. I take one last glance at the monitor and see Skye hasn't moved. Let's see what Bob has to say. It's too soon for him to notice he's missing a shipment and it will take him weeks to realize that all his suppliers in Russia have stopped doing business with him.

I wouldn't answer the door, but I don't want him to raise a racket and alert Skye that he's here. With quick strides I make it to the front door and swing it open just as he goes to press the doorbell again.

"To what do I owe this pleasure, Bob?" I say with a sneer.

"Oh, you're home..." his voice trails off.

"Don't sound so surprised, Bob, you're at *my* house." I don't invite him in, he isn't welcome here. The sight of him makes my blood boil, he sickens me.

"Can I talk with my daughter, she's here, isn't she?" He tries to look past me into the house.

"No, Bob, you can't. You aren't welcome here." I move

slightly to block his view into the house.

"Listen here, boy, you will get my daughter. We have some things to discuss," he demands foolishly.

He puts a hand on my chest in an effort to try and move me out of his way. The old man doesn't realize how strong I've become in the last few years. You would think that once he realized I survived Russia, he would've had an epiphany or something.

"You want to take your hand off me before I do it for you?" I raise a brow at him, not giving away how much I want him to push me, so I can take my anger out on him with my fists.

"You better watch it, boy," he snarls.

I bark out a laugh. "Or what, Bob? You already tried to get rid of me, yet here I am. Take a look around you. I'm not the kid you thought you could just erase anymore. It's you who'd better watch it, Bob, not me."

He removes his hand without any further prompting. "I just need to speak with Skye," he says with urgency.

"No." I cross my arms over my chest.

"No? Who the hell do you think you are?" his says with a raised voice.

My hand strikes out quickly and fists in his shirt. I stand taller than him, so I pull him toward me as I lean in. "I get that I'm nothing to you, Bob, but Skye's everything to me. You won't be getting near her again. *Ever.*"

"You can't stop me."

"I know what you did to her." I lean even closer and can smell the coffee on his breath.

His face turns a shade lighter. "What do you mean?" he asks nervously.

"I know about it all, Bob... the drugging, the beatings, the abuse, all of it. You disgust me." With this I fling him back and watch him stumble then catch his balance. I inhale a calming breath. I have to hold it together, he will get what is coming to him, it's all in place. If I go off now, I'll blow it all. "I'd advise you never to come back here. You have no idea of what I want to do to you right now."

"That little whore is a liar!" He comes rushing at me, and I let him push me first.

He's effectively cut off as my fist meets his face. From the distinct crack of bone and spurt of blood, never mind his howl of pain, I'm quite certain that I broke his nose. What I really can't wait for is to break him. "I suggest you run along, Bob, and don't come back on my property. A restraining order will be delivered to you shortly." The look I give him is menacing.

"Son of a bitch. You'll pay for that!" he mumbles under his breath as he backs away.

I lean against the doorjamb, folding my arms across my chest and call out to his retreating form, "Talk about my mother again and you'll be swallowing your front teeth next."

He cups his hand over his nose as he climbs into his car, attempting not to bleed all over the expensive interior. It's entertaining to watch as he struggles. He rummages around for something to wipe his face clean. When his eyes meet mine and I hold their gaze, there is no mistaking his malicious expression. I smile proudly as he pulls away.

"Was...was that my father?" her voice comes very quietly from behind me.

"Yes." I wait until the car is out of the driveway before I shut the door and turn around to see Skye wrapped snuggly in a towel, her cheeks have a tinge of pink to them.

"What did he want?"

"Hmmm, I didn't ask specifically. He wanted to talk to you and I told him no."

"Just like that huh?" She raises a brow.

"Just like that." I smile.

Twenty Two

SKYE

Today is my birthday, and my father's attempted visit with me the other day has me shaken up some. I'm afraid of what he's going to try; everything with him has always been about the money. His venture to obtain Power of Attorney over my Grandmother's estate has continually failed. I've told Preston everything and it hasn't changed us at all. I see the way he watches me, and I think he can tell I'm on edge. How do I explain I'm afraid my father might come and hurt me?

Trying to relax, I'm partaking in my favorite pastime of lying on a raft in the pool, the music is softly pumping through the exterior speakers. The water ripples and sways, but it's too fast to be caused by the breeze. I lean over to see what caused it and suddenly the raft is turned over, flipping me headfirst into the pool. I emerge spitting water and brushing my hair out of my face.

I come eye to eye with Preston and he has that damn devilish smile on his face. "You looked hot." He shrugs.

I fling myself at him and he catches me, before pushing off the bottom of the pool and pulling me under with him. This time

I was prepared and held my breath. I open my eyes under water and see him smile and waggle his eyebrows at me. I laugh and bubbles shoot out of my mouth. He pulls me closer to him and kisses me underwater.

Just when I think I will have to pull away to come up for air he lifts me above the water. I take a deep breath. "Breathe," he says, with that smile again.

"You're so bad." I can't help but laugh.

"Are you ready for tonight my sweet birthday girl?"

He was smart and told me about the party he was planning, he learned from the last surprise that it wasn't wise to spring things on me. "Meh."

He picks me up out of the water and sits me on the side of the pool, stepping between my legs and resting his arms on them, looking up at me.

"What's the matter?" He frowns.

"You know I don't like everyone's attention focused on me. Christ, I can't remember the last time I celebrated a birthday." Even though I wanted to be in the music industry, it's a different kind of attention to that of your closest friends and loved ones. I grew up looking for ways to blend in and be normal. I didn't want to be looked at because more often than not I had bruises to hide. Preston understands this now and it's a relief to have him at my back.

"I know, but that's why I told you. Did you want me to cancel?"

"Actually. No, I don't want you to cancel. It's time I start enjoying life."

"That's my girl." He grins, lifting my hand and placing a kiss on my knuckles.

His words make me proud of myself and how far I've come. I made the steps to work with Shaina on medication and it has been making me feel better. It's time I stopped being afraid I'm going to get thrown into a panic attack.

"It's just a chill dinner at your favorite Japanese steak house," he reassures me. "Lea wanted to take you there since that was where she had one of her parties and you loved it." He breaks eye contact with me and looks off into the mountains.

I cup his face and turn it back toward me. "What's with the guilty look?"

He huffs. "Damn it. You know me too well."

"Spill it, Hart."

He runs a hand through his hair, his telltale sign that he's up to no good. "Okay okay... Lea is going to kill me, so you have to act surprised. Promise me?"

"I promise. Wait! Please tell me she didn't get a stripper. She's still mad she missed my twenty first birthday."

"Hell no! If you want a strip show, then I will be more than happy to do that for you in the privacy of our own home."

I laugh even as my stomach tightens at his words. 'Our' home. Is that how he sees things now? I can't ever see myself anywhere else, but it still floors me to hear him say it so soon after we made 'us' an official thing. "Maybe later, killer." I shove him, acting playful to cover my surprise. "Now spill," I demand.

"While we're at dinner, we have someone coming to set up a karaoke machine and sound system here. So we all can come back and have a good time."

"Oh! That sounds fantastic!" I squeal. "I'm so glad you told me." This really is my idea of the perfect night; good food, friends and I get to sing.

"Thank fuck. I've been shitting bullets for a week. I wanted to tell you but Lea promised you would love this and wouldn't get mad."

"I'm difficult, I know. I'm sorry. But thank you for telling me. Now I can mentally prepare myself for a full night."

Preston blinks, then a slow smile spreads across his handsome face. "Quirks and all, I love you."

Happiness explodes through me. "I love you too," I tell him.

He pushes himself out of the water, balancing himself on the sides of the pool with impressive upper body strength. He leans forward and touches his forehead to mine. "I've always loved you, *Detka*," he murmurs, then whispers... "Always," as he lowers his lips to mine.

Before we spiral out of control, I place my hands on his shoulders and push him back into the pool. I stand up before he can drag me back in with him. He comes up laughing and shakes his head like a wet dog.

"Come on Skye! Come back in the pool." He splashes me as I walk away.

"No way, I only have a couple of hours to get ready. You know how long my hair takes to dry. I'm going to jump in the shower."

"Want me to join you?"

I laugh. "Nuh-uh. I need to look my best, so you just stay away." I blow him an air kiss and walk slowly into the house, making sure I sashay my hips to tease him all the way.

"You're playing a dangerous game there, Skye," he yells after me with his husky bedroom voice.

"Finish your swim, your back will thank you for it later," I call back after him.

We swim daily. For me, working out helps with my anxiety, and for him it helps keep his muscles loose so the scar tissue on his back doesn't tighten up.

"Skye, we're going to be late," Preston yells from the living room.

"Coming!"

I grab my silver clutch and walk down the hallway. I turn into the living room and stop. I have to remember to breathe. Preston is wearing a gray suit that's tailored to fit him perfectly. He turns to look at me and I see he has on a crisp white shirt with a gray tie. My mouth goes dry.

"You look fucking gorgeous," he says, walking toward me.

I look down at the outfit I deliberated over. It's not every day I get a chance to dress up, but I picked out something I'd be comfortable in: a blush maxi dress. The color looks fantastic against my bronzed skin and to finish the outfit off I have a pair of silver gladiator sandals.

My hair turned out too fizzy for my liking so I pinned it up in a low bun with a few wispy pieces framing my face. My makeup is light, just enough to accent my green eyes and make them pop. It was worth all the effort, just for the way he is looking at me now.

"You clean up nicely yourself," I tell him softly.

He has a box in his hand wrapped all pretty with a white satin bow. "I want to give you your birthday present before we meet up with everyone." He reaches me and leans down to kiss my cheek. He places the box in my hand.

"You shouldn't have," I gasp as I clutch the box.

"Open it." He steps back and smiles.

I slowly open the box, and inside, resting on satin is a pair of earrings and a bracelet in the most brilliant shade of green. "Oh my God, Preston, they're beautiful."

"They are demantoid garnets from the family mine. They always remind me of your eyes."

"I don't know what to say. Thank you."

"You're more than welcome. Here, let me help you put them on."

I'm very happy that I decided to wear my hair up now, it's the perfect hairstyle to showcase these earrings. He takes out an earring and fastens it to my ear, making me shiver, then hurries and puts the other one in. Then he takes the box from me and gets the bracelet and setting the box aside, he claps it on my wrist.

"Happy Birthday, *Detka*," he whispers to me.

"Thank you, Preston. You really didn't have to."

"Nonsense, you deserve everything I can give you and more. Now, let's get going before I end up being selfish and we stay in."

We walk into Kobe, the best Japanese steakhouse in the desert. We have a full table reserved for us.

Preston leans down and whispers in my ear, "Remember, don't let on that you know about the karaoke."

"I won't." I groan when I see the table has balloons around it and the whole gang is already here. Lea must have been responsible for that. She is sitting there with a huge grin on her face.

"Who's that sitting next to Lea?"

"That's Harrison, he works for me. He's good people, you'll like him."

"Why is he here?" I wince as I sound super bitchy asking so harshly.

Preston chuckles. "Lea invited him. I think she has a sweet spot for him."

"I see." Now it makes perfect sense.

"Skye!" Lea yells across the restaurant.

I can feel the heat in my face. "Why does she do that?" I whisper to Preston and hold up a hand, half waving, half desperately trying to silence her.

"She's always been like this. You've been away for a long time, you just forgot. We'd better not keep her waiting or she will yell again."

We reach the table and Lea's the first to jump up and give me a huge hug. "Happy Birthday, Skye! We have five years of birthdays to make up for tonight."

"Thank you, but one is plenty to celebrate." I look back to Preston and mouth, "help," and he holds up his hands laughing.

"Leave her alone, Lea. Are you're trying to make sure she stays hidden in Preston's house and never comes out again? We need our girl back out with us," Shaina says, giving me a hug. "Happy Birthday, Skye."

"Thanks, Shaina."

Craig moves between Shaina and me. "Let me have her! Whoop! The last of us to turn twenty-three," he says, picking me up and swinging me around.

"You big oaf! Put me down!" I can't help the giggle that slips through. He puts me down and moves down to the end of the table with Shaina. The table has a grill built into it and they cook your food in front of you, with the two side seats taken I see Preston's friend stand.

Before Preston can introduce him, Lea interjects herself, "Skye, this is my friend Harrison."

He extends a hand and I clasp it with a firm handshake. "Happy Birthday, Skye. Thank you for allowing me to come to the party." He has a slight accent and I can't place which state it's from.

"Any friend of Lea's is a friend of mine," I tell him. "Welcome to the crazy."

He looks down at Lea fondly. "I don't mind a little crazy."

Well holy shit, Lea just blushed. I look over at Preston with wide eyes, shocked by how our over the top friend just freaking turned red like she's twelve and this is her first crush.

I sit down at the corner of the table so I'm between Shaina and Preston, then the waitress comes around taking drink orders. She gets Craig and Shaina's order, then moves on to me.

"Iced tea, no lemon please." She nods and moves on to Preston.

Shaina leans in closer to me. "How are you doing?" she asks quietly.

"I'm feeling really good, Shaina." I smile. "And it's all thanks to you."

"Oh, now, you're the one doing all the work. I'm just handing you the tools. How's the medication working out for you?"

"It's really a life changer. I feel great."

"Good, I'm glad it was able to help you."

The waitress comes back and starts putting drinks down. She drops the house special – the 'Kobe Dragonberry'-- in front of me.

"Oh no, I didn't order this," I tell her, trying to hand it back.

She smiles. "It was ordered for the birthday girl," she informs me, glancing revealingly at Lea.

Lea lifts her drink in salute and calls, "Cheers!"

I take a sip to get her off my back and she returns to her hushed conversation with Harrison.

"I'll finish this for you," Preston whispers, taking the drink out of my hand.

"Thank you." He knows I never really enjoyed drinking. I saw what it's done to my mother and I don't want the same thing for myself. I'm not about that life.

We order our dinner and in no time, the chef is out in front of us slicing and dicing and putting food in front of us. He puts on a great show and we all laugh our way through our meals. As the meal wraps up, I can see Lea getting antsy. She would have blown the surprise herself with the way she's acting. At least now I can pretend I don't know what's going on.

Preston puts a hand on my thigh and gently squeezes. "It's almost over, *Detka*. Enjoy it."

"You just wait for your birthday," I mumble.

With that, the waitress appears and sets a hat on my head and all the staff gather around in a half circle in front of me and start singing happy birthday off key. As all my closest friends sing happy birthday to me I realize how lucky I am to have them all back in my life.

I'm definitely too stuffed for the birthday dessert they gave me. "Do any of you want to share this with me?"

"Too full?" Preston asks, taking a spoonful of the ice cream on the plate.

"I feel like I'm going to pop. This was such a good dinner. Thank you for setting it up."

"I'd do anything to keep that smile on your face." He puts his arm around my shoulder and I lean in breathing in his manly scent.

"Ok, you lovebirds. Break it up," Lea says, rolling her eyes.

Preston grabs the check off the table and throws a black credit card in the check holder, handing it off to the waitress.

"Do you guys want to go dancing?" This is so horrible of me, but I can't resist. I see Lea's eyes go wide, and from the corner of my eye I see Craig's head snap toward me. Preston just sits back with a small smile parting his lips.

"If dancing is what the birthday girl wants, dancing is what she'll get," he says happily.

Lea can't contain her huff of annoyance. I cover my mouth to hold back the giggle. It's not every day we get one up on Lea, Miss Control-Freak.

"No, I was just kidding." I laugh. "I couldn't dance. I've eaten too much."

"I have an early morning at the hospital," Shaina says to me.

"Thank you all for coming and celebrating with me. It really meant a lot to spend my birthday with you all." One would think I was going soft, but something I learned while I was away was not to take friends for granted. I did that for five years, I won't ever do it again.

I'm stronger than I ever thought I was and I'm ready to get the night moving even if it overloads my feels.

"Yeah, I have an early yoga class," Lea says without looking at me. It's almost comical how she can't lie to save her life.

"Okay, we will see you guys later." I stand and give everyone a hug as we leave the restaurant.

The second Preston and I are sitting in the car he busts out laughing. "You are such an asshole, Skye," he says, wiping tears out of his eyes.

"I couldn't help it. Did you see the look on her face as she started panicking? Christ, I wish I had a picture of that."

I see her and Harrison pulling out of the Kobe parking lot, her hands animated as she talks to him.

"Look at her, I'd bet a hundred bucks she's making his ears bleed." Preston laughs even harder.

"No way, I won't be taking that bet. Shall we race them to the house?"

"There isn't a chance in hell you are going to get me to do that. I don't want to hear her bitching all night."

I hold up my hands. "Alright, alright, I've had my fun. We can go now."

Preston drives home slower than a turtle crossing the road. When we pull into the drive there are no cars in sight. He parks the car by the front door in the circular drive.

"Aren't you going to park in the garage?" I innocently ask.

"As much as you're making me laugh, no," he says, getting out of the car and coming around to open my door.

I place my hand in his and step out. "Spoil sport."

We walk up to the door and he places his key in, unlocks it and motions for me to go in first.

"Surprise!" is yelled in unison.

"What?" I say, covering my mouth, acting bewildered.

Lea bounces up and down like a child, thinking she pulled one over on me. "We wanted to have a whole night of fun! You almost blew it with your wanting to go dancing."

I turn back to look at Preston. "Did you know about this?" I give him a huge wink that they can't see.

"Come on Skye, we have karaoke and drinks all ready." She takes my hand and drags me into the living room where speakers are set up with more damn balloons.

There is a man manning the karaoke station and I frown slightly. He looks familiar but I can't place him. Lea follows my line of vision. "Do you remember Robbie?" She directs me toward him.

"He looks familiar." I just can't place him.

"He went to school with us, he was in Shaina's year."

"How would I know him then?" I still can't shake that I know that face.

"He works at Native Foods during the day."

"No shit? Didn't we go there for our peanut butter parfaits?"

"Yes! Well he deejays in his spare time to make some extra cash."

"Hey Robbie, this is Skye, the birthday girl," Lea introduces us.

I shake his hand. "Nice to meet you, Robbie."

"I go by Robert now but Lea doesn't listen." He looks at her with a soft smile.

Oh shit, he likes her. He glances over at Harrison and gives him a once over and my mouth drops. I look over and make eye contact with Preston with raised brows. He shrugs as if reading my mind, well hot damn Lea is working it.

"You can't tell her crap. It's Lea's way or the highway," I agree.

Lea just laughs.

"Don't I know it? Well, tonight is all about celebrating your birthday. I've a karaoke book on the table. Do you want to go first?"

"Oh no, by all means let Lea go first. I'll take a look at the book."

I take a seat on the sofa and start thumbing through the book. I look up to see Craig and Preston knock back a shot. Shaina's standing by them and pours another when they slam the glasses down. I haven't seen Preston this relaxed and carefree since he left. In fact, it was on our graduation day when he and Craig were goofing around, before everything changed.

Lea claps her hands. "Can I get everyone's attention?" She waits until the talking stops. "Before we start singing, we have some presents for you, Skye."

"I don't need any presents, spending the evening with you all has been the best birthday present."

Preston walks over to me and sits beside me, putting an arm around my shoulders. "You didn't think we would miss this part, did you?"

"Jesus guys, you really know how to make a girl feel special."

Lea puts a box in my lap. "Here open this one first, it's from me."

I carefully tear open the paper because I want to save it and use it in something to remember this night by. I lift the lid on the box and find that it's filled with all the latest and greatest makeup.

"Lea, this is fantastic!"

"I figured you'd have none of your good makeup left."

"I don't, I only have a few little things. Thank you, this is much needed."

She smiles as Craig hands me a card. I open it and read it to myself. He wrote me a touching message about how much he has missed me and there is a gift card for Macy's inside.

"Thank you, Craig."

He raises a beer and takes a long swig from the bottle. Shaina then hands me a package, wrapped in different shades of purple.

Opening it, I gasp. It's a leather bound journal. The smell of the new leather fills my nose. Then I see my name engraved into the leather front.

"This is beautiful, Shaina. Thank you."

"It reminded me of you. I thought you could use it for writing songs or something."

I open the journal and press my fingers into the indentation of my name. I don't know why I never thought of writing my songs down. Or writing period. It takes me a moment to swallow past the lump in my throat.

"Thanks, Shaina, I think I'll start doing just that."

The last box is the smallest and Preston hands it to me. My heart starts hammering in my chest because the box is the size of a ring box. He wouldn't, we aren't there yet.

"You already gave me my gift," I argue.

Preston shrugs like this is of no relevance. "And now I'm giving you another one. You should probably get used to it."

I open the lid on the box, almost afraid to look.

"Go ahead and look, Skye, there's nothing to freak out over in there," Preston says with a laugh.

I narrow my eyes at him. Damn him for knowing me so well. Lifting the lid, I see a copper guitar pick. I take it out and study it. It's engraved with a flowy heart. I pause as grief over the loss of my guitar hits me.

"It's so you think about me when you play," Preston says softly next to me.

"Thank you, I love it."

"There's a but in there somewhere, isn't there?"

I bite my lower lip, feeling guilty for spoiling his thoughtful gift. "It's just...I don't have a guitar anymore."

He takes my hand in his. Oh God, if he gets down on one knee I just might vomit all over him.

"Craig?" His eyes are focused behind me.

"It's all set, Preston," Craig replies.

Huh? What's all set? Preston stands up and guides me up with him. "Come with me, *Detka*." He walks me across the living room and out through the sliding glass doors and I stop in my tracks.

"Where are we going?" The last time we went into where his mother lived was the day she passed away. I've been trying to work up the courage to go in there and pack up some of her things.

"My Mama loved it here," he tells me. "She loved you and having you here. She would have wanted you to have this. Come look." He gently tugs my hand and opens the door.

I take a step into the doorway and gasp. I feel Preston's hands on my shoulders as I look into this amazing room.

"When did you have time to do this?" I ask, amazement clear in my voice. The room has totally been transformed from an extra living space to a recording studio. A white baby grand piano has centerstage and a new guitar is leaning up against it.

"It took a little working out, but we were able to sneak workers in. Do you like it?" he whispers in my ear.

"How can I not?"

"Go look at the guitar." He guides me with a hand at my lower back.

Liliya's carpets are gone, the room now hardwood floors, and pretty floral paintings are on the walls. It's pristine, with clean lines and warm accents. Walking up, I run my hand along the piano and pick up the acoustic guitar, this one way better the junk piece I had broken in Hollywood.

I strum my fingers over the strings and find that he's had it tuned. I examine the pearl inlay of the neck, and up to the headstock where I see "*Detka*" engraved. He didn't spare any expense as I notice all the tuning hardware is also custom made with scrolling lines.

"I'm speechless," I whisper.

"Is that good?" Preston asks from the doorway.

"Of course it's good," Lea says, smacking Preston's arm.

"Thank you, really this means so much to me." I set the guitar down and walk over to Preston and wrap my arms around his waist. I hug him so damn tight. He doesn't hesitate and returns the hug and kisses the top of my head.

"Okay you lovebirds, can we get this party rolling? We all know if Skye starts tinkering with her new toys in here, we won't see her the rest of the night."

I roll my eyes. "Let's go, I can come in here tomorrow."

We all head back into the main house, Preston and I walking side by side, holding hands. It really takes me back to when we first met, he still can make me feel like jelly and fireworks. "Thank you," I whisper just for him and he grins.

Preston lets go of my hand when we get back inside the house and he and Craig do another shot. "*Za zdaróvye,*" Preston says as they tip them back, this time Craig wheezes after it.

"Shit, Preston, what the fuck was that one? It was sweet at first then burned like hell."

Preston laughs. "Bread wine, we should really be sipping it and not knocking it back."

Lea is grabbing the microphone from Robbie and she nods her head signaling that she's ready for the song to start. That reminds me to flip through the book again to find a fun song.

The song starts with a thunder crack and I frown trying to place it, the second she starts singing, my eyes open wide and I don't know If I should laugh or have her committed. Probably both if I'm being honest. She starts belting out the chorus and I crack up. She's singing "It's Raining Men," while looking at both Harrison and Robbie in turn. She is playing with fire but thankfully she has given me a great idea.

I quickly thumb through the songs and find the one I was

looking for. I almost giggle. I write the song down and have to keep myself from skipping to Robbie. I get to him just as the song is coming to a close.

"Craig's up next," Robbie says.

I see Craig lean down and whisper into Preston's ear. He shakes his head and starts laughing. They've been knocking back the shots non-stop. It's evident they're a bit tipsy, but we have enough rooms for everyone to stay the night, so we don't have to worry about them driving home.

We...us...home...it's coming more naturally by the day and I should be freaked out but I just feel happy.

"Oh for fuck's sake," I groan as Craig starts belting out "Man! I Feel Like a Woman!"

Shaina claps her hands like a baby seal, laughing her ass off and smacking Craig's ass as he struts by her. The minute the song is over, Shaina jumps up and grabs the microphone. She's usually so serious and worried about her public image that she rarely lets loose, but she starts singing right in front of Craig and his mouth drops as she sings "I Kissed a Girl."

I bust out laughing. The look on his face is priceless as she sings as dances in front of him. I want to see if Preston is going to sing. Once she is done Robbie looks to me, since he has my song, and I subtly shake my head, indicating that he should ask Preston first.

"Harrison? Preston?" he asks.

Harrison immediately shakes his head and Robbie rolls his eyes thinking he's got one over on his competitor.

"I'm a lover not a singer," Preston replies, lifting his glass of whiskey and silently toasting us.

"I'll go." I giggle, barely containing myself as I walk over to Robbie.

"You're a pretty funny lady, Skye." Robbie laughs as he hands me the mic.

The music starts and I close my eyes getting myself into performance mode. I don't need to look at the monitor to know the words. I'm a huge fan of the band's music and have listened to it enough I could even play it on the piano. The opening notes of "Death of a Bachelor" start playing and I start to sing. Changing a word here and there, Preston looks like he's about to choke on his drink, while Craig shoots his through his nose. I keep singing with a straight face and sit down in Preston's lap as I sing about the demise of his bachelorhood.

When the second the song is over, both Shaina and Lea squeal with laughter. Preston hugs me laughing.

"You are trouble, *Detka*," he whispers and nips my earlobe.

"It's one of my charms."

Karaoke was over from that point on, the rest of the night was spent just chilling out and it felt damn good being with my friends again. I don't know why I was so hesitant about hanging out with everyone, it's like we were never apart.

Robbie didn't drink, so he drove Harrison and Lea home at the end of the night and Craig and Shaina stayed over.

"Preston, that was the best party ever!" I tell him as I fall back onto the bed, exhausted.

He crawls on top of me. "I'm so glad you had a good time. It was fun."

I run my fingers through his hair and stare up into his glossy eyes.

"*Detka*," he slurs on top of me with his whiskey breath.

"You're drunk, Preston." I withhold the giggle that's about to erupt.

"*Detka*, there are ninety-six words for love. How about we flip those numbers and I show you how I feel?"

I bust out laughing. He begins scooting down my body as I laugh and lays his head on my stomach. He stills and seconds later, loud snores vibrate on my belly.

Twenty Three

PRESTON

I wake with a start, my eyes popping open in a sudden alert stare. I listen to the silence of the house trying to think what could have disturbed my sleep. It takes a few moments to confirm that nothing is wrong. Skye's sleeping in my arms and softly snoring. It's cute, she doesn't think she snores.

The muscles in my back are cramping up and my head is pounding, so I slide away from Skye, putting a pillow in my place. She grumbles and then snores into the pillow. I roll my shoulders, trying to loosen up some. This happens sometimes when I overexert myself. Shaina examined me when I came home, ran a series of tests on me to see if I had any torn ligaments or tendons. The results showed I just have scar tissue and it will probably never go away.

With each pull of my stiff muscles I fight not to get lost in the past. I walk down the hall and softly close the door behind me. I need to give Harrison a quick call. I punch his number in from memory and the phone rings a couple times before he answers.

"This'd better be good, Preston, it's six am and some asshole had me doing shots last night..." he groans into the phone.

Quietly, since the rest of the house is silent, I chuckle, scrubbing a hand over my face and wincing at my hangover. Sucks to be him today if he feels like this. "Where are we with the plan?"

Harrison groans. "Same place we were when I saw you five hours ago."

"Well then, rise and shine. I want things happening today."

"You're a sick bastard, Preston," he mutters, but I can hear him getting up, which is what I wanted.

As Harrison grumbles in my ear, a sleepy Skye comes shuffling into my office with one of my shirts on, her curls wild and all over the place. She gives me a sleepy smile and comes right over. I twist around in the chair and she climbs up in my lap. I cradle her as she rubs her temples, fighting to keep her eyes open.

"Call me when you have the next update," I tell Harrison and hang up the phone. It's a pet peeve of his, but I get a little thrill out of hanging up on him each and every time I do it.

"Delivery problems again?" she asks in a sleepy voice.

"Something like that." I shift, my muscles tensing again.

"What's the matter?"

"My back's a little sore today, it's nothing. Do you want to go back to bed?" I shift her again.

She frowns and sits up, then slides off my lap. "Is it your scars? Maybe I can rub it out."

"It's okay, a dip in the pool should help work it out." I'm usually good about putting a shirt on first thing in the morning so that she doesn't have to see them, but I thought I would be in the pool and out again before she even woke. "Why are you awake so early?" I ask her softly, she has been doing well at sleeping in when I get out of bed.

She shrugs her shoulders. "I woke up."

The way she shrugged it off has me curious. "*Detka*, look at me."

"Yes, Preston?"

"Tell me why you're awake," I ask gently

She swallows then says, "I had a nightmare."

"Has anything happened in the last few days to trigger that?" As soon as I say the words, I remember her father's visit.

"My father, you know he always triggers them."

"You know he can't get to you here, right?" I ask as she climbs from my lap.

"Yeah, old habits." She shrugs. "Now, let me see if I can help your back." She rubs her hands together and has this cute little grin on her face.

I feel my muscles tighten and I try not to wince in pain, but now that she knows the details of my ordeal, it was only a matter of time before she would want to try and help me.

"Maybe straddle the chair?" she says, looking around the room for an alternative and coming up short.

I stand up and grab her hand. "I have the perfect place, come on."

"Where are we going?" she asks, following me out of the office.

"My gym."

"I've been keeping away from this room like the plague." She giggles.

"Really, why?"

"Exercise? Come on. Preston, I hate working out."

"You're missing out," I tell her.

The sound of our bare feet slapping against the tile floor echoes off the walls as we approach and I open the door for her, ushering her inside. "Welcome to my sanctuary." I smirk.

She opens her mouth to say something and nothing comes out. She slowly closes her mouth and with a pleasantly shocked look on her face she glances at me and then back to the room. I place my hand at the small of her back and apply gentle pressure, encouraging her to go in.

I watch Skye's face as she takes it all in.

"Holy shit, Preston. You've been holding out on me," she gasps, eyeing the jacuzzi and beyond it, the steam room and sauna. The room is also filled with the best workout equipment and weights I could find and a massage and therapy area for those times when working out isn't helping and I have to call my masseuse.

The full sliding glass doors open up into the backyard when it's hot. I keep them closed and the air on, which is why she's never seen in here before. The windows are tinted for privacy.

"Do you like it, *Detka*?" Her face says she loves it, but I want to hear her tell me. I know it's just a workout room but this is where I find my peace of mind and work off my anger.

"It's awesome!" she says in awe.

I chuckle while I sit on the table with my back facing her. "Is that back rub still in the cards?" I watch her reaction in the mirrors on the other side of the room.

She takes one more look around then turns toward me and looks at my back. "Of cou—" The rest of her sentence is cut off as she stares at me, not at my face but my back.

It takes all my willpower not to stiffen and go in search of a shirt. It's not that she hasn't seen glimpses, I don't exactly hide it. But now that it's all out in the open I feel more exposed somehow. I watch over my shoulder as her mouth presses into a thin angry line. The silence drags on, and she hasn't taken her eyes off my back. It's scarred fairly well, but it isn't disfigured. Her eyes scan all of the old wounds and finally stop just below my shoulder. The scarring on the outside looks bad, but it is those muscles underneath that pain me and tighten up.

"God this pisses me off. I want to knock those two bastards' heads together."

Her touch is featherlight as she follows each scar with her fingertips.

"It was a long time ago, Skye." Her fingers still trail along my back, her touch so soft and light, comforting. Thoughts of her are what got me through that time.

Her lips press into my shoulder where my muscles twitch and burn. I watch her in the mirror, the sight would bring me to my knees if I were standing. She has an enraged look on her face, yet her lips are soft. Her eyes meet mine in the mirror, and she lifts her head and says in my ear, "I could kill them for this."

She walks around the table and bends down in front of me. I cradle her face in my hands. "They have made things right, Skye. It wasn't their fault."

"Well someone needs to pay. I want to find the person who sent you there and kill them with my bare hands." She's breathing hard just at the thought.

I stroke her face, softly. "I'll get my revenge, *Detka*. You don't need to get your hands dirty."

She opens her mouth to speak, but I take full advantage of my position and capture her lips in a swift kiss. When I pull away she has a glazed look in her eyes and it doesn't escape my notice that she is wearing just a t-shirt. I have to chant to myself *down boy, down boy, down boy*. I'm trying to take things slow and when it finally happens, I don't want to give her a school boy quickie romp. I'm no two pump chump.

I push her up off my lap before I cave and smile innocently. "How about that massage?" Not waiting for a response, I give her my back. She doesn't waste any time and starts working my shoulders out. Her fingers go straight into the knot, and I grunt in pain and hold my breath waiting for her to release the muscle. Christ, is she digging her knuckle into it?

"Breathe through it, Preston." Her voice is soft behind me.

I take a shaky breath and listen to her as she starts counting down.

"Five, four, three, two, one."

She does this a few more times. When she finally releases the hold she has on me, I swear the muscle has loosened up. I roll my shoulders and find it doesn't feel as tight.

"How does it feel?" she asks from over my shoulder.

"It feels awesome, where did you learn that?" I again roll my shoulders and it is just a mild ache that's left.

"I used to rub out my own muscles. It made them feel better." she says with a grin.

"You amaze me." I stand up before her. "Thank you."

"We better go get dressed before Craig and Shaina get up," she says, pulling away from me.

Twenty Four

PRESTON

I feel bad that I got so drunk on her birthday, so I was thinking about taking her out tonight to make it up to her. We've been lazy the last few days, just lounging around, enjoying each other's company. She has her nose stuck in her latest novel that she'll finish by the end of the night. I have no idea how that woman breathes in so many novels. She gives my Amazon account a workout, that is for sure.

"*Detka?*" I interrupt her.

She looks up over her device as if I just murdered someone. "What?"

"What? Is that code for *yes, Preston?*" I say with a sarcastic tilt to my head.

"I am at a good part, so no. It means *what do you want?*"

"Come here," I demand.

She frowns and raises a brow blinking at me.

I roll my eyes. She never does as she is told. "Fine, stay there then. I was going to ask if you would like to go to Las Casuelas tonight?"

"Oooh! Yes!!" In her excitement she jumps up then looks

down at me. "I've missed that place so much." A smirk plays about my lips as I watch her excitement. "I was going to make us some lunch, but cancel that, I'm saving the bandwidth for Mexican food." She places a hand on her belly and rubs it licking her lips at the same time.

"Why don't you finish your book? I have some things to take care of before we go." I stand and place a kiss on her forehead and head off to my office.

———

The restaurant is bustling when we walk in. Being a local has its advantages as I spot a familiar face at the host's podium. She was in most of our classes growing up. I take Skye's hand into mine and move through the crowd of people pulling her behind me to the podium.

"Hello, two for dinner."

She hasn't looked up from her seating chart yet as she asks, "Do you have a reservation?"

"No, but I was hoping you'd be able to accommodate us anyway," I tell her. "The name is Hart." I look down at Skye and she has a smirk on her face as she recognizes her too.

She looks up at us and a look of surprise crosses her face as she sees who it is. "Preston? Well I'll be damned! How the hell are you?" She looks to my side and sees who I'm with. "Skye? Oh my God girl...This is a blast from the past! I haven't seen you in forever." She walks around the podium and doesn't give her a chance to reply before she throws her arms around her, hugging her.

The look on Skye's face is priceless, she is definitely not the hugging type. Her eyes are huge and pleading with me to rescue her.

"Hey, Maryann, how've you been?" she asks as she slowly pulls herself out of her arms.

Maryann steps back. "Oh, girl, you know, kids, a man, and all that." She then looks toward me and realizes we are holding hands.

I give her a slow grin.

She's never been one with a filter on her. Skye's hand tightens in mine and I squeeze back in reassurance. "Yes, we are, do you think you have a private booth available?"

She straightens and goes right back into work mode, catching the hint that we want to be alone. "Oh sure, I can fit you two in. One second, let me check something."

She is gone for a few seconds and then turns the corner and crooks her finger at us to come. We follow her around to a booth that can sit at least four, and she places two menus down across from each other. I gesture for her to sit in the booth and as she slides in, I sit down beside her. She opens her mouth to say something when Maryann cuts her off.

"Oh my God! You two were always adorable!" She picks up the other menu and sets it in front of me, giving us a wink. "Your server will be right overt. Enjoy guys."

I can't help but smile, since neither of us pick up the menus. She always orders the same thing. "Are you going to try something new?" I can't help but tease with a laugh.

"Hell no, why mess with perfection?"

The waitress shows up to our table. "Can I get y'all something to drink?"

I don't show my irritation at the use of y'all. I turn to her and plaster a smile on my face.

"For you, ma'am?" She looks at Skye.

"I'll have an iced tea, no lemon please.

She looks at me. "Can I have a Coke? Also, we're ready to order."

She takes out her little pad of paper. "Oh, for sure, what can I get for you, sir?"

I glance at Skye. "Do you want me to order for you?" I ask with a grin.

She smiles. "Sure, if you remember what I have."

Challenge accepted. I turn to the waitress. "We'll have the guacamole appetizer to share and then I'll have the chimichanga entree, rice and beans are fine. The lady will have a bean and cheese burrito enchilada style, no rice, with a side of sour cream."

"Alrighty," the waitress says, scribbling furiously.

"Is that right?" I ask Skye with a smirk.

"Yes, perfect."

"Anything else, perhaps a soup or salad?"

"No, that will be all."

She nods and tucks her pad of paper back into the front pocket of her apron, then she sets off to get our order placed. I turn back to Skye and she has a smile playing about her lips.

"What?" Her smile is infectious, and I give her one in return.

"Are we going to be *that* couple?" she tasks, trying to control her laughter.

"What do you mean?"

"Ordering for each other, sitting side by side..."

I slide closer to her and her automatic response is to give me space by moving over until there is nowhere else for her to move. I lean in closer. "I wouldn't be able to do this from across the table." I lean down and kiss the tip of her nose, then pull away slightly smiling down at her. I tuck one of her curls behind her ear, scanning her face, noting the slight blush on her cheeks.

"Preston, I..." She abruptly presses her lips together stopping herself from finishing.

"What is it, *Detka*?" My brow raises, confused by the uncomfortable look on her face.

"It's nothing, never mind." She lowers her eyes breaking eye contact.

The waitress returns with chips and salsa, our drinks, and appetizer. "Your dinner will be up shortly. Can I get you anything else?"

"No, thank you." I give her a slight smile not wanting to appear rude as she walks away and turn my attention back to Skye.

Skye's taking her time unwrapping her straw and putting it in her iced tea, staring into her glass.

"Skye, what is it?" I ask again. Her eyes flash up to mine, then she looks off to the side and takes a deep breath.

"Nothing," she mutters.

I place a finger under her chin and lift her back up. "Look at me, *Detka*."

She slowly raises her gaze to meet mine, and I see the vulnerability deep within her eyes. "What?" she says with a touch of snark, her defenses on standby.

"*Lyubov moya*, you can tell me anything." I cup her face and use my thumb to caress her lips.

She furrows her brows. "*Lyubov moya*? What does that mean?"

"It means, my love." This time it's me who breaks the eye contact, feeling suddenly self-conscious. I'm surprised to feel her soft skin on my face, her fingers lifting my chin. I meet her eye and only see warmth.

"Preston, all I wanted to say is that I want you. That's it. You hold me, you kiss me, you stroke me, but I want back what we had. I know you've been holding yourself back, but I won't break, I promise you."

When I see her smile, something melts deep within me. "Oh, *Detka*, I love you so much."

She turns and frames my face with her small hands. "I love

you more." She pulls my face down to hers giving me the sweetest kiss yet. When she pulls away, I press my forehead to hers.

"I want you so much, Skye. So much I want to just get the check and take you home right now."

She lets out a throaty laugh. "I haven't eaten decent Mexican food in five years, you can hold out through this meal."

Just as I lean in for another kiss the waitress clears her throat. I give Skye a guilty smirk and move back as our plates are set down in front of us.

Our dinner passes with comfortable conversation, despite my burning need. There has always been an easy way with us. We don't even need to speak sometimes, we can just look at each other and know what the other is thinking.

Finally, she slows down eating and quietly watches me finish.

"Need me to ask for a box?"

She scrunches her nose. "Leftovers? No thank you."

I roar with laughter, she is so picky. "Ok, if the waitress comes back can you get the check? I will be right back."

"Alright, do you want dessert?"

"Yes, you." I lean in and kiss her flaming cheek. It makes me chuckle that I can make her blush so fiercely and I can't wait to get home and see that blush spread everywhere. I slide out of the booth to find my way to the washroom.

As I walk back to our table, I see that Skye is gone from the table and our bill has been left. She must have gone to the restroom too.

"I will be right back with this," the waitress says, taking the check from the table.

"Have you seen the lady I was with?"

"No, sir," she says and stops at the table across from us, clearing off some dishes.

I look down at my watch, a good ten minutes has passed since I came back to the table. I've paid the bill and I'm ready to go home. I furrow my brows in concern, about to flag down a waitress to check the bathrooms to make sure she isn't sick in there, when a sudden chill goes through my core as Bob sits down across from me. My lips tighten into a firm line.

"What are you doing here?" I say between my clenched teeth.

"I was having dinner and saw my daughter sitting here alone."

I smack my palms on the table. "I swear if you did anything to her I will kill you."

Bob just lets out a boisterous laugh.

I reach my arm across the table and fist his shirt in my hand pulling him toward me, not caring who notices. "What did you do to her?"

"I didn't lift a finger, words were enough." He laughs again, his eyes filled with malicious joy.

"What happened? Where is she?" I release his shirt, I can't trust myself not to wrap my hands around his neck.

"You should have warned me that my daughter didn't have a clue you were working for me in Russia."

"Fuck!" I mumble under my breath.

"Guess I put my foot in my mouth, assuming you told her about it. By the look on her face when I told her, it was a shock." His eyes crinkle in the corners as he laughs again.

"I swear I will kill you if anything happens to her." I don't spare him a moment extra. *Bastard!* I scream in my head, I have to find her and explain.

I run out of the restaurant and check each way. Nothing. I break out in a run to the back where we are parked thinking, no hoping, that she is waiting by the car. I get to the car and there is no sign of her. Fuck!

I speed away from the restaurant with a clenched jaw the entire way home, hoping she is there waiting for me. The car hasn't come to a stop before I slam it in park and jump out, running toward the house. The front door swings open with a force, and I run in shouting her name, "Skye! Skye! Where are you?"

I search the house running from room to room, finding each one empty. Heaviness settles deep within my chest. "She's gone," I whisper into the empty living room. My neck muscles are corded as I brace myself on an end table. Breathing hard I hang my head, tears freely flowing down my face as the reality of the situation hits me. I pick up a crystal decanter to pour myself a glass of whiskey and in a rage, I pull my arm back and send it flying through the air, smashing it against the wall.

The amber liquid drips down the walls, mimicking the tears on my face as I fall down to my knees.

Twenty Five

SKYE

It's been thirty-three days since I saw my father and *him*. My chest still tightens with pain as I think about them working together. I was going to pull a Houdini and disappear again; it was sheer luck that Lea found me at the bus station.

I was a hysterical wreck. I saw her car drive by and then slam on the breaks. She threw the car into reverse and came to me. Thankfully there were no other cars around.

I didn't really say much, the fact that I had tear stained cheeks was enough. She peppered off questions faster than an automatic weapon, none of which I remember. I was in no shape to answer them. I felt too betrayed. Preston was working with my father.

Lea shook when she helped me into her house, yet she said nothing. She was angry at me, or at Preston, who knew? But still she held me tight that first night as I cried myself to sleep.

Lea's place is a cozy two-bedroom house; there's no questioning if or how long I'm going to stay. She wouldn't have it any other way. The sound of her walking in the door from work brings me out of my thoughts.

"Hey, Skye, how was your day?" She kicks her shoes off at the door.

"It was okay."

"Did you call Preston today?"

I sigh, it's the same thing every day. "No, I sat here all day binge watching *American Horror Story*."

She nods, walks past me with her back stiff and throws her keys and purse on the kitchen table, then turns back to me and tilts to her head. "Can we cut the shit?"

I groan. I knew this was coming, but in all honesty, she's given me a few weeks longer than I thought she would. "Sure...umm, what's up?" I reply innocently.

She flops down on the sofa across from me. "Oh you know damn well what's up." She scowls.

I slump back on the couch. Here it comes.

"What the fuck are you going to do about Preston?"

I feel my throat tighten. "Nothing. It's over. He works with my father," I say flatly.

She shakes her head. "I know you don't get along with your dad but, is that so bad? I mean, Preston's making a living, right?"

I bite the inside of my lip. "It's more than not liking my father. I fucking hate him and what he's done to me." I press my lips firmly together.

Her eyes narrow slightly and her foot stops moving. "I know he's an asshole, but God Skye, why do you hate him so bad?"

"Sometimes you're an asshole, Lea."

"What the hell did I do?"

I sigh. "It's just your matter-of-fact tone. You don't know the hell I went through."

"I'll only know if you tell me, Skye."

"The thought of Preston working with him after all he did..." I mutter, not really hearing what she's saying.

"Just freaking tell me! Quit tiptoeing around it, I'm your best friend."

"He used to abuse me," I say quietly. "He beat me most of my life and that was some of the easier stuff to get over." Lea is silent and I can't bring myself to look at her. She's my best friend and I've kept a part of me hidden from her for so long.

"Skye...why didn't you ever say anything?"

The tone in her voice makes me look up at her through my lashes; the look on her face is unexpected. She has a fist covering her mouth and tears freely falling. "How could I? Everyone was always so happy, and well, you all made me forget what a nightmare it was at home."

She sniffles. "But we could have had one of our parents help you."

I laugh bitterly. "And what? Have my father ruin you all? He was, well *is* good at that, Lea."

"Oh my God. We are such idiots," she says angrily.

"What?" I look at her slowly raising a brow.

"Is that why you would never change in front of any of us girls?"

"Yeah. He was careful not to leave any evidence where anyone could see." I roll my shoulders, thinking I can still feel some of those bruises.

"Fuck, it all makes sense now. You could have told me."

"I know that now, but then I wanted my friends safe and you, Shaina, Preston, and Craig have always been a safe place for me."

"I understand, but I wish I could have helped."

I shake my head. "Please don't... you did help, I don't know how to explain it."

"But you left me without a word," she says with a sad pitch to her voice.

I look down to the floor, the pain in her voice clear. How do I make her understand? I swallow hard. "The truth? When he left

I didn't want to give anyone another chance to hurt me. I couldn't stand for that to happen. I had to take back control of my life."

"But..."

I hold a hand up to stop her from talking. "I was wrong, Lea. I know I shouldn't have left and there were many times I wanted to talk to you but I would lose my nerve. I was afraid you would be hurt by him somehow if I did. Seeing Preston in Hollywood made me see that I was wrong, I should have stayed here and faced my fears."

She sits up, and her eyes widen slightly. "Wait, you were afraid for me?"

"Yes." I look down at the floor.

"Did someone threaten me?"

I nod. "My father."

She stiffens. "What did he say?"

"It doesn't matter now. They were all lies, everything is lies."

"How does this all tie into Preston?"

"My father told me he and Preston are working together."

"What did Preston say when you asked him, did he deny it?"

"I didn't ask." I swallow past the thickening in my throat willing myself not to cry.

"What?!" she screeches.

"You heard me. I left before he could lie to me."

"Jesus, listen to yourself. Have you ever known Preston to lie to you?"

"What did you expect me to do? My father said he worked for him."

"How about talk to him? That's what grown-ups do," she says, shaking her head.

I'm silent for a few seconds. "But he's working with my father..." I repeat.

"You don't know that for a fact. Do you have any clue how much he hates your father? Do you?"

"I mean I thought he did, but then my father said they work together. How do you know he hates him?"

"When you left..." She shakes her head and closes her eyes, takes a deep breath and starts again. "You didn't see him when he came back, when he found out you were gone. He wanted your father's blood. It was Craig and Harrison who convinced him to be smart and put his energy into finding you." She pauses and looks at me sadly.

"He left me, without a word. He didn't trust me enough to tell me he wasn't leaving for good." I clench my teeth. Call me selfish but what about me?

"He was different when he came back, a piece of him was gone. Let me call Craig to come over," she pleads.

"No. Craig is his best friend. He's biased."

"You're so damn stubborn, Skye. When he came back he was a broken man. When he found you and brought you back, that spark came back to him."

I wince. "What about me, Lea? Does anyone wonder what it did to me?"

She gets up off the sofa and paces the room for a moment, she then sits down and turns toward me and takes my hands into hers. "Of course we did. Every fucking day I thought about you."

My throat and chest feel thick. There is a stinging behind my eyes and I open my mouth to say something and can't seem to choke out any words.

Lea pulls me toward her and wraps her arms around me. "Oh, Skye, come here."

I fall into her and rest my head in her lap. My vision gets blurry and I swipe my eyes with the back of my hand. I hiccup and try to stop the flow of tears, only now that the floodgates have opened, I uncontrollably sob in her lap. When will the pain lessen? When will I stop hurting?

I feel a hand moving my hair back off my face, my eyes feel

like there is sand in them. I'm not too sure how much time has passed, I sniffle and realize she's talking to me. "We all worried so much Skye, but Preston... he was the one that was truly broken. He wouldn't risk losing you again."

"Tell me the truth. Do you think he's in with my father?" I shift slightly so I can see her face.

"No. In fact, fuck no. I promise you, Skye, it's not what you think. I don't know what your father was trying to pull, but the Preston I know hates that man."

My heart swells with hope. "Lea?" I croak out.

"Yeah?"

"Has he been looking for me?"

She's silent and her hand stills in my hair.

"Lea?"

She sighs.

"Has he been looking for me?" I ask her again.

Her jaw clenches, and it takes her a few seconds to answer. "No."

I sigh heavily.

"No one has been able to get a hold of him," she says softly.

I sit up and frown at her as she sets her hands down in her lap. "What do you mean?"

"Craig has been to his house a couple times and he won't answer the door."

"Are you sure he's there?"

"Yes, he yells at him to go away."

My chest hurts. "Do you think I was wrong to leave him?" I'm afraid I already know the answer.

"I don't think you should have run," she says faintly.

I nod and bite my lower lip. "I don't know what to do."

"No?"

"I'm afraid, Lea."

"It will be ok, trust me." She gives me an encouraging smile. "Just talk to him."

"Should I call him?" I frown, trying to figure out the right thing to do. "Wait no... I need to talk to him in person." I nod my head as soon as I say it out loud. It sounds like the right decision.

"Thank fuck, it's only taken you a month," she says and leans back on the couch.

"Sorry." I slowly smile at her.

I walk up to the house and stop just out of sight of the windows. The lights in the living room are on and when I glance over at the driveway, only his cars are parked there. Oh God, can I do this after leaving him again? What if he has moved on and someone is in the house with him. It's always the fucking 'what ifs' that mess with my head. Lifting my chin, I take a deep breath, and give myself a pep talk. *You can do this!*

Before I can talk myself out of it, I walk resolutely to the front door and firmly knock three times. I can hear the TV blaring. My heart sinks as I wait outside, my resolve fading with each passing moment. I've come this far, and I can't leave without at least seeing him. Curling my hand into a fist, I pound on the door. The TV goes mute and then I hear him yell, "Go away!" My eyes pop back open, and I question myself. Does he know it's me? No, of course not.

I bang a few more times on the door and hear something smash against the wall and the pounding of his feet as he stomps to the door. It swings wide open, my breath catching at the sight of him. He looks like complete shit standing in the doorway. He's shirtless, and in his worn Levi's that he's had since high school, his comfort pants. His face looks like it hasn't seen a razor in a month, his hair looks as if his hands have been the only comb in recent days.

My heart breaks as it hits me that I did this to him, or I should say, we did this to each other. His silence claws at my belly, grating on my every nerve. It takes all my strength to not start yelling at him and demanding answers, but I know that would be the quickest way to get the door slammed in my face. After many long moments I finally get the nerve to meet his eyes, as he whispers, *"Detka?"*

Twenty Six.

PRESTON

My voice feels hoarse as I use the name meant only for her. I scrub the back of my hand over my face. I look up at her and stagger backwards, unable to believe that she is standing at my front door. The wall stops me retreating any further and I sink down onto my haunches. Finding it hard to swallow, I lower my head into my hands. Shaking my head I whisper, "Please be real...please..." I lift my face to look at her and find that she's still there.

I watch her step cautiously into the house and close the door behind her. My vision becomes blurred. I use my fingers to clear the tears. I can see the hurt in her eyes, they are the brightest green they have ever been and glossy with unshed tears. It's like a punch to my gut. I did that to her.

She takes a step closer and I hold out my hand to stop her and rise to my feet. "I can explain. Please, *Detka*... I need to explain everything to you." My voice cracks with emotion.

She doesn't say anything, she just brushes my hand out of her way and then she steps closer to me and caresses my face. I briefly close my eyes, her touch feels like home. When I open my mouth about to speak, she places a single finger across my lips, shushing me.

She pulls her hand back and searches my face, for what I don't know. Whatever it is, I think she finds it, because she slips her arms around my waist and lays her head on my chest. My body tenses, then she squeezes me and I finally release the breath I had been holding.

My arms crush around her and my shoulders curve into her. I cup the back of her head as I hold her to me. We stand like this for a few long moments, then I finally get up the nerve to pull back and brush the hair out of her face. A fat tear starts rolling down her cheek. I brush it away with the pad of my thumb.

"Don't cry, *Detka*." I wipe another tear away and my throat feels as if it's going to close.

"You should follow your own advice," she says as she sweeps her knuckles across my face and they come back wet.

"Where have you been?"

"I was at Lea's. No one told you?" She arches a brow.

I think back to all the times Craig was banging on my door or calling the house. "No, I had no clue." I ignored all their attempts to contact me and try to talk to me to see what happened. I'm so stupid sometimes.

I look down at her and find her smirking through the tears. "What?"

"You look like crap." She chuckles.

"You look beautiful, so fucking beautiful."

She blushes and looks down at the ground. "I have to ask you something, Preston." She slowly brings her gaze back up to mine, her eyes have narrowed, and she is chewing on her bottom lip.

"I will answer all your questions," I tell her. "But before I do, can you promise me you'll hear me out and not run?" I take her hands into mine and squeeze them, brushing my thumbs over her knuckles.

She looks away and blushes again, then looks up at me. I see the pain behind her eyes and that hits me low, like a kick to the balls. I have to remove my hand from her face, the skin contact is clouding my thoughts and I can't afford to screw this up.

She squeezes my hand. "I'm willing to try," she says softly, and then glances at the floor.

"Come on." I take her hand and walk through the foyer and into the living room and as I do the sickening feeling in my stomach that has been there for weeks feels like it's getting worse. I walk directly over to the large sofa, the corner spot where we both can sit comfortably. We sit down and turn toward each other and once we are settled, I pull one of her hands into mine and hold on to it. "Ok, what is your question?" I ask cautiously.

"Are you working with my father?" I can see her pulse jumping in her neck.

I watch as she tenses as if she is bracing herself for the answer. "I was, but you have to hear the reasons why."

She slowly pulls her hand away from mine and then opens her mouth to speak.

I hold up my hand, the palm facing her. "Let me tell you everything and then you can ask all your questions."

She hesitates, then finally nods.

I rub my temples, figuring I just need to tell it from that first minute her father started manipulating us. "Your father caught me slipping out of your window one morning at dawn. I thought he was going to kick my ass, but instead he offered me a job. One which would give me enough money to start a life with you. He wanted me to go to Russia..." I look up at her. "Well...you know the rest." She opens her mouth to object. "Before you say anything," I interrupt her. "I told him no. I couldn't figure out his angle, but I just knew he was being shady. Anyway. I said no and prepared for him to start making my life hell. But it never happened.

"For weeks he left me alone. I had all but forgotten it had even happened. Then graduation day changed everything. Mama got sick and you know I couldn't provide the care she needed. Then Bob just appeared out of nowhere in the hospital hallway, like he had been circling and smelled blood. He offered me the help I so desperately needed. The money he promised and Mama's medical bills paid on top. I had no choice, Skye. I couldn't let her die. So I agreed."

She seemed to war with emotions inside, but she didn't say a thing and let me continue. "One of the conditions for working for him was I couldn't tell anyone. This job was going to be a means to be able to provide for you and my Mama. The kind of life you both deserved. I tried to get him to change his mind about telling you, but with my mother in the hospital, he really had me by the balls."

I take in a shaky breath, her wide glossy eyes flash with hurt and the tears start to fall.

"When I got to Russia and nobody met me, at first I thought I was unlucky. Bob was a busy man, I just kept missing him. But when I was taken, and the Volkovs were so convinced I'd stolen their shipment, I started realizing he'd set me up. Unbeknownst to me, he had informed them I would be delivering the shipment from the US. But he never gave me anything to hand over. I had no clue what they were talking about.

"But the brothers figured it all out when they found your picture in my bag. Bob wanted me gone. He knew if he set me up, the Volkovs would put me in a shallow grave and I wouldn't be there to stop him getting to you."

I take a breath and keep on going. "After we figured it out and I healed, I came home with a plan to take him down, but when I got here you were gone. Fuck Skye, a piece of me died that day."

She swipes the tears off her face but keeps silent as I keep going. The sight of her so upset has me standing up and pacing the area in front of the sofa. I turn back, and her eyes are wide and I realize she is scared I might walk away from her. With a couple quick steps, I am standing before her and I drop to my knees so that I am eye level with her and I grasp her hands.

"I went crazy, Skye. I searched and searched for you and I couldn't be certain he didn't have some part in your disappearance. I feared you might be dead, Skye. I lost my mind. For a while I was still that kid who left you. It took a while to pull myself together and be the man you needed. I had money all of a sudden and it took time to fully realize what that meant for me. Once I found my feet, I hired someone to help me search for you. It was only when my PI found out that Bob had people looking for you too that I finally began to hope you might still be safe, just far away."

I release her hands and rub my temples and then take a shaky breath to finish what I need to tell her.

"As time went by I couldn't just sit and watch while Bob got richer. So I started trading, building up a business. The Volkovs favored me, obviously, and it wasn't long before I was taking business from him. I hired Harrison to front it for me. I didn't want Bob knowing I was behind it. I didn't want him to know I was Volkov blood. I wanted him to still think he was above me, so that he would have further to fall when I could bring him down." For a moment I fall silent and she watches me reflecting on the past few years.

"He's never acknowledged the fact that I came back from Russia you know. I'm sure it freaked him the fuck out the first time he saw me. He'd tried to get me killed after all and I'd somehow survived. When I came back I was going to head straight round there and fuck him up. But you were gone and everything changed. So instead, I kept my head down and focused on more important things. He passed me in the street once and stared. But until that morning at breakfast, the day

Mama..." I catch myself before I go to yet another dark place and get back to my story. "We'd never had any contact."

She takes both my hands and opens them from where they were tightly clenched into fists then she pulls them into her lap. I look up at her, hoping she can forgive the mistakes I have made. "With that being said, the answer is yes. Yes, I worked for your father. He had me backed into a corner and I didn't have any other options. I couldn't have imagined what it would do to me, to us. But that is in the past now. I can only change what is in front of me." I stroke a curl from her face. I stay on my knees before her, my jaw tight as I wait for her rejection.

She drops my hands from her grasp and my eyes look down to where my skin still burns from her touch. I can't face her. I'm terrified that I will see a look of disgust on her face.

"Preston?" she says softly.

I thought I would be all cried out by now, but another teardrop lands on the back of my hand. "Yes?"

She leans forward and my heart sinks, I can't watch her leave or see the scorn on her face. I feel her soft hands cup my face. "Preston look at me."

I swallow and look up, her face is blotchy from crying and her eyes... damn her eyes get me every time. Huge green eyes that are glossy with the remnants of unshed tears. "Preston, I love you."

The relief is agony and I groan from the pain of it slamming into me as I cup her face and bring her forward to press my lips roughly to hers. I part my lips and tears spill as she lets me kiss her deeply, almost savagely. I never thought I'd have this again and I can't seem to part from her. Eventually I have to let her go so we can both breathe. "I love you so much," I gasp.

Breathing hard, she strokes my face and smiles through her tears. For a long while we just stare and soak in the closeness we have both missed so much.

"He needs to pay," she says darkly out of nowhere.

"He will," I confirm. "We've been working hard, Skye. We are almost ready to ruin him. I've been buying up small gem companies that buy from him and his sales have been slowly dwindling. Add to that supplies in Russia have been drying up due to 'competitors.' Things have been getting bad for him for a while now and he can't touch most of the money he's always had behind him to create the illusion of wealth. That money doesn't belong to him, it belongs to you. It was always enough to just have it in the family, he was able to use the power it gave him to build his empire and generate a healthy disposable income. But with business taking a sudden turn for the worst, he's had to borrow money." I laugh, mirthlessly. "Lucky for him he has wealthy contacts with Russian money." I smile slyly. "I believe the Volkov brothers have generously invested to help him secure a deal which will get him out of this hole he's in."

"But they're—" She looks horrified.

I shake my head and take her hand. "It's okay, *Detka*, he has no idea we are related. It's something we've been very careful about. We have been planning his downfall for five years. They are as hellbent on his ruin as I am. Don't forget, Bob sent Vasily's only nephew, son of his beloved missing sister, to his death at the hands of the Volkovs no less! Vasily wanted his blood right there and then, but he has trusted me to take the lead on this. He understands that my vendetta is primary here."

"I want to help."

I frown. "Help with what?"

"I want to be involved in his takedown."

"No, absolutely not." My jaw clenches at the thought of her near him or even saying his name.

"Preston, I have to be a part of it," she says softly.

My hands slide into her hair so I can tilt her face to look at me. "No, I can't stand the thought of you in danger, and it might get dangerous, Skye. The Volkovs have invested a substantial sum to bail Bob out and when he finds out it's a set up things could get nasty. We have plans in place, but there's always a chance things could go awry and I want you far away from it."

Her eyes flash with anger. "You don't understand. I have to be part of his demise." She grabs onto my forearm. "I have to have some justice for what he's done. So please, Preston, let me have this."

I pull my hand back and fist it. My skin crawls at the thought of her having any dealings with him at all. "I don't know if I can allow it, *Detka*. What if something happens to you?" My voice cracks.

"A whole lot of shit has happened to me already. Damn it, Preston... I will be part of his takedown." I feel the bite of her nails into my forearm as she stares at me.

I sigh. "Under one condition, otherwise I will call it all off."

"What's that?" She raises a brow at me.

"You are never alone with him, no matter what."

She moves her hand back to my face. "Agreed. We will take him down together." She kisses me softly in stark contrast to the edge to her tone.

I inhale her sweet scent and sigh, happily. "I want us to have no more secrets between us," I murmur against her skin.

I feel her tense and pull back to study her.

"Skye? Look at me," I plead. It takes her a moment to move her eyes back up to mine. "What aren't you telling me?"

I see her lip wobble and then she sits up a little straighter.

"Whatever it is, we can get through it," I promise her.

"When your mom got sick, the first time, after they told us they were going to transfer her." She stops and takes a big breath.

"It's ok, Skye, go on," I assure her.

She nods. "I called my father and begged him to come and pay for her care."

I scowl. "What do you mean? When?"

"They had just told us that without insurance she would have to be moved to County and I knew we...I...had the money to pay for her to stay at Desert where she would have a better chance."

I still as I soak this in. "So he came to the hospital...because you called him?"

"Yes. I wanted to help."

"So...I didn't need to go to Russia?" I'm shocked, even though I shouldn't be.

"No." She fidgets with her hands. "I had to beg him. He told me it would cost me, but I didn't care, Preston. I would do anything for you."

"He screwed me over," I mutter, shaking my head. Then I realize I'm only thinking of myself. Skye put herself on the line for us. My blood runs cold at the thought of her 'owing' Bob. "Wait, what did he mean, it would cost you?"

Her body language gives me the answer I need, but I wait calmly to hear her say it.

She looks down at her hands. "He said I would owe him, if he helped you," she snaps.

I raise a brow. "Has he tried to collect?"

Skye nods. "About a week later. He tried to drug me, but my mother took the drink that he made for me. He broke into my room and was furious to find me alert and awake, he was going to give me to one of his friends. He said he still would, that his friend would probably pay a bonus if I fought him. I ran and didn't look back, Preston." She takes a shaky breath.

I stand and pull her fiercely into my arms, squeezing her as she lays her head on my chest. I can't get close enough to her. I need to physically feel that she is safe now. "Good girl," I whisper, feeling murderous as she relaxes against me.

She sighs and I rest my chin on top of her head, my mind on revenge.

"We'll make him pay, *Detka*, he'll wish for death by the time we're done with him." I kiss the top of her head and hug her tighter.

She pulls back and lifts her head. "Promise me he won't come between us anymore."

"He won't, I promise." I hug her to my chest and bring my hands around her back. "I've missed you so much."

Her eyes sparkle. "I've missed you too." She grins at me.

Twenty Seven

PRESTON

I wake with a contented smile and stretch out. I reach as always across the bed searching for Skye and my stomach drops when, as they have been for the past month, the sheets are cool to the touch and empty. Rolling over I sigh. I still forget each morning for a moment, that she's gone. That I fucked everything up and lost her.

It must have been a beautiful dream I had last night, the first in a long time. Usually my dreams are full of my mistakes tormenting me and of torture and endless suffering. I lay back breathing deeply, trying to deal with the disappointment and gather the strength to face another day without her. Eventually, I flip the blankets off me and get out of bed, stepping into a pair of board shorts and heading for my bathroom.

I feel empty. Lost. Then I open my bedroom door and an aromatic scent fills the air...bacon. I frown. How...? And then it hits me. Maybe it wasn't a dream.

I walk down the hallway cautiously, not wanting to allow myself to hope. I turn the corner into the kitchen slowly and gasp when I see her. Her hair is a wild, beautiful pile of wayward curls, her bronzed skin a stark contrast to the white of one of my shirts she must have borrowed when she got up. Her back is to the stove and she is chewing on the end of a pen as she stares at the paper she is holding, a frown of concentration creating an adorable crease above her nose. Her eyes go wide and she starts writing on the paper with purpose, then without missing a beat she turns and flips the bacon.

She's really here.

I take a moment to watch her, greedy for every second I can soak up. I remember it all now. She came back to me. We talked. It was all real. And so was the breathless, sweaty night we spent wrapped in each other. I grin, remembering how she moved beneath me, urging me on as we lost ourselves and all the demons of the past fell away.

I still feel overwhelmed with emotion and need to get it in check. I can't go weeping with joy every time I see her in my kitchen. When I can trust my voice, I greet her as casually as possible. "Morning."

She jumps at the sound and turns around, her smile matching mine. Relief and happiness. "Morning, I hope I didn't wake you."

"No, you didn't." I move toward her. "Did you sleep okay?"

Her smile is shy, but it betrays her thoughts. She is remembering too. "I always sleep well when I have you beside me."

"Then you will never sleep badly again," I promise her as I wrap her in my arms. I lean down and press my forehead to hers, just gazing into her eyes.

"Is everything okay, Preston?"

I lean over her, and she tilts her head back to look up at me. "It is now." I bend down and kiss lips.

"What are you making? It smells fantastic."

She pulls away from me and smiles brightly, turning back to the stove. "Bacon and pancakes, are you hungry?"

"Starved." I move in close behind her and nuzzle her neck, placing a teasing bite there as she wriggles. She tries to resist me and places the bacon on a paper towel. I stay close behind her as she works. I love the way my shirt looks on her. I wrap my arms around her waist and rest my chin on her shoulder. "I believe this shirt belongs to me."

"First rule of bacon... Don't cook naked." She reaches down to turn off the heat and the grease pops.

"Shit." I pull my arm back.

She quickly turns grabbing my arm. "Are you ok?"

"Yeah." I study her as she is checking my arm out with concern. I use my free hand and lift her chin up. "I'm fine, *Detka*. Now, about those pancakes." I flash her a grin.

She quirks a brow and points to the seats at the counter. "Go sit."

I return her look of incredulity. "Are you ordering me around?"

She tilts her head. "If you want your pancakes, then yes, I am."

"Touché." I step back and take a seat obediently.

I watch as she lights the stove under the griddle. She moves with ease around the kitchen and I hear the hiss of the batter hitting the pan. Mama would be so happy to see Skye back at home where she belongs, especially if she's feeding me the way Mama liked to. She was old fashioned at heart, my mama. She always believed that the way to a man's heart is through his stomach. Skye has other ways to my heart, but I'm not going to fight her if she wants to use pancakes once in a while.

She stacks up a plate for me and just like my mom did, she pre-butters them for me. Fuck I love this woman. She turns to me and sets down the plate, placing the syrup next to the plate.

"Eat," she says and points at my dish.

"I'll wait until yours is ready."

"But they will get cold." Her brows furrow and her lips tighten.

"Not if you hurry." I smile patiently at her.

She opens then closes her mouth, deciding not to argue and hurries and puts more batter on the griddle. She has her smaller stack ready in just a couple of short minutes then grabs the plate of bacon and comes and sits across from me at the counter.

"Okay, dig in," she says as she pours a little pool of syrup on the side of her plate and begins to cut a small piece of pancake to dip into it.

I smile at her quirky ways. "Why don't you just dump syrup on them and eat?"

Her eyes widen in slight horror. "I can't eat them like that."

"Why?"

"Because then the syrup soaks into the cakes making them soggy and all the flavors become a big soppy mess," she tells me with a tilt to her head as if that makes perfect sense.

Laughing I shake my head and I pour the syrup all over my pancakes with a smirk.

"So gross."

I put a generous portion on my fork and shovel it in my mouth and the flavors hit. Home, these taste exactly like my mama's. "Jesus," I manage after I swallow my first bite.

"What? Are they okay? I followed Liliya's recipe exactly." She looks worried.

"Oh my God, *Detka*. They're perfect," I say as I stuff another forkful in my mouth.

She shyly smiles. "Yeah? They came out good?"

"More than good, perfect. Now eat." I motion to her plate with my knife. "You lost weight again and I don't want to see you pushing food around. You are home now and this is where you are going to stay." I look into her eyes, shifting from my playful tone to something I hope she knows is sincere. "It's just you and me from now on, *Detka*."

"Yes, sir." She grins and mock salutes me with her fork.

I raise a brow. "Are you being sassy?"

She is silent as she carefully puts a bite on her fork and dips it into the syrup, then she looks up at me with a smirk. "Me? Never!" She takes the bite and groans, a sound that travels straight to my shorts. It takes me back to the dim light of my bedroom last night and the ecstasy of finally losing myself to her for the first time in five years. I feel whole again. "You're right, they came out good," she says, digging in for another taste and dragging me back to the present.

I chuckle. "I usually am."

"Mmmhmmm sure..." she says, chewing.

"You *are* being sassy." I stare at her aghast. She hasn't been so playful since...before all of this happened.

"Maybe." She shrugs.

I watch her eat and try to do the same, although the pancakes come second to the raging torrents of relief, joy, and gratitude I'm feeling. I know I will get past this phase of disbelief, but right now, it's all I can do not to keep pinching myself. Trying to behave normally, I glance on the counter and see the pad of paper she was writing on when I walked into the room. "What were you writing down when I came in?"

She looks over to the paper. "Oh, I was making a to do list."

"To do list? Are there things you need?" I ask, knowing I will give her anything.

"Yes, I need to take my father down." She grabs the paper and pushes it my way.

I scan the list and read the first one out loud. "Get a lawyer??"

"Yes, I'm going to claim what's mine. I'm twenty-three. His

time as guardian of my inheritance has ended and he only has what he has because I have yet to take it from him. But that is going to change." She presses her lips together in a line and her shoulders drop slightly.

"I think that's a good idea, Skye. But why does it seem like you are having second thoughts?"

She looks up with guilty eyes. "Because, I sound just like him. Greedy. Should I just let the money go? Oh God, Preston... am I my father's daughter?" She covers her face with her hands.

I get up and walk around the counter to her side. "*Detka*, look at me."

She takes a deep breath and looks up. I can see the self-loathing in her eyes. "Don't let me be like him." She swallows hard.

I brush my knuckles down her face. "You are nothing like him, this isn't about the money for you. This is about what's yours."

"Isn't it all the same?" she whispers.

"No, it's not and you know that." Pushing her hair out of her face and tucking it behind her ear, I cup her face. "Dig deep, *Detka*, don't let his poison taint what a beautiful person you are."

I could kill him with my bare hands for what he's done to her. She thinks the shattered pieces of her soul are ugly and grotesque. How do I show her it's the most beautiful mosaic I've ever seen?

"Is it worth it? All of this for money?" she asks with a snarl of disgust playing about her lips.

"Do you want your father to have wealth and comforts that your grandmother set aside for you and with it all the power it brings?"

"No."

Putting a finger under her chin and holding her gaze with

mine, I soothe her. "Don't ever doubt your reasons, *Detka*. This has nothing to do with money."

She nods her head. "Sometimes when I talk about money, I…I just feel like I sound like him and it makes me sick to my stomach."

"Well, I will have to convince you you're not. You've got me now to remind you of your self-worth."

After a few moments of silence, she straightens up and sets her jaw.

She points to her list. "I need a lawyer."

"Do you know any?"

She sighs. "I don't know any that aren't in my father's pocket."

"Would you like me to call mine?" I take a small step back and watch her face.

"Is he trustworthy?" She scrunches her nose up.

I chuckle. "I trust him as much as I trust Craig and you trust Craig, right?"

She nods. "Okay, call him. I need to get things started."

"Yes, the sooner the better," I agree.

She narrows her eyes. "Yes, we need to move forward. Finish this."

I pull her to me and wrap my arms around her. "You are so amazing." I kiss the top of her head and feel her arms squeeze around me.

She pulls back slightly to look up at me. "When do you think he will be able to see him?"

"He is actually on my calendar for tomorrow morning. Would you like me to see if he can come today?"

"Tomorrow should work," she says slowly.

I give her a crooked smile. "I will call him now and see if he can come this afternoon."

Her eyes light up. "Thank you."

"Don't be afraid to tell me what you really want, Skye. Ever."
I place a kiss on her forehead and pull away.

"I will work on it, Preston."

"Good girl, now I need to get some work done. I will be in my
office if you need anything." The minute I let her go I miss her
warmth.

Twenty Eight

SKYE

I'm soaking in the sun, the heat has always had a calming effect on me. The doorbell rings and my heart skips a beat and pounds in time with the chime. Ever since Preston found me in Hollywood and brought me home, any time we get an interruption from the world beyond this house, I always think it might be my father trying to find some way to drag me off. It should stop scaring me, I have never felt so safe. Old habits are just hard to break.

I can hear the patio door open. "Skye, the lawyer is here. Want to get dressed and meet us in my office?"

I cover my eyes to block the sun, seeing his shadow in the doorway. "I'll be right there."

The door shuts and I get up and walk around the pool. I don't use the same door to get into the house, instead I go through the sliding glass door that leads to the master bedroom. I'm completely dry already so I just throw a summer dress over my swimsuit. I pause in front of the mirror and silently curse the slight pink tinge of my skin. I even had on sunblock, damn sensitive skin. I will have to look for a higher SPF.

My palms are sweaty and I wipe them down the front of my dress as I walk down the hallway to Preston's office. I pause when I place my hand on the door handle. I hear them talking but can't make out the words. I swallow hard and lift my chin up and remove my hand from the handle and softly knock twice on the door.

"Come in," Preston calls out.

As I walk in the room my eyes immediately go to Preston, he has a warm smile which calms me. Out of the corner of my eye I can see the man standing across from him.

"Did you enjoy the sun, *Detka?*" Preston says as his eyes examine me.

"Uh... yes, we need stronger sunblock though."

"We can go to Target later." He gives me a small smile.

"Ohh Target run, sounds like a plan." I dart a glance at the stranger in the room. He is standing, quietly watching the exchange.

"Skye, this is Jason Carey, my good friend and lawyer," Preston says gently.

I turn to him and give him a small smile. "Hello."

He steps closer and holds a hand out. I hold out mine and he gives it a firm shake and cups my hand with both of his. "It's a pleasure to finally meet you," he says with a very proper English accent.

I look back at Preston, my brow raised.

"Jason is well aware I was looking for you, everyone knows about you, Skye."

I press my face into Preston's side, leaving just enough room to take a peek at his friend. He has a huge grin on his face but is looking at Preston. "She's good for you mate, it all makes sense now."

Preston squeezes me and then starts rubbing my arm,

relaxing me. "Skye, I briefly told Jason about your inheritance. Before we get too far into the details let's all sit down."

He puts his hands on the small of my back and guides me to the sofa. I sit down and he sits right next to me, pulling one of my hands into his. Jason follows us and unbuttons the jacket of his three-piece suit as he takes a seat across from us. Classy.

Bending down, he reaches into his briefcase, pulls out a pen and paper, then looks up and looks directly at me. "Now, first do you know who your father's lawyer is?"

"Yes, it has been Dillan MacDonald for as long as I can remember." Just saying his name makes me want to vomit. My father taught me a few lessons with his backhand while Dillon watched and did nothing. Preston squeezes my hand and brushes his thumb over the top, his touch strengthens me.

"Yes, I know of him," Jason says with a small frown and writes on the pad of paper. "This inheritance is from your grandmother, correct?" He stops taking notes and looks up at me.

"Yes, she passed away when I was nine," I say softly.

"I'm sorry for your loss," he says gently.

"Thank you, it was a long time ago." I fight back the lump in my throat at the thought of her.

"Time doesn't always take away the pain of losing a loved one." He presses his lips together and looks down at his notes and continues writing.

"No, I never really mourned for her." I quickly close my mouth and look up at Preston.

He gives me a smile. "She would be proud of the woman you've become, *Detka*."

I swallow hard and give him a small nod, choking down all my emotions.

"Do you know any of the particulars of the will?' Jason gets us back on the subject at hand.

"All I know is, I get control of her entire estate when I turn twenty-three."

"When do you turn twenty-three?" he asks.

"I already did, a few weeks back."

"Good, I will petition the courts for a copy of the will and also to start the transfer of funds into an account in your name."

"How long does something like this take?" I ask quickly.

"It all depends on how clearly the will is written. This could be quick and simple, that's the outcome I am hoping for." His pen is moving across the paper a bit quicker now.

"Can my father fight this?" I blurt out, wondering if it will be worth it.

"Am I correct in thinking he isn't of blood relation to your grandmother?"

"Yes, that's right. She was my mother's mom."

"Then I doubt your father has a leg to stand on, but I need to get hold of the will to be certain." He pauses his pen as he answers me then goes right back to scribbling notes down.

"Okay, is there anything that I need to do?"

"I will need you to give me your bank account number so I can set the transfer of funds in motion."

"Oh... I don't have one. I mean I know my father has my name on the main account, but I don't have access to those numbers." I look up nervously at Preston.

His smiles softly. "We will set you up with one. Is there anything else we should prepare for, Jason?"

He looks down at his notepad and then back up at Preston. "No, I can handle everything else." Jason picks his case up off the floor and puts his pad of paper in it. Standing up he moves toward us. "I will get back to you both when I have a copy of the will."

"Thank you, Jason." Preston stands and shakes his hand.

"Anytime, it was a pleasure to finally meet you Skye." He

extends his hand to me. Standing, I pull mine free from Preston and place it in Jason's.

"It was nice meeting you too and thank you."

"Don't thank me just yet, I'll be in touch," he says as he releases my hand and leaves the room.

We stand in silence for a few seconds as I watch the doorway where Jason just left, Preston's soft touch down my arm brings my attention back to him.

"*Detka?*"

"Mmm?" I reply absently.

"Are you ok? Is this all too much for you?" He brushes his knuckles down the side of my face.

"Is this all worth it? My father always finds a way to win." I look away and bite my lower lip.

"He won't win this time. We're together, we are strong and my family is more than a match for him."

I furrow my brows. "It's so weird hearing you talk about family referring to the Volkovs."

He gives me a crooked smile. "I know, it's still strange sometimes for me and I've had a few years to get used to it."

"Do they hate me because of my dad?"

"No, of course not, *Detka*. They know what you mean to me and that is enough to make you family in their eyes, but..." he drifts off and I panic at the word but.

"What is it?" I plead.

Preston sighs. "I want your permission to tell them the truth about all that Bob has done to you," he asks gently.

I take a step back. "No." My eyes break from his and I look down to the floor.

"*Detka*, look at me."

A second passes and I bring my eyes up to his, unable to find the words for how I feel at the moment.

"None of it was your fault. They don't need every detail, but

I think they need to know just how low he really is." He takes a step closer and cups my face, using his thumbs to swipe away tears I didn't realize were falling.

"Why do they have to know anything?" I whisper, shame still at the forefront of my warring emotions.

"Because they have a lot on the line to help me bring him down. I think they need to know what we know. He is not only a crooked businessman who tried to get me killed, he is also a vile child abuser. The Volkovs hold family above everything, especially now that my grandfather doesn't run the family anymore. They should know who they are dealing with."

A terrible show reel of some of the lowest times of my life flashes through my head and my stomach rolls at the thought of anyone knowing those things. But Preston is right. If they are willing to help us take my life back, they deserve to know what kind of man they are taking down. "Okay, as long as they don't know the specifics. I want the details buried in the past where they belong."

Preston nods and leans down to kiss my forehead. "I'll handle it."

I wrap my arms around his waist. "Thank you."

Twenty Nine

PRESTON

The phone call to my cousins went as expected, they were furious. It's well known that Bob was into anything that would make him a quick buck, but to put your child out there like that is just sickening. It was a good thing I called them when I did. Apparently they were going to come and knock down my door. I guess that's what happens when you go dark and off the grid, your friends and family come to pull you out, whether you want them to or not.

I assure them I'm fine. More than fine now that I have Skye back. I fill them in on Skye's plan to reclaim the inheritance Bob has been sitting on for years. They agree that everything is in place to make our move and we just need to wait for Bob to discover that his shipment was stopped.

Hanging up my phone, I get up from the desk and walk across the room. Opening my office door, I still. Skye's laughter rings through the house. I smile at the carefree sound as I go in search of her to find out what is making her laugh. I find her in the living room laying on the sofa with her legs over the side, her feet swinging back and forth. There is a commercial on the television, I walk around the sofa and see the phone to her ear.

I stop just out of her sight, watching her.

She smacks her forehead. "Oh my God, Lea. You are so horrible." She says laughing into the phone.

I step into her view and her eyes go wide, I quirk a brow at her. Before I say anything her eyes pop and she busts out laughing. I step closer and run my palm up her shin, she moves her feet together on the arm of the chair and tenses. I smile at her.

"Lea, I have to go."

I can't make out the words, but I can hear Lea talking faster, trying to finish her conversation before she loses Skye to me. I move my hand around and squeeze her calf.

"Mmmhmmm... I really should go." Skye keeps her eyes locked on mine.

I caress her gently and can feel the goose bumps on her soft skin. I tenderly trail my fingers over her knee and place my open hand on her inner thigh. She squeezes her knees together keeping my hand in place. I watch as she licks her lips looking at me with hooded eyes.

I step to the end of the sofa and place both hands behind her knees and in one swift movement I pull her to me, so I am standing between her legs.

She lets out a big breath. "Lea..."

I look down at her with her pink cheeks, her green eyes sparkling like a grassy field after rain. She is so beautiful. Her dress is bunched at her waist and I move a hand to cup her mound, placing the other hand on her belly to still her. I slip my fingers into her panties and brush my knuckles across her tender flesh, she gasps.

"Pres..."

The look I give her stops her from speaking and sure as shit I can hear Lea still talking in her ear. I lean over her and pluck the phone right out of her hand.

"Lea?" I say into the phone.

"Uhh... Preston? What happened to Skye, I was in the middle of a story," she says impatiently. I can hear her heels clicking on the pavement as she walks.

"Yeah... she's busy right now. We will see you later."

"Wait Preston, I'm at the mall and need to get Skye's advice on an outfit," she rushes out.

"Send her a picture, she'll answer in a few."

"But..." I don't let her finish and hang up, tossing the phone on a nearby chair.

Without breaking eye contact, I again stroke my finger over her sensitive flesh, this time watching her quiver with need.

She sighs and lifts herself to meet my hand.

I use my other hand to press her back down on the sofa. Her response to me is immediate. My fingers explore her as her body dances in time with my touch, her eyes not leaving my face. She opens her legs wider, begging for my touch.

The ring of the phone covers her gasp, and her eyes glance over to where I threw it. "Are you going to answer that?" Her voice has an aroused edge to it.

"No, she can leave a message." I manage to keep the growl out of my voice. The phone stops ringing and I listen to see if a message is being left and hear the phone click off. I grin down at her as if to prove my point. "Now, where were we...?"

The phone starts ringing again and I groan. Then a feeling of unease has me walking over to the phone and picking it up to look at the caller ID.

"Who is it?" she asks, the arousal gone from her voice.

I sigh and hand her the phone. "It's Lea."

Her brows furrow as she answers. "Hello?"

I watch as the color leaves her face and her eyes snap to mine. "What's the matter, *Detka?*"

"My..." She pauses. "My father bumped into Lea and wants to talk to me."

I take the phone from her. "Lea, the answer is no, stay where you are and let me come get you."

"It's too late for that. He already asked me to go with him to his house," she says in a monotone voice, not showing any emotion.

I hear Bob in the background. "Tell my slut of a daughter to hurry up and meet us, I haven't got all day."

"Lea, listen to me for a second. Can you get away?" I look down at Skye. She is biting her fingernails, now sitting up on the sofa. I try and give her a reassuring smile.

"No, I tried, he forced me," she hisses. I hear a scuffle through the phone and what sounds like a smack. Lea yelps in pain as the phone is taken from her. "You bastard!" she spits. "Don't come! He is going to hurt you!" she screams into for me to hear.

"Hurry up and come home, Skye," Bob growls down the line, "before I hurt your little friend here." I hear another thud and Lea's grunt before the phone goes dead.

I squeeze the phone in my hand and look down into Skye's eyes that are wide with worry. "What does he want Preston?" she asks with a hitch to her voice.

"He wants you to meet him at his house."

"Is Lea okay?"

"I hope so." I grit my teeth, a bad feeling in my stomach. I can't bring myself to tell her what I just heard.

"I have to go. We can't just leave her." She stands up and searches the room blindly.

I firmly grab her by the shoulders and give her a slight shake. "I'm going to call my cousins and we will go get her together. You need to stay here."

"No. I can't just leave her there, it's me he wants. I won't allow anyone to get hurt because of me." She looks at me with narrowed eyes.

"You need to stop for a second, *Detka*." She has a stubborn tilt to her chin that I know very well, there won't be any stopping her.

"You should think as well, you call your cousins and it won't end pretty." She narrows her eyes.

I sigh. "You're right, we will go. But give me a minute to gather some things, and when we get there, you need to follow my direction and stay out of his way. Can you do that?"

"I can try," she says softly.

I nod. "Okay, we need to get you into some jeans and a long sleeved shirt. I want you to be comfortable and able to run if you have to."

She looks down at her sundress and steps out of my grip. "We need to hurry, Preston, I have a bad feeling, I'll be back quick."

She turns and walks to our bedroom to change. I have a change of heart. Bob is unpredictable, I need to let someone know where we are going. I won't put Skye in more danger. I scrub a hand over my face and dial the number.

It rings three times before he answers. "Preston?"

"Dimtri? Bob has made a move and has Skye's friend."

"Okay, I'll get Evgeni and we will be at your house in a few minutes." He has a calmness to him that settles me, he is used to this sort of job.

"No, I'm calling as a courtesy. Now isn't the time to make our move. If you go in with us it will blow five years of keeping our connection a secret. I just needed someone to know that we are going to get her out." As I talk I'm walking into my office and going directly to my wall safe. I punch in the combination and take out my Beretta, setting it on my desk, before also retrieving the box of ammunition.

Dimitri lets out a frustrated growl. "Okay, be smart cousin. Stay safe and call us in an hour or we are going in," he says sharply and hangs up the phone.

Checking the gun and loading it, then locking the safety on it, I put it in the back waistband of my pants.

"Skye?"

I frown at the silence. "Skye?" I call again as I open up our bedroom door, I quickly scan the room to find it empty.

"Fuck." My curse echoes off the walls as I turn and take off at a run to her parents' home.

Thirty

SKYE

I curse myself the whole way to my parents' house. Why did I think he would leave me alone if I just stayed away? I stop at the end of the drive and look at the house, trying to remember just one good time spent here. Nothing comes to mind, this place was my hell. I straighten and swallow hard, the thought of Lea in there with him gives me the courage to walk up the drive.

I bite my lip as I reach for the handle, my mind screaming for me to run. The door swings open before I have a chance to open it, and the surprised squeak escapes before I can compose myself.

"Skye," my father says in a cold voice. "Come in."

I stare at him, keeping still, controlling the urge to clutch my hands. His eyes almost look sane, I am in deep shit. Cold dread sits at the pit of my stomach. I should have waited for Preston.

He doesn't wait for me to cross the threshold. He turns and walks away. The door is left open, he knows I won't leave Lea here. A classic scare tactic that he has used before, I glance over my shoulder hoping to see Preston. He is nowhere in sight. I swallow hard, straighten my shoulders and walk into the house, gently closing the door behind me

The house is eerily silent. Other than his footsteps pounding on the Spanish tile, marking his way to the living room, there is no noise. I stop in the doorway and see Lea, gagged and bound to a chair, indignant fury in her eyes. Any other time I would laugh at how pissed she looks.

"Let her go," I demand, surprised at how strong my voice sounds.

He turns by the bar and places an elbow on the polished surface, leaning onto it. This sickens me. He has always perched himself there, at the bar. King of his castle. Entertaining his disgusting friends and holding court in MY home. Using MY money to get fat and hold me prisoner. Using MY body however he saw fit. I wish I had a gun. I would finish him right there on his precious throne.

Lea starts grunting, trying to talk through the piece of fabric in her mouth.

"Shut up, or I'll shut you up," he snarls at her.

Lea scowls at him, her eyes narrowed and filled with hate. He takes a step toward her, and she reacts. I have to get him away from her.

"Where's mom?" I blurt.

He stops and turns back to look at me. "Who knows." He leans back onto the bar, Lea forgotten for now. When he puts his arm up I see the big sweat stain on his shirt, he isn't as calm as he appears.

"What do you want Dad?" I hold myself still in the doorway.

"Don't you dare call me that," he says with his face all scrunched up and spit flying from his mouth.

"I'm sorry." The apology comes automatically and makes me sick at how weak I sound. I don't know what else he wants me to call him.

"Pathetic little Skye," he chides, then takes a sip of his scotch on the rocks.

"I'm here now, let Lea go. She isn't who you want," I say without making eye contact with Lea.

"Oh, Miss Mouth over here is my collateral," he says with a smirk.

I sigh. "I won't leave, just let her go. You have me, you don't need her."

"Nice try, Skye. She can sit there. I won't have her running to get help for you." He gives her a calculating smile.

"What the hell do you want from me?" I scream at him, my patience running on empty.

"You will show me some respect," he bellows, turning purple with the effort. "Now try asking nicely," he says with a firm set to his jaw.

I grit my teeth and inhale through my nose, trying to calm the burning anger before I answer. "Why did you request this meeting?"

"Why do you think?" he says as he takes another drink, the ice clinking in the glass grates on my nerves. He stares into the bottom of his now empty glass and pushes his big bulk off the bar, walking around it to fix another.

I hear a noise to the side of me and my eyes dart over to the shadows, where I see my mother standing silently, watching. Always a part of the darkness. She doesn't even hold up a finger to silence me anymore. I still to this day try and protect her.

"Are you going to answer me, girl?" my father says as he perches himself back on his throne.

"I have no clue," I reply through gritted teeth.

"Really? Here I thought you were smarter than you look," he says with a mirthless laugh.

I glance over at Lea and take a step inside the room. She shakes her head and looks at my father. I pause, she's right. It's best to keep some distance between us.

"Don't be coy, Skye. I hear you've had a nice little visit with a lawyer," he sneers.

My face flushes.

"You never could lie, you're so easy to read, Skye."

"So what if I did? Haven't you kept my inheritance for long enough?" I stand up a little straighter, proud for once to be standing my ground.

His eyes flash with rage. "That old bitch! She changed her will and didn't tell anyone. It was all supposed to go to your mother."

"Why didn't it then? Why would she give it all to me?

"The old cow took a disliking to me and apparently decided to cut your mother out and hand it all straight to you."

"Maybe she knew you'd get your hands on it and piss it all away if she left it to mom."

"Watch your tongue, Skye," he roars, slamming his glass on the bar and both Lea and I flinch. "I put a decent roof over your head; funded you and your mother's endless shopping."

"I never wanted any of this." I wave a hand around the room.

"Oh, cut the 'poor me' act, always sounding like a sniveling little brat." He has a crazed look about him as he turns back to the bar and tosses back another scotch.

"Bastard," I hiss. He says these things just to get a rise out of me, I should know better but I'm done letting him win.

"Takes one to know one," he spits and lifts his glass in salute.

My brows furrow. "Okay… I'm done stooping to your level. Enough of the name calling. Why am I here?"

"Why? You ask me why?" He emits a crazed cackle and pushes off the bar and walks over to a side table. He shakes his head as he opens the drawer and takes something out, slowly turning back to me.

I look from the look of cold steel in his eyes, to the cold steel of a gun, pointed at me.

I glance over to Lea and her eyes are wide and focused on the gun. Then they snap to me. She can't say anything, but I understand what she's trying to convey, her eyes say run.

"You asked me why?" he repeats as the gun gently sways in his hand.

"It doesn't matter. I don't need to know." I see out of the corner of my eye that my mother has moved closer to the door way. Coward.

"Oh? But I want you to know," he says and takes a step closer.

"Fine Dad, have it your way... tell me why?" I'm surprised at the impatience in my voice given that my life is being threatened.

"Don't you ever call me that again. I'm not your goddamn father!" he yells with spittle coming out of his mouth.

My mouth opens but the gasp doesn't come from me, it comes from my mother beside me, still hiding in the shadows.

"That's right, your mother thought to trap me with a baby that wasn't mine." His hand is steady even as he shakes with rage.

"So why take this out on me?"

"I was happy taking it out on your mother, until her bitch of a mother ruined my plans." His beady little eyes focused directly on me.

Out of the corner of my eye I see my mom shuffle.

When I focus back on my father, my eyes are drawn straight past him to the patio. Preston is standing in the doorway and raises a finger to his lips, then he steps out of sight.

"All I had to do was sit tight and wait for the money to be ours and then I could take what I deserved for putting up with this family for far too long. But she wrecked it. So now I'm going to take what is owed to me."

"Enough, Bob!" My mother finally finds her voice.

"Oh look who it is, hiding in the shadows as always. Hello Victoria," he says with a sneer.

"You want the money, Bob? Just take it and end all of this," she says, her voice shaking with anger.

"The little mouse has finally found her voice," he says and takes another step closer.

"Just stop this insanity," she says in a voice I've never heard.

I look over at my mother, gone is the timid woman, she is standing up straight, determined.

"You thought I didn't know didn't you, thought you'd played me for a fool all these years. Ever wonder why I didn't put another brat in you? No? I'm sterile, you stupid bitch!"

My mother presses her lips together and turns to me. "I'm so sorry, Skye."

She looks back at my father. I catch myself before I say it in my head. His face is contorted with rage. "You apologize to her? I'm the one that deserves an apology."

"No, Bob, after the hell you made our life, you deserve to rot in hell and that's about it." She clenches her fists to her side.

"With both of you dead, it will all be mine." He lifts the gun, pointing it at me.

My mother laughs. "You aren't thinking straight. Put the gun down, Bob."

He looks at her, but doesn't take his aim off me. "You're going to watch your brat die, then I'll deal with you."

The next few seconds happen in slow motion. He turns back to face me and tightens his grip on the gun. "Just know that everything that's happened to you is your mother's fault."

He braces the gun with both hands, and I hear the click. I don't take my eyes off his as he pulls the trigger. The next thing I know, I hit the floor. My head cracks hard on the tile and the wind is knocked from my lungs. I don't know where I was hit, I feel nothing but where I hit my head and a great weight on my chest. As I focus I realize the weight is my mother. I'm just starting to figure out that she must have thrown herself in front of me, when she moves. She turns her head slightly and says, "Please forgive me."

Before I can answer her, he steps into view and I look up into the barrel of the gun. He stares into my eyes and smiles as he pulls the trigger.

An animalistic roar fills the room, and his hand waivers as the shot goes off. Sharp searing pain in my head blinds me momentarily and when I focus again I seed Preston tackle Bob, another shot going off in the process. I feel my mother stop moving on top of me and this kicks me into action.

Preston is yelling, "You asshole..." I can't hear the rest.

I roll my mom off me and look down and see a bullet hole in her temple. My vision goes blurry and I touch my temple, bringing my hand down covered in blood. I must have hit my head pretty hard. "Shit shit shit," I hiss, wiping my hand down my pants and seeing the front of my shirt covered in blood too.

Preston's guttural cry has me looking for him. He is screaming as his fists meet flesh. Bob is trying to block the punches when Preston suddenly stops and reaches down beyond Bob's head and picks up the gun.

He points it directly at Bob's forehead and presses it in. "You son of a bitch, you killed her," Preston cries.

"Go ahead, shoot me you little bastard," Bob dares him.

I can see Preston's hand shaking. So not to startle him I speak softly. "Preston..."

"Oh my God. I can still hear her voice." He has tears streaming down his face. "I'm going to fuck you up, Bob. You're going to beg me to kill you."

"Preston. I'm here." I stand and waver for a moment, slightly dizzy, then take the few steps over to him. "Preston?"

"*Detka?*" he croaks.

I set my hand on his shoulder and he jumps from the contact. "I'm okay," I soothe. "I'm right here."

Preston snarls down at Bob, then takes the gun away from his forehead and slams the butt into the side of his head, knocking him out cold. He tosses the gun to the side and scrambles to his feet. "*Detka*, are you hurt? Is that your blood?" he pleads, looking me over.

"Umm, I don't know." I raise a hand to my head where it is throbbing. "I hit my head."

"Come here," he says softly, opening his arms.

I touch my head again and look at my fingers. I take a step toward him. "I think this might be my blood," I tell him, and the dizziness overcomes me.

Beep...beep...beep... the constant sound of the alarm cuts through my sleep. I reach out to try and press snooze and my hand is instantly engulfed in strong hands.

"*Detka*, open your eyes for me." The soft plea comes as my hand is squeezed tighter.

I slowly open my eyes, the light hurting them. I gasp and quickly try to sit up, groaning. I look around me and realize I am in a hospital bed, with Preston by my side. I search my mind for my last memory. "My father...?" I turn my head and look into Preston's worried face.

He frowns and stands up. "He was arrested. You don't have to worry about him anymore."

I nod and bring a hand to my head. "And my mother?"

He sits down on the side of the bed. "She's gone, *Detka*. I'm so sorry."

My eyes swell with tears and I squeeze his hands. "She was a horrible mother," I blurt out as I start to cry.

He wastes no time climbing into my bed with me and pulling me into his arms. I let him hold me. "Yes she was, *Detka*, but she was also your mom."

I nod, sniffling into his chest. "Lea?" I ask as I fist his shirt in my hand.

"Fine and as feisty as ever and waiting outside for you to wake up," he says as he brushes the hair from my face.

"Thank God, I'm glad she wasn't hurt because of me." I swallow hard.

He cups my face and brings my head up to look into his eyes. "This wasn't because of you."

"But..." I try to argue.

He silences me with his lips, then presses his forehead to mine. I let out a hiss of pain. "Shit," he murmurs and pulls away and skims his fingers over a bandage on my head. "I was so goddamn scared, *Detka*."

I slightly shrug. "I only hit my head on the floor."

He shakes his head. "That bastard shot you," he tells me and hugs me closer. I saw that gun pointed at you and thought I'd lost you again." He takes in a shaky breath.

"I'm here, Preston," I say softly.

"The bullet only grazed your head, a flesh wound the doctor says. You will have one hell of a headache though. Are you in pain? Want me to get a nurse?" he questions.

I lift a hand and press a finger to his mouth. "I'm okay, I'm here with you."

His eyes fill with tears. "I can't stand the thought of losing you." He swallows hard, his jaw is in a firm line.

"You won't, I will be just fine," I say as I gently wipe a tear off his cheek. "I love you."

His eyes light up. "Say it again, please...I need to hear it again." He cups my face, tilting it so we are looking in each other's eyes.

"I love you, Preston Hart." Truer words I have never spoken and felt.

He releases my face and captures my hands, bringing them to his chest. "Finally, Miss Divine, I can show you what a beautiful mosaic you truly are."

Epilogue

PRESTON

I'm woken by the soft strings of her guitar. I listen with my eyes closed and wait for her to start singing softly. It makes me so happy. I smile from the bed and listen to her finish the love song she's been working on.

When she stops, I lean up on my elbow and look over at her, her eyebrows scrunched with concentration. She stops playing and sets her guitar down.

"What's the matter?"

She looks at me and her face automatically brightens with a carefree smile. "Just stuck on the next verse."

"Come back to bed, I'll help you find the words."

She laughs. "Come on, get up, I have coffee ready."

I groan. "Does that mean you're not coming back to bed?"

She walks back over to the bed, leans down and grabs the corner of the blanket. Before she can pull it off I launch myself up and grab her around the waist. She shrieks and I twist, pulling her down under me.

I frame her face with my hands and hold her still. Leaning down I kiss her. "We can make the melody from here, *Detka*."

She laughs. "Are you being a pervert?"

I waggle my eyebrows at her. "I can be if you want me to be."

"All night wasn't enough for you?" she asks, caressing my face.

"It will never be enough."

"Every day I fall even more in love with you. Now how are you going to help me find the melody?"

"Listen, *Detka*, what do you hear?" I ask her as I brush the hair away from her face.

Her brows furrow for a moment, then he brightest smile lights up her face. "The ocean, I hear the water."

"Yes, what else do you hear?" I trace her lips with the pad of my thumb, vowing to myself to keep that smile there.

"Our heart beats."

She nips at my thumb and then whispers, "It's really over, isn't it?"

"Murder, kidnapping, and attempted murder are just a few of the charges he was proven guilty of. I don't think he will outlast the two life sentences. Do you?"

"No," she whispers, her eyes wide with happiness. She slides out from under me and gets out of bed. She spreads her arms, and twirls while she laughs. "I'm free, we're free," she sings, then walks to the window and opens up the blinds and gasps.

I smile as I am captivated by her rare form. "It's beautiful, isn't it?"

"It's stunning. When we arrived last night you couldn't tell. The view is amazing. You should come see." She turns to me and is outlined by the bright sunshine. She walks back over to the bed and I hold out a hand, she puts her hand in mine and my heart swells. I pull her back into the bed.

"Fiji can wait, *Detka*. This view is all I need." I smile down at her.

She caresses my face. "I love you, Mr. Hart."

I take her left hand in mine and press a kiss to her knuckles. "I love you too, Mrs. Hart."

Acknowledgements

It takes a village to raise a book and I want to thank my tribe.

About the Author

Heather Shere is a wife of twenty some odd years and wants you to know that you get less for murder. She's also the mother of two adult shaped kids, who she thinks she messed up just enough to make them highly successful individuals, who are also hilarious.

She has a masters degree in snark and nothing entertains her more than someone who can word battle with her. She considers herself an awesome cook and an expert baker but wants to eat out most days, however nothing is made 'the right way' unless she makes it herself.

When she gets bored she likes to tinker with different hobbies like crocheting, scrapbooking, stamping and card making. Her newest and most fulfilling passion is writing and she welcomes you into the deep dark depths of her mind.

30577539R00167

Printed in Poland
by Amazon Fulfillment
Poland Sp. z o.o., Wrocław